CS

OF

nghorne Clemens (1835–1910), drew his identity from life along the Mississippi River during the years immediately preceding the Civil War, which inspired the characters and incidents in his best-known works, including *The Adventures of Tom Sawyer* (1876) and *Adventures of Huckleberry Finn* (1884). Born in Florida, Missouri, but raised in Hannibal, Clemens first trained as a printer, but in 1857 he became an apprentice pilot on the great river. At the start of the Civil War, he went to Nevada with his brother Orion, and was briefly involved in mining ventures before taking up a journalistic career (under the name Mark Twain) which eventually carried him to California and Hawaii, experiences recounted in *Roughing It* (1872). He next travelled to Europe and the Holy Land with an excursion party, the basis for *The Innocents Abroad* (1869), a humorous narrative that quickly established his reputation and launched his career as a comic lecturer. After marrying Olivia Langdon in 1870, Clemens abandoned the lecture circuit and moved to Hartford, Connecticut, where he wrote most of the books by which he is known, in a period of great prosperity that was ended in 1894 by bankruptcy resulting from incautious investments. Returning to the lecture circuit, Clemens recovered his fortune but his later life was darkened by tragedy, including the deaths of his favourite daughter, Susy, and his wife. Another daughter, Jean, suffered from epilepsy and died in 1909, followed shortly by her father.

LEE CLARK MITCHELL is Professor of English at Princeton University, where he has also served as Director of the Program in American Studies. He teaches courses in American literature and has written *Determined Fictions: American Literary Naturalism* (1989) and *Witnesses to a Vanishing America: The Nineteenth Century Response* (1981). He has published essays on Stephen Crane, Henry James, and Mark Twain, and his present project is a book-length study of the formula Western from Cooper to Peckinpah.

OXFORD WORLD'S CLASSICS

*For almost 100 years Oxford World's Classics have brought
readers closer to the world's great literature. Now with over 700
titles—from the 4,000-year-old myths of Mesopotamia to the
twentieth century's greatest novels—the series makes available
celebrated as well as lesser-known writing.*

*The pocket-sized hardbacks of the early years contained
introductions by Virginia Woolf, T. S. Eliot, Graham Greene,
and other literary figures that enriched the experience of reading.
Today the series is recognized for its fine scholarship and
reliability in texts that span world literature, drama and poetry,
religion, philosophy and politics. Each edition includes perceptive
commentary and essential background information to meet the
changing needs of readers.*

OXFORD WORLD'S CLASSICS

MARK TWAIN

The Adventures of Tom Sawyer

Edited with an Introduction and Notes by
LEE CLARK MITCHELL

OXFORD
UNIVERSITY PRESS

OXFORD

UNIVERSITY PRESS

Great Clarendon Street, Oxford OX2 6DP

Oxford University Press is a department of the University of Oxford.
It furthers the University's objective of excellence in research, scholarship,
and education by publishing worldwide in

Oxford New York

Athens Auckland Bangkok Bogotá Buenos Aires Calcutta
Cape Town Chennai Dar es Salaam Delhi Florence Hong Kong Istanbul
Karachi Kuala Lumpur Madrid Melbourne Mexico City Mumbai
Nairobi Paris São Paulo Singapore Taipei Tokyo Toronto Warsaw

with associated companies in Berlin Ibadan

Published in the United States
by Oxford University Press Inc., New York

Introduction, Note on the Text, Select Bibliography,
Chronology, and Explanatory Notes
© Lee Clark Mitchell 1993

The moral rights of the author have been asserted

Database right Oxford University Press (maker)

First published as a World's Classics paperback 1993
Reissued as an Oxford World's Classics paperback 1998

British Library Cataloguing in Publication Data

Data available

Library of Congress Cataloging in Publication Data

Data available

ISBN 0–19–283389–8

5 7 9 10 8 6

Printed in Great Britain by
Cox & Wyman Ltd.
Reading, Berkshire

CONTENTS

INTRODUCTION

When Samuel Clemens married Olivia Langdon on 4 February 1870, he stood at the midpoint of his life, with an established reputation as popular humorist, lecturer, and author. The prospect of further success fuelled his expectations of supporting 'Livy' in the affluent style she had become accustomed to as the daughter of a wealthy merchant. Yet Clemens, as ever, harboured doubts. His rough-hewn Western background as printer's devil, steamboat pilot, journalist, and Nevada silver miner posed a rude contrast to the refined society into which he was marrying—a contrast whose significance for his literary future prompted him to mull over his past. Only a few days after his wedding, he wrote a letter to his closest boyhood friend, Will Bowen, admitting: 'The fountains of my great deep are broken up & I have rained reminiscences for four & twenty hours.'[1] Then in one interminable sentence, he spewed out a list of vignettes recalled from their childhood together in Hannibal, Missouri—of the 'town drunkard', Jimmy Finn, who slept in a vat; of playing Robin Hood 'in the woods on Holliday's Hill'; of the day when the whole town feared he had drowned; and over a dozen other experiences which, transformed, would find their way into *The Adventures of Tom Sawyer*.

A few months later, feeling again the tug of memory, Clemens indulged recollections of Hannibal more elaborately in 'A Boy's Manuscript'—a fragment written in dramatic form that contains, once again, the germs of characters and situations to be recast in his first novel. Charles A. Norton has argued that Clemens felt at the time of his marriage 'abnormally sensitive' about his family's early poverty and needed to redeem himself in his in-laws' eyes by inventing an 'acceptable past'.[2] That need drew him for the first time to what Henry

---

[1] Cited by Charles A. Norton, *Writing Tom Sawyer: The Adventures of a Classic* (Jefferson, NC: McFarland & Co., 1983), 49.

[2] Ibid. 59.

Nash Smith termed the 'Matter of Hannibal', the biographical source of so many other narrative explorations undertaken by Clemens in his persona as Mark Twain. For the first time as well, he was prompted to venture a long work of fiction, moving beyond the tall tales, short stories, and epistolary travel accounts that had won him considerable renown, in order to craft a more sustained, more complex narrative structure. It is important, in other words, to recognize how misleading was the prefatory claim to *The Adventures of Tom Sawyer*: that most of the events had 'really occurred'. For not only was much of the point of this fictive invention to divorce Mark Twain from an embarrassing past, it represented a turn in his career towards more deliberately artful narratives.

Mark Twain began writing *Tom Sawyer* no later than February 1873, scrawling a rough outline at the top of the opening page that promised to take his young hero well into adulthood. With only a vague initial idea about where his imagination would lead (a routine state for Twain in the early stages of composition), he worked steadily and completed 118 manuscript pages by May before returning to *The Gilded Age*, the novel he was co-authoring with Charles Dudley Warner. Twain, Livy, and their daughter Susy then sailed to England for a round of lectures and sight-seeing which prevented his return to *Tom Sawyer* until the following February. Writing through the summer of 1874 in Elmira, New York, he finished about five hundred pages before discovering he had 'pumped myself dry'. So, in September, he 'knocked off, and went to playing billiards for a change'.[3] Returning again to the novel soon after moving to Hartford, Connecticut, he continued writing through 5 July 1875, when he proudly announced to William Dean Howells that he had 'finished the story & didn't take the chap beyond boyhood'. Whatever notable uncertainties he harboured over the conventional narrative voice ('I perhaps made a mistake', he admitted, 'in not writing it in the first

---

[3] Cited in Justin Kaplan, *Mr. Clemens and Mark Twain: A Biography* (London: Jonathan Cape, 1967), 179.

person'), he was adamant about the genre of his first novel: 'It is *not* a boy's book, at all. It will only be read by adults. It is only written for adults.'[4]

The first adult other than Livy to read the novel, however, forcefully disagreed: Howells argued instead for marketing the book as 'a boy's story', and offered suggestions for revision that included dropping a final chapter depicting Huck Finn's life with the Widow Watson. After hemming and hawing, Twain dryly concurred: 'Mrs. Clemens decides with you that the book should issue as a book for boys, pure and simple—and so do I. It is surely that correct idea.'[5] Correct or not, this marketing decision had little effect on the novel's reception. For despite Twain's hopes to have the book appear in early spring, his American publisher, Elisha Bliss, was unable to produce copies until December 1876. Among other things, the result was that Howells's enthusiastic May review appeared far too early to be of much help. And Twain's increasing disappointment in the novel's delay was confirmed in its unexceptional American sales: barely 13,000 copies bought in the first two months, and only 10,000 more purchased through the rest of the year. If the actual numbers are hardly as bad as Twain believed them to be, it is true that American critics largely ignored the book, leaving him ever after with the feeling that the novel was a relative failure.

That perception of failure none the less did little to alter Mark Twain's ambitions. Like other strong artists keen for approval yet faced with popular disfavour, he put his reception behind him as he began to grasp innovative possibilities in the materials newly unearthed. Even before the end of *Tom Sawyer*, we can discern a turn from its conventional narrative ploys towards the singular first-person sequel conceived the following year: *Adventures of Huckleberry Finn*. In the process of writing

---

[4] *Mark Twain–Howells Letters: The Correspondence of Samuel L. Clemens and William D. Howells, 1872–1910*, ed. Henry Nash Smith and William M. Gibson (Cambridge, Mass.: Harvard Univ. Press, 1960), 91.

[5] Ibid. 62.

his first novel, Twain had already sensed a way to master his streak of writerly exhibitionism—a way to control the skewed attitudes and fiercely incompatible energies that generated so much of his narrative power. Sensing mastery, of course, is far from the same as achieving it, and no one would confuse the accomplished style of *Huckleberry Finn* with that of its predecessor. Yet, curiously, it is *Tom Sawyer* that lays claim to being America's most popular novel, which raises the question of why readers continue to respond to the book as they do. What is it about Twain's conflicted voices in the novel—his peculiar blend of lyric and sardonic modes, his mix of elevated diction and vernacular expressions—that continues to elicit such an enthusiastic response? What, in short, does the novel suggest about an America that has made it one of its favourite texts?

Despite disappointing sales on first appearance, *The Adventures of Tom Sawyer* has remained continuously in print ever since—translated into countless languages, abridged in versions from Reader's Digest to comic books, reproduced in plays, musicals, movies, and assorted dramatic adaptations. Long before Twain's death, it had surpassed all his other books in total sales, and catapulted the diminutive figure of Tom Sawyer into a firm position as national icon. Recently, an American bicentennial stamp depicted Tom in front of a whitewashed fence; commemorative plates and pictures reveal him carrot-topped and barefooted, in chequered shirt and overalls, outwitting his kind, primly bespectacled Aunt Polly—all to the glorification of life in small-town America. How could Mark Twain's nostalgic reminiscence of ante-bellum years in Hannibal, Missouri have produced a set of characters and scenes that have become so firmly fixed in America's cultural imagination—of boys whitewashing a fence, disrupting school, attending their own funeral?

Certainly, the novel is winsomely comic, confirming Twain's skill as popular entertainer. And in the vein of contemporary Southwestern humorists, the most uproarious scenes match his earlier tendency (in 'The Celebrated Jumping Frog of

Calaveras County', say, or *Roughing It*) to focus on exotic forms of animal locomotion: a poodle in church sitting down on a 'pinchbug', then 'sailing up the aisle' (p. 46); Peter the cat, dosed by Tom with pain-killer that is 'simply fire in liquid form', prompted in 'a frenzy of enjoyment' to 'throw a few double summersets' before sailing through the window (p. 95); or later, an alley cat lowered from the school stage onto Mr Dobbins's head, snatching his wig to reveal a bald and gilded pate to the citizens of St Petersburg. Elsewhere, the narrator himself injects a wry note of humour, caricaturing ill-bred church choirs, or openly deriding the style of Examination Day essays. Yet engaging as it continues to be for each new generation of readers, the novel's humour seems by itself insufficient to have attracted so loyal a readership.

Perhaps it is Twain's larger paean to childhood that has helped to spur the novel's success, by soliciting the reader's yearning for a sunny, pre-industrial, pre-adult world that appears somehow inimitably American. But if so, just as many questions remain as before, such as why it should be boyhood behaviour that is so elaborately celebrated, or why appeals are so often specifically made to the male reader: 'The reader probably remembers how to [whistle] if he has ever been a boy' (p. 13). As William Dean Howells straightforwardly remarked in his early review: 'The story is a wonderful study of the boy-mind, which inhabits a world quite distinct from that in which he is bodily present with his elders.'[6] Whether or not an accurate description, Howells's remark suggests how often the novel portrays girls as merely the objects of boys' delight and distress. Becky Thatcher exists as little more than a narrative foil for Tom, the goal of his mercurial affections and hyperthyroid athleticism.

Given this relegation of women to largely subsidiary narrative roles, it is notable that the social context of the novel is all but exclusively matriarchal—in sharp contrast, as

---

[6] William Dean Howells's unsigned review in *Atlantic*, 37 (May 1876), 621–2; repr. in Frederick Anderson (ed.), *Mark Twain: The Critical Heritage* (London: Routledge & Kegan Paul, 1971), 61.

Cynthia Griffin Wolff .has observed, to the distinctively patriarchal enclaves that Huck Finn encounters in his own novel. Moreover, St Petersburg's matriarchy embodies the most cloying of genteel virtues, suffocating Tom in strict but lifeless standards of dress and decorum. The central figure in a narrative peopled largely by girls and single women, he clearly lacks any models of appropriate adult male behaviour. Yet the triumph of Tom's delinquent sensibility over the town's emasculating ethos is registered in the fact that his conduct is always finally found to be above reproach.

If neither the novel's focus on boyhood nor its humour alone explain its appeal, the fact that both these elements are checked by contrary forces may help to do so. Think of the tension that results from the violence abruptly imaged in certain scenes—as the gentle, patronizing narrative tone is unexpectedly punctuated by Doc Robinson's murder in the cemetery, or the horrifying figure of Injun Joe suddenly looms out of the moonlit shadows, or the sunny picnic excursion of Tom and Becky is transformed into a gruesome burial alive in a cave. Early reviewers were especially concerned with the effect on young people of the 'brutality' of these scenes, registering how fragile a balance existed between the presumed readerships of the novel—those adults for whom Twain thought he was writing, and the boys that Howells convinced him were his true audience. What Howells tacitly understood, however, was that children would delight in the novel's unexpected outbursts of violence.

The point is that such abrupt tonal shifts—of humour spicing scenes of horror, of 'model' behaviour from 'bad' boys, of adults vying with children as readers—hardly detract from the novel, but form instead an essential part of its narrative appeal. Particular scenes, motifs, characters, indeed the novel's style itself are all strangely ambivalent, pitched against themselves without appearing to be so, arrayed together in ways that mask the conflicts they embody. Nothing could be further from the truth, in other words, than Twain's later categorical claim that 'Tom Sawyer is simply a hymn, put into prose form to give it a worldly air.'[7] On the contrary, for every glowingly sunlit scene of childhood reminiscence that lightens the novel, its opposite number lurks, nightmarish and crass, drawing into question the very premisses of the lost world of St Petersburg. And that inconsistency is itself at the heart of the novel's perennial appeal.

This powerfully ambivalent tension extends to the novel's protest of the genre it invokes: the 'model boy' literature that had been widely published long before Mark Twain's own youth.[8] In explicitly announcing that Tom is *not* a 'model boy', Twain aligned himself with a more recent movement of 'bad boy' literature that satirized the moral philosophy of model-boy stories. That alignment proved unstable, however, if only because the novel itself confirms the behaviour it otherwise claims to spoof. The very delight with which Twain imagined his characters' mischievous idiosyncrasies has the effect of dislodging any clear distinction between 'good' and 'bad' behaviour—a distinction illustrated, on the one hand, through Tom's brother Sid and 'the Model Boy, Will Mufferson', and, on the other, through Tom Sawyer, Joe Harper, and Huck Finn, the 'juvenile pariah of the village, [and] son of the town drunkard' (pp. 42, 51). As ever for Twain, abstractions were inadequate to the roiling turmoil of life he envisioned. And not until eight years later, in *Adventures of Huckleberry Finn*, would he be able to define the contorted implications of 'bad' behaviour— behaviour that paradoxically appears most ethical in its capacity to subvert the morally 'sivilized' premises of a slave-holding South.

[7] *Mark Twain's Letters*, ed. Albert Bigelow Paine (New York: Harper & Brothers, 1917), 477.

[8] For an overview of this genre, which includes William Mumford Baker's *Carter Quarterman* (1876), Thomas Bailey Aldrich's *Story of a Bad Boy* (1869), Thomas Hughes's *Tom Brown's School Days* (reissued in 1876), and Horatio Alger's *Ragged Dick* (1867), see Walter Blair, 'On the Structure of *Tom Sawyer*', *Modern Philology*, 37 (1939), 75–88; Judith Fetterley, 'The Sanctioned Rebel', *Studies in the Novel*, 3 (1971), 299; and John Seelye, 'What's in a Name: Sounding the Depths of *Tom Sawyer*', *Sewanee Review*, 90 (Summer 1982), 420–1.

Recent critics have increasingly explored the novel's darker reaches, including the sinister economics of St Petersburg's devotion to what William James would refer to as the 'cash nexus'. Even Tom's peerless sister, Mary, bribes him with a Barlow knife in the hope of encouraging him at Sunday-school lessons, exemplifying the terms of almost every other exchange in the novel—from the school's elaborate system of 'ticket' transactions for winning a prize Bible, to Huck's more straightforward method of upgrading a dead cat. From this perspective, the novel's conclusion comes to seem ironically appropriate, rewarding Huck and Tom with a fortune invested at 6 per cent a year. After all, work and knowledge can hardly be touted as their own rewards in a community where the most celebrated episode pivots on nothing more than a sales tactic: Tom's persuading others that whitewashing is not really work but play.

That sales tactic significantly lay at the heart of a new consumer culture in America, which emerged in the 1870s in tandem with an advertising industry that altered forever public attitudes towards goods and services. Tom represents the emergence of this newly speculative psychology (associated more with Madison Avenue than small-town Missouri), and his behaviour anticipates many of the techniques we accept today as commonplace business ploys. Circuitously playing on others' aspirations and desires, secretly buying up tickets for the Sunday-school prize, openly baiting his friends into remaining on Jackson's Island, slyly diverting the schoolmaster from his lessons: Tom wins his way by wheedling modest concessions from others that result in considerable gains for himself. It is a seductive, highly speculative style that only Huck knows how to thwart, as when he defends his pet tick against Tom's disparagement: 'Oh, anybody can run a tick down that don't belong to them. I'm satisfied with it. It's a good enough tick for me' (p. 55). In three brief sentences, Huck exposes the entire logic of the whitewashing scene, showing how thoroughly mere assertion alters the terms of any exchange. His stalwart resistance to that logic, moreover, leads to one of Tom's few economic failures, compelling Tom finally to offer his newly loosened tooth in trade for the tick.

Yet the strain of economics that dominates life in St Petersburg no more fully defines the experience of reading *Tom Sawyer* than Twain's description of the novel as 'a hymn'. Or rather, life as Tom lives it is at the same time whimsical *and* crass, both ludic *and* exploitative, and therefore gay as well as forbidding. Few authors have evoked as skilfully as Twain the wide-eyed state of childhood ignorance, revealing it as an unstable blend of confident innocence and fearful bewilderment. Anticipating Freud, he shows how coming of age entails learning once again a civilization that we feel we already know at the price of a discontent we know we already feel. That trade-off is adumbrated throughout his first novel, imaged most starkly by Tom in his Sunday-best suit, looking 'exceedingly improved and uncomfortable' (p. 33). And throughout, the novel's mix of contrasts matches the contradictions many have felt about coming of age in Amercian culture. That match has more than anything else contributed to the novel's popularity, which like most popular texts, appears at once to defy and yet to augment convention. *Tom Sawyer* appeals to readers precisely through this contradictory mix, invoking horror as well as humour, indulging high and low styles, satirizing yet championing the venal impulse of wanting something for nothing. In the process, it celebrates an apparently characteristic American figure of rags-to-riches success.

The difficulty of finding a category for Tom Sawyer was pinpointed early by William Dean Howells, whose shrewd critique appeared before the novel was even published:

He is mischievous, but not vicious; he is ready for almost any depredation that involves the danger and honor of adventure, but profanity he knows may provoke a thunderbolt upon the heart of the blasphemer, and he almost never swears; he resorts to any stratagem to keep out of school, but he is not a downright liar, except upon terms of after shame and remorse that make his falsehood bitter to him. He is cruel, as all children are, but chiefly because he is ignorant; he is not mean, but there are very definite bounds to his generosity; and his courage is the Indian sort, full of prudence and mindful of retreat as one of the conditions of prolonged hostilities. In a word, he is a boy, and merely and exactly an ordinary boy on the moral side.[9]

More sensitive to the nuances of Tom's character than most commentators since, Howells none the less hedges his bets so fully by a whittling-down process of negation that readers can only at last wonder how to take Tom. Cruel but not mean, adventurous yet prudent, likeable yet in notable ways unappealing—Tom strikes us as an intensely ambivalent figure, with contradictions that run as deep as Mark Twain's own tumultuous personality. He's kind, if also a bully; sometimes honourable, but also unscrupulous; ready to jeer at others in order to get his way, or to vow a solemn blood-oath that he breaks without a second thought.[10]

Indeed, Tom's desires themselves emerge only *as* contradictions, in response to the web of family constraints and social taboos that define a child's experience in St Petersburg. If obligation kills desire, as Tom duly learns both at home and at school, it can none the less acquire a compelling allure when transformed into opportunity—a lesson he masters to considerable profit in the whitewashing episode. That lesson is parsed more meticulously in a later scene, when he joins the Cadets of Temperance (having been attracted by their sartorial elegance) only to find that the enforced abstention, which is the manifest price of membership, has the effect of heightening his appetite for things he had never craved before. Quickly resigning, however, he discovers once again the law of appetite: 'The simple fact that he could took the desire away, and the charm of it' (p. 159).

These contradictions in Tom's psychology serve as a foil to

[9] Howells, unsigned review in *Atlantic*, 37 (May 1876); repr. in Anderson (ed.), *Mark Twain: The Critical Heritage*, 60.

[10] A more obvious contradiction involves Tom's bookish love of Romance and flagrant ignorance of the Bible (even the story of David and Goliath, a model for his own behaviour). Though presented as a dunce at school, Tom acts out a fencing battle with Joe Harper according to 'the book', and later explains what pirates must do and say.

his most prominent tendency, itself conspicuous for being so entirely unshaded: his flagrant exhibitionism. Like his creator in this as well, Tom is perpetually on stage, ever prepared to give a performance, 'always showing off'.[11] Whether aspiring for 'the glory and the *éclat*' of a Bible prize (p. 35); or yearning to be the Biblical 'little child [who] should lead' his promised people (p. 45); or imagining himself a 'gaudy' pirate returning 'at the zenith of his fame' to the town's collective admiration (p. 68): Tom cannot resist any occasion, real or imagined, large or small, to assert himself in another's gaze. His various antics throughout the novel to attract the eye of Becky Thatcher simply reflect this larger hope 'to live for glory'. And when he does in fact return to town at last a conquering hero, the narrator informs us equivocally that 'it gratified all the vicious vanity that was in him' (p. 138).

Nor is St Petersburg averse to Tom's antics or niggardly in its admiration, and the adulation has a predictable effect of further inciting Tom, prompting him during the murder trial to break his deepest vow to Huck, by confessing Injun Joe's guilt: 'Tom was a glittering hero once more—the pet of the old, the envy of the young' (p. 169). Later again, after Tom trumpets their discovery of buried treasure: 'Wherever Tom and Huck appeared they were courted, admired, stared at' (p. 241). This, perhaps the most frequently repeated theme in the novel, offers only a faintly veiled dramatization of Twain's own yearnings for success, as well as an apt anticipation of his transformation into white-suited public persona: 'they had evidently lost the power of doing and saying common-place things' (p. 241). Over and over, Tom is caught up in others' expectations, transformed by their gaze into a 'hero' who acts always for the presumed effect he will have, moving with 'a

[11] James M. Cox has written: 'Thirty years after the writing of *Tom Sawyer*, Mark Twain observed that Theodore Roosevelt was a political incarnation of Tom Sawyer. "Just like Tom Sawyer," he remarked of Roosevelt's eagerness to keep the public eye; "always showing off".' See *Mark Twain: The Fate of Humor* (Princeton, NJ: Princeton Univ. Press, 1966), 137.

dignified swagger, as became a pirate who felt that the public eye was on him' (p. 137).

The only mistake lies in seeing Tom as essentially different in this regard from anyone else in St Petersburg, since everyone shares much the same propensity as him. They are simply less successful. On the novel's opening page, Aunt Polly searches for Tom by peering first over, then under her fashionable spectacles, 'her state pair, the pride of her heart . . . built for "style", not service—she could have seen through a pair of stove-lids just as well' (p. 9). Vanity dictates ineptness as well as discomfort, for Aunt Polly and nearly everyone else 'consumed with envy', all of whom are given over to pretension and sundry forms of self-glorification (p. 137). This collective tendency is exemplified nowhere better than in the Sunday-school presentation of a prize Bible, made before Judge Thatcher, with Tom reduced to his characteristic behaviour of ' "showing off" with all his might' to attract Becky's attention (p. 37). So contagious is the mood that soon the rest of the community joins in:

Mr. Walters fell to 'showing off' with all sorts of official bustlings and activities . . . The librarian 'showed off', running hither and thither with his arms full of books . . . The young lady teachers 'showed off'—bending sweetly over pupils that were lately being boxed . . . The young gentleman teachers 'showed off' with small scoldings and other little displays of authority . . . The little girls 'showed off' in various ways, and the little boys 'showed off' with such diligence that the air was thick with paper wads . . . And above it all the great man sat and beamed . . . and warmed himself in the sun of his own grandeur, for he was 'showing off' too. (p. 38).

Everyone is caught in this cycle of pretence, for it is, as James M. Cox has observed, 'the activity which unites the entire community'.[12]

Or rather, almost everyone, since Huck Finn makes it clear that he is unlike Tom in hating special attention—attention the novel itself discreetly refrains from bestowing on him until near

[12] *The Fate of Humor*, 143.

the end. In contrast to the rest of St Petersburg, Huck is embarrassed by accolades, and the acclaim that greets him for saving the Widow Douglas makes him almost forget 'the nearly intolerable discomfort of his new clothes in the entirely intolerable discomfort of being set up as a target for everybody's gaze and everybody's laudations' (p. 239). Only Tom can inveigle Huck into staying behind for more. It is as if the novel were marking Huck as different, reserving him for later elaboration, alerting the reader to his special character by the very resistance he offers to any possibility of standing in the limelight.

The implications of 'showing off' are illustrated fully in the novel's most dramatic moment, the notorious scene when Tom, Huck, and Joe Harper make a surprise appearance at their own funeral. The importance of the scene is confirmed not only by the suspense in which Tom keeps us all (one of the few such narrative occasions in the novel), but by the frequency with which the scene has been anticipated. As early as the third chapter, Tom wonders self-pityingly how Aunt Polly would feel should he die, 'out in the cold world, with no shelter over his homeless head' (p. 29). Three chapters later, as an excuse to play hookey, he convinces first Sid, then himself ('so handsomely was his imagination working'), that he is actually dying and prepared to make a last will and testament (p. 50). In Chapter 8, melancholy over a tiff with Becky Thatcher, he envies another dead boy the peace of his grave: 'and nothing to bother and grieve about, ever any more. If he only had a clean Sunday-school record he could be willing to go, and be done with it all' (p. 67). Even his dream of becoming a pirate is shaped as a death to the life he now thinks he knows too well: 'What if he went away—ever so far away, into unknown countries beyond the seas—and never come back any more!' (p. 68).

This recurrent fantasy of self-annihilation leads to the adventure on Jackson's Island, the high point of which occurs when the three boys observe a ferry-boat booming cannons across the river to raise the bodies of those who have drowned.

Bewildered at first about who it could be, Tom suddenly realizes: 'Boys, I know who's drownded; it's us!' (p. 111). That moment echoed so powerfully in Twain's imagination that he copied it straight into *Huckleberry Finn*, though without the cruel sequel in which Tom returns to overhear his distraught aunt praising the 'dead'. The scene, moreover, sets the stage for Tom's later return with Huck and Joe to attend their own memorial service: 'They had been hid in the unused gallery, listening to their own funeral sermon!' (p. 131). Further to reinforce the moment's clear significance, its description is repeated in Tom's ensuing account of his 'dream of returning', only then again to be reiterated simply to be refuted. Later, when Tom and Becky are 'buried' alive in the cave and presumed dead, the collective mourning in St Petersburg reminds us once more of the centrality of this motif.

The idea of attending one's own funeral epitomizes the paradox of being at once absent yet present, already 'dead' yet still alive to the implications of one's life. Unable to 'die *temporarily*!' (as Tom at one point phrases the wish to himself), he can none the less stand outside his self at the moment of its fullest solicitation, when praise and regret for a self now apparently lost are diminished by no adverse judgements (p. 68). After all, decorum dictates that cruel estimations be publicly silenced, allowing the lost self to appear to itself in its most appealing guise. The moment forms the culmination of Tom's (and of all St Petersburg's) desire for adulation, placing him at the centre of even his own admiring gaze.

Given the intense focus of everyone else's attention on Tom Sawyer, it may come as something of a shock to realize how little he is actually seen or shown, how minimally in fact the novel ever describes or specifically places him. Consider how few questions can be answered about his past (when and how was he orphaned? why is Sid his half-brother?), or even how little we know of his actual physique. Numerous illustrators have created for us the image of a barefoot boy, but no confirmation exists in the novel that he ever dons a tattered straw hat, or sports a chequered shirt, or that his overalls are

INTRODUCTION

either ragged or barely held up by suspenders. We cannot even
be altogether certain of his age. And that may be part of the
novel's point: Tom's very emptiness as a physical signifier
encourages readers to project their separate ideas and fantasies,
to fill in the faceless shape that Mark Twain so vaguely
delineates.[13] If so, the irony of the novel is twofold: that despite
its silence, early illustrators imposed an image of Tom on the
text that remains for most readers vivid enough to make them
forget it is not *in* the text; and yet, that within the novel, Tom's
elaborate dramas of 'showing off' curiously avail him nothing
in terms of either physical or visual description.

Nor are other characters described with any greater precision,
reducing the entire village of St Petersburg to shadowy
gestures and physical types, some signalled only through the
most fleeting of metonymic identifications. Aunt Polly is
simply identified as a pair of spectacles 'built for "style"'
(p. 9), while the new boy in town is likewise equated with the
natty jacket, bright necktie, dainty cap, shining shoes, and
'citified air' he wears (p. 13). While the Widow Douglas
appears as merely 'fair, smart, and forty', Jim, 'the small
coloured boy', is granted no description at all (pp. 42, 11).
Becky Thatcher is portrayed more completely than any other
child, and yet the terms are so stereotypical as to make her
seem not more, but less distinctive: 'a lovely little blue-eyed
creature with yellow hair plaited into two long tails, white
summer frock, and embroidered pantalettes' (p. 26). Joe
Harper, Amy Lawrence, Huck Finn, and the other children,
like Injun Joe, Muff Potter, Judge Thatcher, and most of the
other adults are all equally undefined. Indeed, the novel offers
only a single exception to this descriptive rule, in the painfully
ample depiction of Mr Walters, the school superintendent:

This superintendent was a slim creature of thirty-five, with a sandy
goatee, and short sandy hair; he wore a stiff standing-collar whose

[13] As James M. Cox has observed: 'it is impossible to tell what he looks
like—how tall, how heavy, how handsome or ugly he is. He emerges as the
figure, the *character*, of the Boy.' See *The Fate of Humor*, 133–4.

upper edge almost reached his ears, and whose sharp points curved forward abreast the corners of his mouth—a fence that compelled a straight look-out ahead, and a turning of the whole body when a side view was required. His chin was propped on a spreading cravat, which was as broad and as long as a bank-note, and had fringed ends; his boot toes were turned sharply up, in the fashion of the day, like sleighrunners—an effect patiently and laboriously produced by the young men by sitting with their toes pressed against a wall for hours together. Mr. Walters was very earnest of mien, and very sincere and honest at heart. (p. 36).

It is as if a full physical description were to be invoked only in order to diminish a person, making him vivid as a corporeal presence because so insignificant otherwise.

Supporting this argument is the extremely thin portrait offered of Injun Joe, who serves as something like a grim reality principle for the novel. He too is never described, even though Tom and Huck repeatedly freeze in fear at the sudden sight of his 'stolid face' (p. 89). Within the idyllic world that Mark Twain conjures up as St Petersburg, 'iron faced' Injun Joe represents the existence of unadulterated evil and death, the necessary 'Et in Arcadia Ego' to this pastoral on the Mississippi (p. 167). And if, in a peculiar fashion, he seems to compete with Tom for the town's undivided attention, the difference between the two is imaged in the differences between their two deaths: Tom's repeated false alarms and the fraud of his elaborately staged funeral versus Injun Joe's excruciating experience of burial alive, slowly starved to death on a diet of old candles and raw bats, like something out of Edgar Allan Poe. 'Injun Joe is Tom's shadow self,' Cynthia Griffin Wolff has observed, and his presence in the novel is 'as if one element in Tom's fantasy world has torn loose and broken away from him, roaming restlessly—a ruthless predator—genuinely and mortally dangerous'.[14] What makes Injun Joe's presence all the more menacing, of course, is

---

[14] Cynthia Griffin Wolff, 'The Adventures of Tom Sawyer: A Nightmare Vision of American Boyhood', Massachusetts Review, 21 (Winter 1980), 647–8.

that that presence is no more detailed than Tom's, his psychological 'shadow self'.

Even so, the remarkable feature of Injun Joe's appearance lies less in the vagueness of his physical characteristics than in the frequency with which he is signalled in the novel by sound alone. Tom first recognizes this menacing Other only when he begins to speak: 'Say, Huck, I know another o' them voices; it's Injun Joe' (p. 76). And when the villain is later significantly disguised as a 'deaf and dumb Spaniard', it is his unexpected, angry outburst that betrays him: 'This voice made the boys gasp and quake. It was Injun Joe's!' (p. 182). Inded, many of the novel's characters are denoted by their distinctive voices—from Aunt Polly's opening, stentorian 'Tom' to Huck Finn's closingly ebullient, 'Now, that's something *like*' (p. 245). And the reason that Tom Sawyer seems to us the most vivid character of all is that his personality is conveyed so fully in a characteristic manner of speech. Despite his vague physical features, we hear him come fully alive through the charm of his speech.

Tom Sawyer's most compelling feature is its emergent collection of voices, and the book can be seen as a novelistic step towards the remarkable vernacular speech that we've since come to identify with Mark Twain. As with other aspects of the novel, its own 'voice' is deeply conflicted, registering the ambivalence Twain felt about formal narrative as he came to terms with a more traditional style. Despite his deliberate invoking of dialect speech and regional idioms, despite his satirization of conventional modes of formal address, the novel persistently takes refuge in the settled terrain of standard English.[15] This was not because Twain lacked confidence in his extraordinary ear for inflections of character. It was simply that he had not

---

[15] For a fuller account of the alterations Mark Twain made in the manuscript to both increase and decrease the incidence of vernacular speech, see Paul Baender's 'Introduction' to *'The Adventures of Tom Sawyer' by Mark Twain; A Facsimile of the Author's Holograph Manuscript* (2 vols.; Washington, DC: Georgetown Univ. Library, 1982), esp. i, p. xxxv.

yet discovered the narrative means of forsaking a flattened prose through an entire novel—something only to be achieved in the deft verbal rhythms of *Huckleberry Finn*'s first-person voice.

In any event, no one would have been surprised by the use of dialect, idioms, or vernacular speech, all of which had become familiar features of popular literature by the 1870s. Twain's distinction lay in his gift for finding just the turns of phrase and patterns of speech that define a unique personality. Aunt Polly is inimitably evoked in the opening five words of *Tom Sawyer*: 'What's gone with that boy' (notably changed in the original manuscript from the standard, 'Where can that boy be'). And within a few brief paragraphs, her stern queries about the absent Tom will reinforce that characterization: 'I lay if I get hold of you'; and 'I never did see the beat of that boy' (again, changed from 'I never see such a boy'). All at once, we are thrust into the lively vocal realm of St Petersburg, where characters speak (at least, part of the time) in distinctively Middle American patterns. When Tom instructs Joe Harper in how to play Robin Hood, he concludes, 'Now if you've got the hang, go it lively!' (p. 71). And a few pages later, that night in the graveyard, a fearful exchange between Huck and Tom nicely captures their respectively agitated tones:

'I'll try, but don't you be afeard. They ain't going to hurt us. "Now I lay me down to sleep, I ——".'

'*Sh!*'

'What is it, Huck?'

'They're *humans*! One of 'em is, anyway. One of 'em's old Muff Potter's voice.'

'No—'tain't so, is it?'

'I bet I know it. Don't you stir nor budge. *He* ain't sharp enough to notice us. Drunk, same as usual, likely—blamed old rip!' (p. 76).

In this briefest of dialogues, Twain brings to life the two cowering, chattering boys, themselves petrified by the outburst of other voices.

Occasionally, the narrative voice itself slips into a mode

Twain made his own, adapting language in idiosyncratic ways. Consider the description of St Petersburg's graveyard:

It was a graveyard of the old-fashioned western kind. It was on a hill, about a mile and a half from the village. It had a crazy board fence around it, which leaned inwards in places, and outward the rest of the time, but stood upright nowhere. Grass and weeds grew rank over the whole cemetery. All the old graves were sunken in. There was not a tombstone on the place; round-topped, worm-eaten boards staggered over the graves, leaning for support and finding none. 'Sacred to the memory of So-and-So' had been painted on them once, but it could no longer have been read, on the most of them, now, even if there had been light. (p. 74).

The sentence construction is decidedly simple, the diction thoroughly straightforward, and yet the overall point of view is none the less skewed. In part, the animistic verbs and adjectives succeed in bringing the landscape bizarrely alive, with the graveyard itself transfigured into a shuffling derelict. And the very punctuation of the last sentence, broken up by otherwise unneeded commas, reinforces this impression by confirming the faltering, stumbling collapse of the entire scene in its syntax itself.

Yet set against the new voice that emerges here in the novel's vernacular expression as well as its descriptive idiosyncrasies, are more clearly conventional forms of representation that otherwise govern the whole. The narrator is everywhere calmly patronizing, not only of Tom and other children, but of the adults and the reader as well. Aunt Polly is treated 'like many other simple-hearted souls' with her 'pet vanity' (p. 11), while the Revd Mr Sprague 'turned himself into a bulletin board, and read off "notices" ' (p. 44). Constant editorial asides are made to matters 'the reader probably remembers' (p. 13), although our eyes are decorously averted from whatever may be supposed to embarrass: 'Let us draw the curtain of charity over the rest of the scene' (p. 41). Far-ranging satirical claims are made that intimate the narrator's superior social judgement: 'There was once a church choir that was not ill-bred, but I have forgotten where it was now' (p. 43). Conversely, natural experiences are invoked in tones that sound blandly lyrical: 'Saturday morning was come, and all the summer world was bright and fresh, and brimming with life' (p. 18); or, 'The sun rose upon a tranquil world, and beamed down upon the peaceful village like a benediction' (p. 31).

Certain scenes do anticipate the richness of description in *Huckleberry Finn*, but Twain was not yet prepared to venture so far either narratively or stylistically, as suggested by even a brief glance at the opening of Chapter 14. While Tom marvels wide-eyed at the arrival of dawn on the day following the boys' 'death' on Jackson Island, his awe is hardly justified by the rhetorically tired process of 'Nature shaking off sleep and going to work'. The scene fails as fully as the violent thunderstorm depicted soon after at considerable length, in part because both are rendered through stale tropes and flatly conventional images. Interestingly, both scenes recur in similar narrative circumstances in *Huckleberry Finn*, when Huck is likewise presumed to be dead, having staged his own murder to escape from Pap. But where the earlier novel retreats from a vigorous prose into consoling clichés ('It was a wild night for homeless young heads to be out in'), the later one explores a starkly unconventional perspective through language that remains persistently vernacular.

Indeed, *Tom Sawyer* highlights this battle of discursive modes by adopting, yet disparaging, a classical style, in the process evincing Twain's own uncertainty about where he stood. Following a pompous description of Tom's feelings on being rejected by Becky—'And thus he would die—out in the cold world, with no shelter over his homeless head, no friendly hand' (p. 29)—Twain turns around and mocks this high tone by throwing dishwater over Tom, signalling how wet his phrasings (as well as his feelings) already are. Only pages later, however, the diction is again as sentimentally exalted as that of any St Petersburg orator (he 'picked his pathless way' through 'a dense wood' where 'there was not even a zephyr stirring'). And Tom is once again reduced to a maudlin pose of self-mortification: 'The boy's soul was steeped in melancholy;

his feelings were in happy accord with his surroundings' (p. 67).

Often as Mark Twain revised passages by replacing standard English with vernacular expressions, it is notable how frequently he also did just the opposite, introducing inflated diction back into his drafts ('hither & thither' exchanged for 'here and there', or 'purloined' substituted for 'stolen'). Such moments, as Paul Baender informs us, attest to Twain's striking predilection for more as well as less conventionally elevated discourse. Granted that the bombastic compositions delivered on Examination Day are thoroughly debunked, none the less they are given centre stage and quoted full length, with a footnote attesting to their status as actual extracts 'taken without alteration from a volume entitled *Prose and Poetry, by a Western lady*' (p. 157).

Twain's oddly contradictory view of high and low discursive modes runs through the novel. The narrator spoofs the minister's affected delivery by marking his rising inflection typographically, even though the narrator's own classical style is likewise affected. His balanced rhythms most notably punctuate the text in the form of zeugma: 'he strode down the street with his mouth full of harmony and his soul full of gratitude' (p. 13); 'Aunt Polly was retiring from the field with a slipper in her hand and triumph in her eye' (p. 19); 'they came to jeer, but remained to whitewash' (p. 22), a line itself borrowed from Oliver Goldsmith's poem, 'The Deserted Village': 'fools, who came to scoff, remain'd to pray.' Huck's expressions were altered in manuscript as a means of intensifying its vernacular flavour—from 'because' and 'been' to 'becuz' and 'ben'—but at the same time Twain's narrator indulges in frequently sentimental expressions. Even when Huck, Tom, and Joe are safely on Jackson's Island, when they might well have been discursively freed from the strains of St Petersburg gentility, the narrator opts for a sentimental perspective: 'drowsiness began to steal upon the eyelids of the little waifs' (p. 105); 'an intruder came now that would not "down". It was conscience' (p. 106).

Wavering over the stylistic direction he wants to take, Mark Twain had clearly not yet achieved the discursive breakthrough that was to come eight years later in *Huckleberry Finn*. The calm third-person narrator who organizes the verbal world in *Tom Sawyer* provides the formal security that Twain was still unwilling to forego, even if he was already feeling uncomfortable with the implications of an impersonal narrative voice, and even as his discomfort expresses itself in the abrupt shifts and generic mixes of his narrator's style. Much as he trusted the perspective of omniscience and control, he could not help critiquing the calm diction, the 'sivilized' expressions, the conventional point of view represented by that voice—the way in which certain crass moral assumptions were necessarily reinforced by the very conventional verbal means through which they were expressed. Among other contradictions that make up the novel, its divided voice was the most significant and most troubling—and, in the later novel, the first thing to go.

In a letter written to William Dean Howells after *The Adventures of Tom Sawyer* was completed but yet to be published, Mark Twain admitted that 'since there is no plot to the thing, it is likely to follow its own drift'.[16] That critique helps to explain the novel's unstructured sequence of chapters, which follow one another with very little causal logic. The opening eight chapters consist of brief character sketches, scenes of puppy love between Tom and Becky, and an emergent distinction between 'good' and 'bad' boys. Doc Robinson's murder and its aftermath then occur in Chapters 9–11, before the narrative returns for a chapter to the lovesick state of Tom and Becky. Chapters 13–16 depict the boys' adventures on Jackson's Island, leading up to their funeral service in the following chapter. Tom's rendition of his 'dream' and his renewed relationship with Becky occur in Chapters 18–20, preceding his Examination Day triumph and experience with

[16] The letter, written on 21 June 1876, is contained in *Mark Twain–Howells Letters*, 87–8.

the Cadets of Temperance. Muff Potter's trial occupies Chapter 23, followed by a three-chapter burlesque of the 'blood and thunder' novel contained in the boy's hunt for buried treasure. The school picnic then leads to Tom and Becky's separation as well as Huck's vigil, described in Chapters 29–30, followed by a two-chapter flashback to Tom and Becky's adventures in the cave and their escape. After Chapter 33 details Injun Joe's death, Tom and Huck's discovery of buried treasure is described in the novel's final two chapters.

Weak as is the design of the novel in terms of structural coherence, it differs little in this respect from many of Mark Twain's more mature works. Even at his imaginative best, Twain failed to think in terms of integrated plots, and his forte would always remain the sharp dramatic effect and quick narrative turn that had marked his earliest efforts in the tall tale and short story. Certainly, those effects and turns are present throughout *The Adventures of Tom Sawyer*, but only as a series of episodes whose import is to give voice to a young Midwestern boy. And since the need to authenticate Tom's voice required no single order of events, no special plot, the novel's sequence strikes us as just as arbitrary as it struck Twain himself, with only vague ties linking the episodes together. Critics have sometimes noted that Twain's handling of narrative becomes somewhat more accomplished in the course of the novel. The funeral sequence, for instance, is presented as a 'secret' from readers as well as from friends, after which a flashback describes the boy's earlier preparations. Later, this technique of heightening suspense is repeated in the cave-burial sequence, when Tom and Becky's ordeal is recounted only after the town's reaction is given—narratively linking the whole of St Petersburg together. But in general, the novel's chain of otherwise unrelated incidents corresponds to the minimum episodic plotting characteristic of the picaresque.

Sheer succession is all that defines the order of events in the picaresque mode (things simply happen to happen, with no apparent connection to each other); there is little of the binding narrative causality common to strongly integrated plots. One curious effect of the arbitrariness with which incidents are represented as occurring is not to diminish, but rather to accentuate the importance of time itself. That may help explain why the passing of time is foregrounded in *Tom Sawyer*, mentioned specifically in each of the opening sentences of well over half the chapters. In part, of course, these allusions serve as a means of moving the story along, lending the appearance of holding a plotless narrative together ('Saturday morning was come'; 'At half-past nine that night'). This heightening of the reader's consciousness of time, however, occurs in a novel where moments of greatest misgiving involve the loss of an accurate sense of time passing. Or as Tom thinks to himself, following the 'agony' of his impatient night-time vigil for Huck, 'at last he was satisfied that time had ceased and eternity begun' (p. 73).

Indeed, the worst aspect of Tom and Becky's experience adrift in the cave is their confused inability to know what time it actually is, which only makes them excessively conscious of time's passage: 'they could not tell how long' they have been there, and 'the hours wasted away' as they watch their candle melt (pp. 218, 220). Forced to 'bear the weight of the heavy time in idleness', both find themselves obsessively recurring to the question first of what time, then what day it is: 'Tom believed that it must be Wednesday or Thursday, or even Friday or Saturday, now' (p. 222). The fact that the following chapter opens with the explicit announcement that 'Tuesday afternoon came, and waned to the twilight' accentuates the degree to which Tom and Becky no longer share in the novel's normal world of relaxed time-consciousness—especially since they are saved that very night, far sooner than Tom had expected. Moreover, their time-obsessed wait provokes, for the first time in the novel, the adverbial gesture that will become ubiquitous in the timeless narrative realm of *Huckleberry Finn*: 'By and by' (p. 220)—as if to register the shift from St Petersburg's mechanical clock-time to a temporal order far less tyrannical.

INTRODUCTION

As it happens, the cave enforces a disablingly timeless alternative to the timebound regularities of life in St Petersburg—an alternative from which Tom and Becky are all too happy to be rescued. Yet when Tom returns with a crowd to stare at a starved Injun Joe, the narrator breaks from his usual mode to describe a stalagmite near the corpse, and does so in terms quite unlike those invoked through the rest of the novel. The stalagmite was formed by slow drops:

that fell once in every three minutes with the dreary regularity of a clock-tick—a dessert-spoonful once in four-and-twenty hours. That drop was falling when the Pyramids were new; when Troy fell, when the foundations of Rome were laid, when Christ was crucified; when the Conqueror created the British Empire; when Columbus sailed; when the massacre at Lexington was 'news.' It is falling now; it will still be falling when all these things shall have sunk down the afternoon of history and the twilight of tradition, and been swallowed up in the thick night of oblivion. Has everything a purpose and a mission? (p. 228)

Here, for the only time in a novel set vaguely in 1844, where even the faintest direct allusion to ante-bellum events is never permitted, recorded history is formally, all too self-consciously invoked—and invoked in precisely the setting, the cave, where consciousness of time itself had been threateningly impaired. The passage is a strikingly 'eloquent' one, as Henry Nash Smith has observed, 'quite out of keeping with the tone of the book'.[17] And it serves a curious purpose, by paradoxically reinforcing the novel's ahistorical design through an invocation of history itself. The very listing of famous, remote incidents, so many over so long a term, renders the everyday processes of history irrelevant and the varied course of time moot. History, in other words (like religion and education), is invoked only to be suppressed.

This process of invocation and suppression corresponds once again to our conflicted sense of the novel: on the one hand, the

---

[17] Henry Nash Smith, *Mark Twain: The Development of a Writer* (Cambridge, Mass.: Harvard Univ. Press, 1962), 84.

timeless, lyrical quality of a narrative that self-consciously wants to immerse (at least, its male) readers in a dream of what childhood might have been like; on the other, the frequent assertions that events 'really' happened, and that readers will 'recall' them. The novel perpetually teeters on the border between time and timelessness, revealing a recurrent obsession with temporal succession that masks the desire to stand outside of time. At an authorial level, this reflects Mark Twain's own persistent imaginative fascination with the idea of extracting himself from history to stand outside of it—a fascination that led him later to experiment with time travel and dream narratives (something anticipated in Tom's extended conjecture that his experience in the abandoned house was a dream). At this point in his career, however, Mark Twain seems still to have been unself-conscious about the implications of his desire to locate a place in the past that transcended the strictures of time.

As most adult readers of *The Adventures of Tom Sawyer* have observed, usually to their dismay (surprised, perhaps, by rereading in eager expectation a text they had so much enjoyed as children), the contradictions and conflicts in this first attempt to deal with 'the matter of Hannibal' do not quite come off. Mark Twain, American humorist, had not yet become Mark Twain, major American author. In part, this was because he remained undecided about where he stood in regard to his past, and particularly, in regard to the patterns of speech he had learned as a child, and to the Southern mores imbibed with that speech. Such indecision would remain a notorious part of Twain's persona through his career, but it was especially disabling before he discovered the distinctive voice of *Huckleberry Finn*, and learnt how profoundly such a voice itself could embody both homage and critique.

Part of our problem as readers of *The Adventures of Tom Sawyer*, then—and a problem I've deliberately saved till now to discuss—is that it generated a sequel justifiably more famous than itself. *The Adventures of Huckleberry Finn* has attained a status as one of America's few literary classics, and its achievement insistently alters our response to the earlier novel. Indeed, only with difficulty can we catch a glimpse of *Tom Sawyer* that is not somehow altered by the prism of *Huckleberry Finn*. At times, straightforward borrowings from the first novel appear in the second, as in the exchange between Tom and Huck about 'orgies'—'What's orgies?' '*I* dono. But robbers always have orgies, and of course we've got to have them too' (p. 235)—an exchange that anticipates the Duke's more elaborately ludicrous explanation in *Huckleberry Finn*. More generally, the late dialogue in the first novel between Tom and Huck anticipates the conversational tone in the second novel between Huck and Jim—as when Tom exhaustively outlines the romantic logic of buried treasure to Huck, who responds with shrewd common sense (pp. 171–5).

Any such comparison, however, only reveals how far Mark Twain in *Tom Sawyer* had yet to go to achieve the voice, characterization, and moral drama of its sequel. Jim is still only 'a small coloured boy', not the compassionate man we know, and Huck's inquisitive, wide-eyed perspective has barely been tested. Even then, the conventional narrative works against his skewed point of view. When he admits to occasional meals with blacks—'A body's got to do things when he's awful hungry he wouldn't want to do as a steady thing' (p. 195)—the sentiment echoes many he will make in the later novel, but no context exists within which to read it here as narratively ironic rather than simply racist. Twain is only belatedly discovering the possibility of Huck's first-person voice, in the course of writing a novel about Tom Sawyer. In fact, only when Huck is left by himself to stand vigil at Injun Joe's tavern are we given a lingering view of the process of him 'communing with himself' (p. 200). And in the hair-raising episode in which he then tracks Injun Joe to the Widow Watson's, we begin to appreciate in Huck someone who can become more than a mere ancillary to Tom. He alone is able to turn from the narcissistic logic of St Petersburg, by refusing to allow himself to be defined through others' gaze. In so doing, he selects himself out for further narrative treatment. While the calm, third-person perspective of *Tom Sawyer* precludes any sense of psychological immediacy, any feeling of intimate involvement with Huck's point of view, already the possibilities of this compassionate river-rat's perspective is on display.

Tom Sawyer enjoys more popular attention than critical esteem, if only because it poses serious narrative problems that only eager readers can ignore. From a formal perspective, the novel fails as an integrated whole, divided as it is by multiple narrative pressures, conflicted voices, and ambiguous characterizations. Writing the novel allowed Mark Twain to see how just such an integration might be achieved in a very different kind of effort. Yet if the novel will always be seen as the prelude to a later masterpiece, it also stands on its own for reasons directly having to do with the problems it fails to resolve. The novel's extraordinary popularity—more than all but one of its successors—depends at least partly on the very contradictions apparent throughout, in voice, in character, and not least, in temporal theme. The continuing appeal of the book to readers, and perhaps especially young first-time readers, suggests moreover that its contradictions continue to be very much their (and our) own. To listen attentively to the diverse voices of this striking first novel requires more than just a sharp ear for humorous cadences and narrative insouciance. As in almost all his work, America's first author compels the reader to come to terms with the powerfully contested features he felt in American culture. And what particularly surprises those who return to the book as adults is how starkly he already does it in this, his first novel—the first of many he would write in order to transform his past, the first to make all readers feel, at least for the moment, American.

NOTE ON THE TEXT

INTERNAL manuscript evidence makes it clear that Mark Twain began work on *The Adventures of Tom Sawyer* early in 1873, with no clear idea of where it would end. Across the top of the first page, he scrawled an outline that would have taken Tom well beyond boyhood. After finishing more than a hundred pages, he set the manuscript aside in order to finish *The Gilded Age*. A long trip to England for lectures and sight-seeing prevented his completing any more work on the book until the following year. Resuming the project in February 1874, he kept more or less steadily at the novel until September, took a break for some months (in his customary pattern of writing), and started up again later in the year. By the following 5 July 1875, he could write from Hartford to his friend, William Dean Howells, that he had reached the end ('It is about 900 pages of MS., & may be 1000 when I shall have finished "working up" vague places. . . .').[1] About its genre, he was definite: 'It is *not* a boy's book at all. It will only be read by adults. It is only written for adults.'[2]

Howells offered to look at the novel, and late in October Twain sent on a corrected copy, which Howells quickly read and returned at the end of the year. He had made some minor stylistic suggestions, one large proposal for deleting the original last chapter (which would have detailed Huck Finn's life with Widow Douglas), and an earnest argument for publishing it as a boy's book. Twain accepted Howells's suggestions (which mostly involved altering improprieties and vulgar diction) as well as the generic classification of the book. In January 1876 he began arranging for publication and turned to the American Publishing Company of Hartford, Connecticut—who had published his earlier books—as well as commencing negotiations that would lead to an English

[1] *Mark Twain–Howells Letters*, 48.
[2] Ibid.

publisher: all in hopes of a mid-spring publication. Unfortunately, engraved illustrations for the American edition (among other matters) delayed its appearance until December, a full six months after Chatto and Windus had published the unillustrated English edition.

Howells's enthusiastic review of the book, intended to help American sales, appeared in May with the expectation of early publication, and had no effect on sales of the novel. Sales the first year, in fact, amounted to only 24,000 copies, and when Twain sailed with his family to Europe in April 1878, he left convinced that the novel had been a relative failure.

Of the two first editions of the novel, that with greater authority is the American, whose manuscript and copy-text are the basis for the authoritative text included in Volume 4 of *The Works of Mark Twain* (1980).

The present text has been reproduced directly from the Zodiac edition, published in 1962. Several small printer's errors have been silently corrected.

SELECT BIBLIOGRAPHY

Frederick Anderson (ed.), *Mark Twain: The Critical Heritage* (New York: Barnes & Noble, 1971).

Kenneth R. Andrews, *Nook Farm: Mark Twain's Hartford Circle* (Cambridge, Mass.: Harvard Univ. Press, 1950).

Paul Baender, 'Introduction' to *'The Adventures of Tom Sawyer' by Mark Twain; A Facsimile of the Author's Holograph Manuscript* (2 vols.; Washington, DC: Georgetown Univ. Library, 1982), i, pp. xi–xxxvi.

Walter Blair, 'On the Structure of *Tom Sawyer*', *Modern Philology*, 37 (1939), 75–88.

—— *Mark Twain and Huck Finn* (Berkeley and Los Angeles: Univ. of California Press, 1960).

Thomas Blues, 'The Strategies of Compromise in Mark Twain's "Boy Books" ', *Modern Fiction Studies*, 14 (1968), 21–31.

James Cox, *Mark Twain: The Fate of Humor* (Princeton, NJ: Princeton Univ. Press, 1966).

Bernard De Voto, *Mark Twain's America* (Cambridge: Houghton, 1932).

Owen Dudley Edwards, 'Mark Twain: Historian of a Lost World', in Tom Dunne (ed.), *The Writer as Witness: Literature as Historical Evidence* (Cork: Cork Univ. Press, 1987), 197–226.

Joseph J. Feeney, SJ, 'Darkness at Morning: The Bitterness in Mark Twain's Early Novel, *Tom Sawyer*', *Mark Twain Journal*, 19/3 (1979), 4–5.

Judith Fetterley, 'Mark Twain and the Anxiety of Entertainment', *Georgia Review*, 33 (1979), 382–91.

—— 'The Sanctioned Rebel', *Studies in the Novel*, 3 (1971), 294–304.

Leslie Fiedler, 'Duplicitous Mark Twain', *Commentary*, 29 (1960), 239–48.

—— *No! in Thunder: Essays on Myth and Literature* (Boston: Beacon, 1960).

John C. Gerber, 'Introduction', in *The Adventures of Tom Sawyer*, by Mark Twain. Volume 4 of *The Works of Mark Twain*, ed. John C. Gerber, Paul Baender, and Terry Firkins (Berkeley and Los Angeles: Univ. of California Press, 1980).

Hamlin Hill, 'The Composition and the Structure of *Tom Sawyer*', *American Literature*, 32 (1961), 379–92.

SELECT BIBLIOGRAPHY

John Hinz, 'Huck and Pluck: "Bad" Boys in American Fiction', *South Atlantic Quarterly*, 51 (1952), 120–9.

Jim Hunter, 'Mark Twain and the Boy-Book in 19th-Century America', *College English*, 24 (1963), 430–8.

James L. Johnson, *Mark Twain and the Limits of Power: Emerson's God in Ruins* (Knoxville: Univ. of Tennessee Press, 1982).

Kenneth Lynn, *Mark Twain and Southwestern Humor* (Boston: Little, Brown, 1959).

Thomas A. Maik, 'The Village in *Tom Sawyer*: Myth and Reality', *Arizona Quarterly*, 42 (1986), 157–64.

Barry A. Marks, 'Mark Twain's Hymn of Praise', *English Journal*, 48 (1959), 443–8.

Leo Marx, *The Machine in the Garden: Technology and the Pastoral Idea in America* (New York: Oxford, 1967).

Charles A. Norton, *Writing Tom Sawyer: The Adventures of a Classic* (Jefferson, NC: McFarland & Co, 1983).

George Orwell, (Eric Blair), 'Riding Down from Bangor', in *The Collected Essays, Journalism and Letters of George Orwell*, iv, ed. Sonia Orwell and Ian Angus, 2nd edn. (Harmondsworth: Penguin, 1970), 281–7.

Elizabeth G. Peck, 'Tom Sawyer: Character in Search of an Audience', *American Transcendental Quarterly* (September 1988), 223–36.

Robert Regan, *Unpromising Heroes: Mark Twain and His Characters* (Berkeley and Los Angeles: Univ. of California Press, 1966).

Forrest G. Robinson, 'Social Play and Bad Faith in *The Adventures of Tom Sawyer*', *Nineteenth-Century Fiction*, 39 (1984), 1–24.

Franklin Rogers, *Mark Twain's Burlesque Patterns as seen in the Novels and Narratives, 1855–1885* (Dallas: Southern Methodist Univ. Press, 1960).

Louis D. Rubin, 'Tom Sawyer and the Use of Novels', in *The Curious Death of the Novel* (Baton Rouge: Louisiana State Univ. Press, 1967).

John Seelye, 'What's in a Name: Sounding the Depths of *Tom Sawyer*', *Sewanee Review*, 90 (Summer 1982), 408–29.

Henry Nash Smith, *Mark Twain: The Development of a Writer* (Cambridge, Mass.: Harvard Univ. Press, 1962).

Albert E. Stone, Jr., *The Innocent Eye: Childhood in Mark Twain's Imagination* (New Haven, Conn.: Yale Univ. Press, 1961).

Tom H. Towers, ' "I Never Thought We Might Want to Come Back": Strategies of Transcendence in *Tom Sawyer*', *Modern Fiction Studies*, 21 (1975–6), 509–20.

SELECT BIBLIOGRAPHY

John S. Whitley, ' "Kids" Stuff: Mark Twain's Boys', in Robert Giddings (ed.), *Mark Twain: A Sumptuous Variety* (London: Vision, 1985), 72–5.

Cynthia Griffin Wolff, '*The Adventures of Tom Sawyer*: A Nightmare Vision of American Boyhood', *Massachusetts Review*, 21 (Winter 1980), 637–52.

A CHRONOLOGY OF
MARK TWAIN

1835   Samuel Langhorne Clemens, sixth child of John
        Marshall Clemens and Jane Lampton Clemens, born in
        Florida, Missouri, 30 November.

1839   Family moves to Hannibal, Missouri.

1847   Father dies; Samuel Clemens begins work as printer's
        apprentice, but continues schooling for two years.

1852   Publishes 'The Dandy Frightening the Squatter' in the
        Boston *Carpet Bag*; occasionally writes for his brother's
        newspaper.

1853–6 Leaves Hannibal to work as printer in St Louis, New
        York, Philadelphia, Keokuk (Iowa), and Cincinnati;
        occasional journalism.

1857–61 Steamboat pilot on Mississippi River.

1861   Brief service in Marion Rangers, a volunteer Confederate
        militia, before travelling to Nevada with his brother
        Orion. Tries prospecting.

1862–5 Reporter, writer of comic features for Nevada and San
        Francisco newspapers; adopted pseudonym 'Mark
        Twain'; published own version of folk tale, 'Jim Smiley
        and His Jumping Frog'.

1866   Travelling correspondent in Hawaiian Islands; began
        career as lecturer; travels to New York.

1867   Publishes *The Celebrated Jumping Frog of Calaveras County,
        and Other Sketches*; travelled to Europe and Holy Land as
        correspondent; lectures at Cooper Union (New York).

1869   *The Innocents Abroad* published.

1870   Marries Olivia Langdon; a son, Langdon, born.

1871   Settles in Hartford, Connecticut.

1872   Daughter, Susan, born; Langdon dies. *Roughing It*
        published.

1873   *The Gilded Age* (co-authored with Charles Dudley
        Warner) published.

1874	Daughter, Clara, born; new mansion in Hartford occupied.
1875	'Old Times on the Mississippi', series of seven articles, published in the *Atlantic Monthly*.
1876	*The Adventures of Tom Sawyer* published; begins work on *Adventures of Huckleberry Finn*.
1878–9	Travels in Europe.
1880	Jean, a daughter, born; *A Tramp Abroad* published.
1882	Revisited Mississippi River; published *The Prince and the Pauper*.
1883	*Life on the Mississippi* published.
1884–5	Lecture tour with George W. Cable; *Adventures of Huckleberry Finn* published (19 December 1884, in England and Canada; 18 February 1885, in United States).
1889	*A Connecticut Yankee in King Arthur's Court* published.
1894	*The Tragedy of Pudd'nhead Wilson* published; bankruptcy.
1895	Begins world lecture tour.
1896	Susan dies; *Personal Recollections of Joan of Arc* published.
1899	*The Man that Corrupted Hadleyburg* published.
1901	Receives honorary degree from Yale.
1904	Mrs Olivia Langdon Clemens dies.
1906	*What is Man?* privately printed.
1907	Awarded honorary degree from Oxford.
1908	Moves to Stormfield, Redding, Connecticut.
1909	Daughter Jean dies.
1910	Clemens dies on 10 April, in Redding.
1916	*The Mysterious Stranger* published.

The Adventures of
Tom Sawyer

Preface

MOST of the adventures recorded in this book really occurred; one or two were experiences of my own, the rest those of boys who were schoolmates of mine. Huck Finn is drawn from life; Tom Sawyer also, but not from an individual: he is a combination of the characteristics of three boys whom I knew, and therefore belongs to the composite order of architecture.

The odd superstitions touched upon were all prevalent among children and slaves in the West at the period of this story; that is to say, thirty or forty years ago.

Although my book is intended mainly for the entertainment of boys and girls, I hope it will not be shunned by men and women on that account, for part of my plan has been to try to pleasantly remind adults of what they once were themselves, and of how they felt and thought and talked, and what queer enterprises they sometimes engaged in.

THE AUTHOR

Contents

CONTENTS

CONTENTS

CHAPTER I

*Y-o-u-u Tom—Aunt Polly decides upon her
Duty—Tom practises Music—The Challenge—
A Private Entrance*

'Tom!'
No answer.
'Tom!'
No answer.
'What's gone with that boy, I wonder? You TOM!'

The old lady pulled her spectacles down and looked over them about the room; then she put them up and looked out under them. She seldom or never looked *through* them for so small a thing as a boy; they were her state pair, the pride of her heart, and were built for 'style', not service—she could have seen through a pair of stove-lids just as well. She looked perplexed for a moment, and then said, not fiercely, but still loud enough for the furniture to hear:

'Well, I lay if I get hold of you, I'll——'

She did not finish, for by this time she was bending down and punching under the bed with the broom, and so she needed breath to punctuate the punches with. She resurrected nothing but the cat.

'I never did see the beat of that boy!'

She went to the open door and stood in it, and looked out among the tomato vines and 'jimpson' weeds that constituted the garden. No Tom. So she lifted up her voice at an angle calculated for distance, and shouted:

'Y-o-u-u *Tom*!'

There was a slight noise behind her, and she turned just in

9

time to seize a small boy by the slack of his roundabout*and arrest his flight.

'There! I might 'a' thought of that closet. What you been doing in there?'

'Nothing.'

'Nothing! Look at your hands, and look at your mouth. What *is* that truck?'

'*I* don't know, aunt.'

'Well, *I* know. It's jam, that's what it is. Forty times I've said if you didn't let that jam alone I'd skin you. Hand me that switch.'

The switch hovered in the air—the peril was desperate.

'My! Look behind you, aunt!'

The old lady whirled round, and snatched her skirts out of danger. The lad fled, on the instant, scrambled up the high board-fence, and disappeared over it. His Aunt Polly stood surprised a moment, and then broke into a gentle laugh.

'Hang the boy, can't I never learn anything? Ain't he played me tricks enough like that for me to be looking out for him by this time? But old fools is the biggest fools there is. Can't learn an old dog new tricks, as the saying is. But my goodness, he never plays them alike two days, and how is a body to know what's coming? He 'pears to know just how long he can torment me before I get my dander up, and he knows if he can make out to put me off for a minute or make me laugh, it's all down again, and I can't hit him a lick. I ain't doing my duty by that boy, and that's the Lord's truth, goodness knows. Spare the rod and spile the child, as the Good Book says. I'm a-laying up sin and suffering for us both, *I* know. He's full of the Old Scratch*, but laws-a-me! he's my own dead sister's boy, poor thing, and I ain't got the heart to lash him, somehow. Every time I let him off my conscience does hurt me so; and every time I hit him my old heart most breaks. Well-a-well, man that is born of woman is of few days and full of trouble, as the Scripture says, and I reckon it's so. He'll play hookey this evening,[1] and I'll just be obleeged to make him work to-morrow, to punish him. It's mighty hard to make him work Saturdays, when all the boys is having holiday, but he hates work more than he hates anything else, and I've *got* to do some of my duty by him, or I'll be the ruination of the child.'

Tom did play hookey, and he had a very good time. He got back home barely in season to help Jim, the small coloured boy, saw next day's wood, and split the kindlings before supper—at least he was there in time to tell his adventures to Jim while Jim did three-fourths of the work. Tom's younger brother (or rather, half brother) Sid was already through with his part of the work (picking up chips), for he was a quiet boy, and had no adventurous, troublesome ways. While Tom was eating his supper and stealing sugar as opportunity offered, Aunt Polly asked him questions that were full of guile, and very deep—for she wanted to trap him into damaging revealments. Like many other simple-hearted souls, it was her pet vanity to believe she was endowed with a talent for dark and mysterious diplomacy, and she loved to contemplate her most transparent devices as marvels of low cunning. Said she:

'Tom, it was middling warm in school, warn't it?'

'Yes'm.'

'Powerful warm, warn't it?'

'Yes'm.'

'Didn't you want to go in a-swimming, Tom?'

A bit of a scare shot through Tom—a touch of uncomfortable suspicion. He searched Aunt Polly's face, but it told him nothing. So he said:

'No'm—well, not very much.'

The old lady reached out her hand and felt Tom's shirt, and said:

'But you ain't too warm now, though.' And it flattered her

[1] South-western for 'afternoon'.

to reflect that she had discovered that the shirt was dry without anybody knowing that that was what she had in her mind. But in spite of her, Tom knew where the wind lay now. So he forestalled what might be the next move.

'Some of us pumped on our heads—mine's damp yet. See?'

Aunt Polly was vexed to think she had overlooked that bit of circumstantial evidence, and missed a trick. Then she had a new inspiration:

'Tom, you didn't have to undo your shirt collar where I sewed it to pump on your head, did you? Unbutton your jacket!"

The trouble vanished out of Tom's face. He opened his jacket. His shirt collar was securely sewed.

'Bother! Well, go 'long with you. I made sure you'd played hookey and been a-swimming. But I forgive ye, Tom. I reckon you're a kind of a singed cat, as the saying is—better'n you look —*this* time.'

She was half sorry her sagacity had miscarried, and half glad that Tom had stumbled into obedient conduct for once.

But Sidney said:

'Well, now, if I didn't think you sewed his collar with white thread, but it's black.'

'Why, I did sew it with white! Tom!'

But Tom did not wait for the rest. As he went out at the door, he said:

'Siddy, I'll lick you for that.'

In a safe place Tom examined two large needles which were thrust into the lapels of his jacket—and had thread bound about them—one needle carried white thread and the other black. He said:

'She'd never noticed if it hadn't been for Sid. Confound it! sometimes she sews it with white, and sometimes she sews it with black. I wish to geeminy she'd stick to one or t'other— I can't keep the run of 'em. But I bet you I'll lam Sid for that. I'll learn him!'

He was not the Model Boy of the village. He knew the model boy well enough—and loathed him.

Within two minutes, or even less, he had forgotten all his troubles. Not because his troubles were one whit less heavy and bitter to him than a man's are to a man, but because a new and powerful interest bore them down and drove them out of his mind for the time—just as man's misfortunes are forgotten in the excitement of new enterprises. This new interest was a valued novelty in whistling, which he had just acquired from a negro, and he was suffering to practise it undisturbed. It consisted in a peculiar bird-like turn, a sort of liquid warble, produced by touching the tongue to the roof of the mouth at short intervals in the midst of the music. The reader probably remembers how to do it if he has ever been a boy. Diligence and attention soon gave him the knack of it, and he strode down the street with his mouth full of harmony and his soul full of gratitude. He felt much as an astronomer feels who has discovered a new planet. No doubt, as far as strong, deep, unalloyed pleasure is concerned, the advantage was with the boy, not the astronomer.

The summer evenings were long. It was not dark yet. Presently Tom checked his whistle. A stranger was before him— a boy a shade larger than himself. A newcomer of any age or either sex was an impressive curiosity in the poor little shabby village of St. Petersburg. This boy was well-dressed, too—well-dressed on a week-day. This was simply astounding. His cap was a dainty thing, his close-buttoned blue cloth roundabout was new and natty, and so were his pantaloons. He had shoes on—and yet it was only Friday. He even wore a necktie, a bright bit of ribbon. He had a citified air about him that ate into Tom's vitals. The more Tom stared at the splendid marvel, the higher he turned up his nose at his finery, and the shabbier and shabbier his own outfit seemed to him to grow. Neither boy spoke. If one moved, the other moved—but only sideways, in a circle; they

13

kept face to face and eye to eye all the time. Finally, Tom said:

'I can lick you!'

'I'd like to see you try it.'

'Well, I can do it.'

'No, you can't, either.'

'Yes, I can.'

'No, you can't.'

'I can.'

'You can't.'

'Can.'

'Can't.'

An uncomfortable pause. Then Tom said:

'What's your name?'

''Tisn't any of your business, maybe.'

'Well, I 'low I'll *make* it my business.'

'Well, why don't you?'

'If you say much I will.'

'Much—much—*much*! There, now.'

'Oh, you think you're mighty smart, *don't* you? I could lick you with one hand tied behind me, if I wanted to.'

'Well, why don't you *do* it! You *say* you can do it.'

'Well, *I will*, if you fool with me.'

'Oh, yes—I've seen whole families in the same fix.'

'Smarty! You think you're *some* now, *don't* you? Oh, what a hat!'

'You can lump that hat if you don't like it. I dare you to knock it off; and anybody that'll take a dare will suck eggs.'

'You're a liar!'

'You're another!'

'You're a fighting liar, and dasn't take it up.'

'Aw—take a walk!'

'Say—if you give me much more of your sass, I'll take and bounce a rock off'n your head.'

'Oh, of *course* you will.'

'Well, I *will*.'

'Well, why don't you *do* it, then? What do you keep *saying* you will for? Why don't you *do* it? It's because you're afraid.'

'I *ain't* afraid.'

'You are.'

'I ain't.'

'You are.'

Another pause, and more eyeing and sidling around each other. Presently they were shoulder to shoulder. Tom said:

'Get away from here!'

'Go away yourself!'

'I won't.'

'*I* won't either.'

So they stood, each with a foot placed at an angle as a brace, and both shoving with might and main, and glowering at each other with hate. But neither could get an advantage. After struggling till both were hot and flushed, each relaxed his strain with watchful caution, and Tom said:

'You're a coward and a pup. I'll tell my big brother on you, and he can thrash you with his little finger, and I'll make him do it, too.'

'What do I care for your big brother? I've got a brother that's bigger than he is; and, what's more, he can throw him over that fence, too.' [Both brothers were imaginary.]

'That's a lie.'

'*Your* saying so don't make it so.'

Tom drew a line in the dust with his big toe, and said:

'I dare you to step over that, and I'll lick you till you can't stand up. Anybody that'll take a dare will steal sheep.'

The new boy stepped over promptly, and said:

'Now you said you'd do it, now let's see you do it.'

'Don't you crowd me, now; you better look out.'

'Well, you *said* you'd do it—why don't you do it?'

'By jingo! for two cents I *will* do it.'

The new boy took two broad coppers out of his pocket, and held them out with derision. Tom struck them to the ground. In an instant both boys were rolling and tumbling in the dirt, gripped together like cats; and for the space of a minute they tugged and tore at each other's hair and clothes, punched and scratched each other's noses, and covered themselves with dust and glory. Presently the confusion took form, and through the fog of battle Tom appeared, seated astride the new boy, and pounding him with his fists.

'Holler 'nuff!' said he.

The boy only struggled to free himself. He was crying—mainly from rage.

'Holler 'nuff!'—and the pounding went on.

At last the stranger got out a smothered ''Nuff!' and Tom let him up, and said:

'Now that'll learn you. Better look out who you're fooling with next time.'

The new boy went off brushing the dust from his clothes, sobbing, snuffling, and occasionally looking back and shaking his head, and threatening what he would do to Tom the 'next time he caught him out'. To which Tom responded with jeers, and started off in high feather; and as soon as his back was turned the new boy snatched up a stone, threw it, and hit him between the shoulders, and then turned tail and ran like an antelope. Tom chased the traitor home, and thus found out where he lived. He then held a position at the gate for some time, daring the enemy to come outside; but the enemy only made faces at him through the window, and declined. At last the enemy's mother appeared, and called Tom a bad, vicious, vulgar child, and ordered him away. So he went away, but he said he ''lowed' to 'lag' for that boy.

He got home pretty late that night, and when he climbed

cautiously in at the window, he uncovered an ambuscade in the person of his aunt; and when she saw the state his clothes were in, her resolution to turn his Saturday holiday into captivity at hard labour became adamantine in its firmness.

CHAPTER II

Strong Temptations—Strategic Movements—The Innocents beguiled

SATURDAY morning was come, and all the summer world was bright and fresh, and brimming with life. There was a song in every heart; and if the heart was young the music issued at the lips. There was cheer in every face, and a spring in every step. The locust trees were in bloom, and the fragrance of the blossoms filled the air. Cardiff Hill, beyond the village and above it, was green with vegetation, and it lay just far enough away to seem a Delectable Land, dreamy, reposeful, and inviting.

Tom appeared on the side-walk with a bucket of whitewash and a long-handled brush. He surveyed the fence, and all gladness left him, and a deep melancholy settled down upon his spirits Thirty yards of board-fence nine feet high! Life to him seemed hollow, and existence but a burden. Sighing he dipped his brush and passed it along the topmost plank; repeated the operation; did it again; compared the insignificant whitewashed streak with the far-reaching continent of unwhitewashed fence, and sat down on a tree-box discouraged. Jim came skipping out at the gate with a tin pail, and singing 'Buffalo Gals'.* Bringing water from the town pump had always been hateful work in Tom's eyes before, but now it did not strike him so. He remembered that there was company at the pump. White, mulatto, and negro boys and girls were always there waiting their turns, resting, trading playthings, quarrelling, fighting, skylarking. And he remembered that although the pump was only a hundred and fifty yards off, Jim never got back with a bucket of water under an hour;

and even then somebody generally had to go after him: Tom said:

'Say, Jim; I'll fetch the water if you'll whitewash some.'

Jim shook his head and said:

'Can't, Mars Tom. Ole missis, she tole me I got to go an' git dis water an' not stop foolin' roun' wid anybody. She say she spec' Mars Tom gwine to ax me to whitewash, an' so she tole me go 'long an' 'tend to my own business—she 'lowed *she'd* 'tend to de whitewashin'.'

'Oh, never you mind what she said, Jim. That's the way she always talks. Gimme the bucket—I won't be gone only a minute. *She* won't ever know.'

'Oh, I dasn't, Mars Tom. Ole missis she'd take an' tar de head off'n me. 'Deed she would.'

'*She!* She never licks anybody—whacks 'em over the head with her thimble, and who cares for that, I'd like to know? She talks awful, but talk don't hurt—anyways, it don't if she don't cry. Jim, I'll give you a marvel.* I'll give you a white alley!'*

Jim began to waver.

'White alley, Jim! And it's a bully taw.'*

'My! Dat's a mighty gay marvel, *I* tell you! But, Mars Tom, I's powerful 'fraid ole missis——'

'And besides, if you will I'll show you my sore toe.'

Jim was only human—this attraction was too much for him. He put down his pail, took the white alley, and bent over the toe with absorbing interest while the bandage was being unwound. In another moment he was flying down the street with his pail and a tingling rear, Tom was whitewashing with vigour, and Aunt Polly was retiring from the field with a slipper in her hand and triumph in her eye.

But Tom's energy did not last. He began to think of the fun he had planned for this day, and his sorrows multiplied. Soon the free boys would come tripping along on all sorts of delicious expeditions, and they would make a world of fun of him for having to work—the very thought of it burnt him like fire. He got out his worldly wealth and examined it—bits of toys, marbles and trash; enough to buy an exchange of *work*, maybe, but not half enough to buy so much as half an hour of pure freedom. So he returned his straitened means to his pocket, and gave up the idea of trying to buy the boys. At this dark and hopeless moment an inspiration burst upon him! Nothing less than a great, magnificent inspiration.

He took up his brush and went tranquilly to work. Ben Rogers hove in sight presently—the very boy, of all boys, whose ridicule he had been dreading. Ben's gait was the hop-skip-and-jump—proof enough that his heart was light and his anticipations high. He was eating an apple, and giving a long, melodious whoop at intervals, followed by a deep-toned ding-dong-dong, ding-dong-dong, for he was personating a steamboat. As he drew near he slackened speed, took the middle of the street, leaned far over to starboard, and rounded-to ponderously and with laborious pomp and circumstance—for he was personating the 'Big Missouri,' and considered himself to be drawing nine feet of water. He was boat, and captain, and engine-bells combined, so he had to imagine himself standing on his own hurricane deck giving the orders and executing them:

'Stop her, sir! Ting-a-ling-ling.' The headway ran almost out, and he drew up slowly toward the sidewalk.

'Ship up to back! Ting-a-ling-ling!' His arms straightened and stiffened down his sides.

'Set her back on the stabboard! Ting-a-ling-ling! Chow! ch-chow-wow! Chow!' His right hand meantime describing stately circles, for it was representing a forty-foot wheel.

'Let her go back on the labboard! Ting-a-ling-ling! Chow-ch-chow-chow!' The left hand began to describe circles.

'Stop the stabboard! Ting-a-ling-ling! Stop the labboard! Come ahead on the stabboard! Stop her! Let your outside turn over slow! Ting-a-ling-ling! Chow-ow-ow! Get out that head-line! *Lively*, now! Come—out with your spring-line—what're you about there? Take a turn round that stump with the bight of it! Stand by that stage now—let her go! Done with the engines, sir! Ting-a-ling-ling! *Sh't! s'h't! sh't!'* (trying the gauge-cocks).

Tom went on whitewashing—paid no attention to the steam-boat. Ben stared a moment, and then said:

'Hi-*yi*! *You're* up a stump, ain't you?'

No answer. Tom surveyed his last touch with the eye of an artist; then he gave his brush another gentle sweep, and surveyed the result, as before. Ben ranged up alongside of him. Tom's mouth watered for the apple, but he stuck to his work. Ben said:

'Hello, old chap; you got to work, hey?'

Tom wheeled suddenly and said:

'Why, it's you. Ben! I warn't noticing.'

'Say—*I'm* going in a-swimming, *I* am. Don't you wish you could? But of course you'd druther *work*—wouldn't you? Course you would!'

Tom contemplated the boy a bit, and said:

'What do you call work?'

'Why, ain't *that* work?'

Tom resumed his whitewashing, and answered carelessly:

'Well, maybe it is, and maybe it ain't. All I know is, it suits Tom Sawyer.'

'Oh, come now, you don't mean to let on that you *like* it?'

The brush continued to move.

'Like it? Well, I don't see why I oughtn't to like it. Does a boy get a chance to whitewash a fence every day?'

That put the thing in a new light. Ben stopped nibbling his apple. Tom swept his brush daintily back and forth—stepped back to note the effect—added a touch here and there—criticized the effect again—Ben watching every move, and getting more and more interested, more and more absorbed.

21

Presently he said: 'Say, Tom, let *me* whitewash a little.'

Tom considered—was about to consent; but he altered his mind:

'No, no; I reckon it wouldn't hardly do, Ben. You see, Aunt Polly's awful particular about this fence—right here on the street, you know—but if it was the back fence I wouldn't mind, and *she* wouldn't. Yes, she's awful particular about this fence; it's got to be done very careful; I reckon there ain't one boy in a thousand, maybe two thousand, that can do it the way it's got to be done.'

'No—is that so? Oh, come now; lemme just try, only just a little. I'd let *you*, if you was me, Tom.'

'Ben, I'd like to, honest Injun; but Aunt Polly—well, Jim wanted to do it, but she wouldn't let him. Sid wanted to do it, and she wouldn't let Sid. Now, don't you see how I'm fixed? If you was to tackle this fence, and anything was to happen to it——'

'Oh, shucks; I'll be just as careful. Now lemme try. Say—I'll give you the core of my apple.'

'Well, here—No, Ben; now don't; I'm afeard——'

'I'll give you *all* of it!'

Tom gave up the brush with reluctance in his face but alacrity in his heart. And while the late steamer 'Big Missouri' worked and sweated in the sun, the retired artist sat on a barrel in the shade close by, dangled his legs, munched his apple, and planned the slaughter of more innocents. There was no lack of material; boys happened along every little while; they came to jeer, but remained to whitewash.* By the time Ben was fagged out, Tom had traded the next chance to Billy Fisher for a kite, in good repair; and when *he* played out, Johnny Miller bought in for a dead rat and a string to swing it with; and so on, and so on, hour after hour. And when the middle of the afternoon came, from being a poor poverty-stricken boy in the morning, Tom was literally rolling in wealth. He had, beside the things before mentioned, twelve marbles, part of a jew's-harp, a piece of blue bottle-glass to look through, a spool-cannon,* a key that wouldn't unlock anything, a fragment of chalk, a glass stopper of a decanter, a tin soldier, a couple of tadpoles, six fire-crackers, a kitten with only one eye, a brass door-knob, a dog-collar—but no dog—the handle of a knife, four pieces of orange-peel, and a dilapidated old window-sash. He had had a nice, good, idle time all the while—plenty of company—and the fence had three coats of whitewash on it! If he hadn't run out of whitewash, he would have bankrupted every boy in the village.

Tom said to himself that it was not such a hollow world, after all. He had discovered a great law of human action, without knowing it—namely, that in order to make a man or a boy covet a thing, it is only necessary to make the thing difficult to attain. If he had been a great and wise philosopher, like the writer of this book, he would now have comprehended that Work consists of whatever a body is *obliged* to do, and that Play consists of whatever a body is not obliged to do. And this would help him to understand why constructing artificial flowers or performing on a treadmill is work, while rolling ten-pins or climbing Mont Blanc is only amusement. There are wealthy gentlemen in England who drive four-horse passenger-coaches twenty or thirty miles on a daily line in the summer, because the privilege costs them considerable money; but if they were offered wages for the service, that would turn it into work, and then they would resign.

The boy mused a while over the substantial change which had taken place in his worldly circumstances, and then wended toward head-quarters to report.

23

CHAPTER III

Tom as a General—Triumph and Reward— Dismal Felicity—Commission and Omission

TOM presented himself before Aunt Polly, who was sitting by an open window in a pleasant rearward apartment, which was bedroom, breakfast-room, dining-room, and library combined. The balmy summer air, the restful quiet, the odour of the flowers, and the drowsing murmur of the bees, had had their effect, and she was nodding over her knitting— for she had no company but the cat, and it was asleep in her lap. Her spectacles were propped up on her grey head for safety. She had thought that of course Tom had deserted long ago, and she wondered at seeing him place himself in her power again in this intrepid way. He said:

'Mayn't I go and play now, aunt?'

'What, a'ready? How much have you done?'

'It's all done, aunt.'

'Tom, don't lie to me—I can't bear it.'

'I ain't, aunt; it *is* all done.'

Aunt Polly placed small trust in such evidence. She went out to see for herself; and she would have been content to find twenty per cent. of Tom's statement true. When she found the entire fence whitewashed, and not only whitewashed but elaborately coated and re-coated, and even a streak added to the ground, her astonishment was almost unspeakable. She said:

'Well, I never! There's no getting round it: you *can* work when you're a mind to, Tom.' And then she diluted the compliment by adding, 'But it's powerful seldom you're a mind to,

I'm bound to say. Well, go 'long and play; but mind you get back sometime in a week, or I'll tan you.'

She was so overcome by the splendour of his achievement that she took him into the closet and selected a choice apple, and delivered it to him, along with an improving lecture upon the added value and flavour a treat took to itself when it came without sin through virtuous effort. And while she closed with a happy Scriptural flourish, he 'hooked' a doughnut.

Then he skipped out, and saw Sid just starting up the outside stairway that led to the back rooms on the second floor. Clods were handy, and the air was full of them in a twinkling. They raged around Sid like a hailstorm; and before Aunt Polly could collect her surprised faculties and sally to the rescue, six or seven clods had taken personal effect, and Tom was over the fence and gone. There was a gate, but as a general thing he was too crowded for time to make use of it. His soul was at peace, now that he had settled with Sid for calling attention to his black thread and getting him into trouble.

Tom skirted the block, and came round into a muddy alley that led by the back of his aunt's cow stable. He presently got safely beyond the reach of capture and punishment, and hasted towards the public square of the village, where two 'military' companies of boys had met for conflict, according to previous appointment. Tom was General of one of these armies, Joe Harper (a bosom friend) General of the other. These two great commanders did not condescend to fight in person—that being better suited to the still smaller fry—but sat together on an eminence and conducted the field operations by orders delivered through aides-de-camp. Tom's army won a great victory, after a long and hardfought battle. Then the dead were counted, prisoners exchanged, the terms of the next disagreement agreed upon, and the day for the necessary battle appointed; after which the armies fell into line and marched away, and Tom turned homeward alone.

As he was passing by the house where Jeff Thatcher lived, he saw a new girl in the garden—a lovely little blue-eyed creature with yellow hair plaited into two long tails, white summer frock, and embroidered pantalettes. The fresh-crowned hero fell without firing a shot. A certain Amy Lawrence vanished out of his heart, and left not even a memory of herself behind. He had thought he loved her to distraction; he had regarded his passion as adoration; and behold it was only a poor little evanescent partiality. He had been months winning her, she had confessed hardly a week ago; he had been the happiest and the proudest boy in the world only seven short days, and here, in one instant of time, she had gone out of his heart like a casual stranger whose visit is done.

He worshipped this new angel with furtive eye, till he saw that she had discovered him; then he pretended he did not know she was present, and began to 'show off' in all sorts of absurd boyish ways, in order to win her admiration. He kept up this grotesque foolishness for some time; but by and by, while he was in the midst of some dangerous gymnastic performances, he glanced aside, and saw that the little girl was wending her way towards the house. Tom came up to the fence, and leaned on it, grieving, and hoping she would tarry yet a while longer. She halted a moment on the steps, and then moved towards the door. Tom heaved a great sigh as she put her foot on the threshold; but his face lit up, right away, for she tossed a pansy over the fence a moment before she disappeared.

The boy ran around and stopped within a foot or two of the flower, and then shaded his eyes with his hand, and began to look down street as if he had discovered something of interest going on in that direction. Presently he picked up a straw and began trying to balance it on his nose, with his head tilted far back; and as he moved from side to side in his efforts he edged nearer and nearer towards the pansy; finally his bare foot rested upon it, his pliant toes closed upon it, and he hopped away with the treasure, and disappeared round the corner. But only for a minute—only while he could button the flower inside his jacket, next his heart, or next his stomach possibly, for he was not much posted in anatomy and not hypercritical anyway.

He returned now and hung about the fence till nightfall, 'showing off' as before; but the girl never exhibited herself again, though Tom comforted himself a little with the hope that she had been near some window meantime, and been aware of his attentions. Finally, he rode home reluctantly, with his poor head full of visions.

All through supper his spirits were so high that his aunt wondered 'what had got into the child'. He took a good scolding about clodding Sid, and did not seem to mind it in the least. He tried to steal sugar under his aunt's very nose, and got his knuckles rapped for it. He said:

'Aunt, you don't whack Sid when he takes it.'

'Well, Sid don't torment a body the way you do. You'd be always into the sugar if I warn't watching you.'

Presently she stepped into the kitchen, and Sid, happy in his immunity, reached for the sugar-bowl—a sort of glorying over Tom which was well-nigh unbearable. But Sid's fingers slipped, and the bowl dropped and broke. Tom was in ecstasies—in such ecstasies that he even controlled his tongue and was silent. He said to himself that he would not speak a word, even when his aunt came in, but would sit perfectly still till she asked who did the mischief; and then he would tell, and there would be nothing so good in the world as to see the pet model 'catch it'. He was so brimful of exultation that he could hardly hold himself when the old lady came back and stood above the wreck discharging lightnings of wrath from over her spectacles. He said to himself, 'Now it's coming!' And the next instant he was sprawling on the floor! The potent palm was uplifted to strike again, when Tom cried out:

'Hold on, now, what're you belting *me* for? Sid broke it!'

Aunt Polly paused, perplexed, and Tom looked for healing pity. But when she got her tongue again she only said:

'Umf! Well, you didn't get a lick amiss, I reckon. You been into some other audacious mischief when I wasn't around, like enough.'

Then her conscience reproached her, and she yearned to say something kind and loving; but she judged that this would be construed into a confession that she had been in the wrong, and discipline forbade that. So she kept silence, and went about her affairs with a troubled heart. Tom sulked in a corner, and exalted his woes. He knew that in her heart his aunt was on her knees to him, and he was morosely gratified by the consciousness of it. He would hang out no signals, he would take notice of none. He knew that a yearning glance fell upon him, now and then, through a film of tears, but he refused recognition of it. He pictured himself lying sick unto death and his aunt bending over him, beseeching one little forgiving word, but he would turn his face to the wall, and die with that word unsaid. Ah, how would she feel then? And he pictured himself brought home from the river, dead, with his curls all wet, and his sore heart at rest. How she would throw herself upon him, and how her tears would fall like rain, and her lips pray God to give her back her boy, and she would never, never abuse him any more! But he would lie there cold and white and make no sign—a poor little sufferer, whose griefs were at an end. He so worked upon his feelings with the pathos of these dreams that he had to keep swallowing—he was so like to choke; and his eyes swam in a blur of water, which overflowed when he winked, and ran down and trickled from the end of his nose. And such a luxury to him was this petting of his sorrows, that he could not bear to have any worldly cheeriness or any grating delight intrude upon it; it was too sacred for such contact; and so presently, when his cousin Mary danced in, all alive with the joy of seeing home again after an age-long visit of one week to the country, he got up and moved in clouds and darkness out at one door as she brought song and sunshine in at the other.

He wandered far from the accustomed haunts of boys, and sought desolate places that were in harmony with his spirit. A log raft in the river invited him, and he seated himself on its outer edge, and contemplated the dreary vastness of the stream, wishing the while that he could only be drowned, all at once and unconsciously, without undergoing the uncomfortable routine devised by nature. Then he thought of his flower. He got it out, rumpled and wilted, and it mightily increased his dismal felicity. He wondered if *she* would pity him if she knew? Would she cry, and wish that she had a right to put her arms around his neck and comfort him? Or would she turn coldly away like all the hollow world? This picture brought such an agony of pleasurable suffering that he worked it over and over again in his mind, and set it up in new and varied lights, till he wore it threadbare. At last he rose up sighing, and departed in the darkness.

About half-past nine or ten o'clock he came along the deserted street to where the Adored Unknown lived; he paused a moment, no sound fell upon his listening ear; a candle was casting a dull glow upon the curtain of a second-story window. Was the sacred presence there? He climbed the fence, threaded his stealthy way through the plants, till he stood under that window; he looked up at it long, and with emotion; then he laid him down on the ground under it, disposing himself upon his back, with his hands clasped upon his breast, and holding his poor wilted flower. And thus he would die—out in the cold world, with no shelter over his homeless head, no friendly hand to wipe the death-damps from his brow, no loving face to bend pityingly over him when the great agony came. And thus *she* would see him when she looked out upon the glad morning— and oh! would she drop one little tear upon his poor, lifeless form, would she heave one little sigh to see a bright young life so rudely blighted, so untimely cut down?

The window went up; a maid-servant's discordant voice profaned the holy calm, and a deluge of water drenched the prone martyr's remains!

The strangling hero sprang up with a relieving snort; there was a whiz as of a missile in the air, mingled with the murmur of a curse, a sound as of shivering glass followed, and a small, vague form went over the fence and shot away in the gloom.

Not long after, as Tom, all undressed for bed, was surveying his drenched garments by the light of a tallow dip, Sid woke up; but if he had any dim idea of making any 'references to allusions', he thought better of it, and held his peace—for there was danger in Tom's eye.

Tom turned in without the added vexation of prayers, and Sid made mental note of the omission.

CHAPTER IV

Mental Acrobatics—Attending Sunday School—
The Superintendent—'Showing off'—Tom lionized

T HE sun rose upon a tranquil world, and beamed down
upon the peaceful village like a benediction. Breakfast
over, Aunt Polly had family worship; it began with a
prayer built from the ground up of solid courses of Scriptural
quotations, welded together with a thin mortar of originality;
and from the summit of this she delivered a grim chapter of the
Mosaic Law, as from Sinai.

Then Tom girded up his loins, so to speak, and went to work
to 'get his verses'. Sid had learned his lesson days before. Tom
bent all his energies to the memorising of five verses; and he
chose part of the Sermon on the Mount, because he could find
no verses that were shorter. At the end of half an hour, Tom
had a vague general idea of his lesson, but no more, for his mind
was traversing the whole field of human thought, and his hands
were busy with distracting recreations. Mary took his book to
hear him recite, and he tried to find his way through the fog.

'Blessed are the*—a—a———'

'Poor———'

'Yes—poor; blessed are the poor—a—a———'

'In spirit———'

'In spirit; blessed are the poor in spirit, for they—they———'

'Theirs———'

'For *theirs*. Blessed are the poor in spirit, for *theirs*—is the
kingdom of heaven. Blessed are they that mourn, for they—
they———'

'Sh———'

'For they—a——'

'S, H, A——'

'For they S, H—— Oh, I don't know what it is!'

'*Shall!*'

'Oh, *shall*! for they shall—for they shall—a—a—shall mourn —a—a—blessed are they that shall—they that—a—they that shall mourn, for they shall—a—shall *what*? Why don't you tell me, Mary?—what do you want to be so mean for?'

'Oh, Tom, you poor, thick-headed thing, I'm not teasing you. I wouldn't do that. You must go and learn it again. Don't you be discouraged, Tom, you'll manage it—and if you do, I'll give you something ever so nice. There, now, that's a good boy.'

'All right! What is it, Mary? tell me what it is.'

'Never you mind, Tom. You know if I say it's nice, it *is* nice.'

'You bet you that's so, Mary. All right, I'll tackle it again.'

And he did 'tackle it again'; and under the double pressure of curiosity and prospective gain, he did it with such spirit that he accomplished a shining success. Mary gave him a brand-new 'Barlow' knife, worth twelve and a half cents; and the convulsion of delight that swept his system shook him to his foundations. True, the knife would not cut anything, but it was a 'sure enough' Barlow, and there was inconceivable grandeur in that —though where the western boys ever got the idea that such a weapon would possibly be counterfeited to its injury is an imposing mystery, and will always remain so, perhaps. Tom contrived to scarify the cupboard with it, and was arranging to begin on the bureau, when he was called off to dress for Sunday-school.

Mary gave him a tin basin of water and a piece of soap, and he went outside the door and set the basin on a little bench there; then he dipped the soap in the water and laid it down; turned up his sleeves; poured out the water on the ground

32

gently, and then entered the kitchen, and began to wipe his face diligently on the towel behind the door. But Mary removed the towel and said:

'Now ain't you ashamed, Tom? You mustn't be so bad. Water won't hurt you.'

Tom was a trifle disconcerted. The basin was refilled, and this time he stood over it a little while, gathering resolution; took in a big breath and began. When he entered the kitchen presently, with both eyes shut and groping for the towel with his hands, an honourable testimony of suds and water was dripping from his face. But when he emerged from the towel he was not yet satisfactory, for the clean territory stopped short at his chin and his jaws like a mask; below and beyond this line there was a dark expanse of unirrigated soil that spread downward in front and backward around his neck. Mary took him in hand, and when she was done with him he was a man and a brother, without distinction of colour, and his saturated hair was neatly brushed, and its short curls wrought into a dainty and symmetrical general effect. (He privately smoothed out the curls, with labour and difficulty, and plastered his hair close down to his head; for he held curls to be effeminate, and his own filled his life with bitterness.) Then Mary got out a suit of his clothing that had been used only on Sundays during two years—they were simply called his 'other clothes'—and so by that we know the size of his wardrobe. The girl 'put him to rights' after he had dressed himself; she buttoned his neat roundabout up to his chin, turned his vast shirt-collar down over his shoulders, brushed him off, and crowned him with his speckled hat. He now looked exceedingly improved and uncomfortable. He was fully as uncomfortable as he looked; for there was a restraint about whole clothes and cleanliness that galled him. He hoped that Mary would forget his shoes, but the hope was blighted; she coated them thoroughly with tallow, as was the custom, and brought them out. He lost his temper, and said he was always being made to do everything he didn't want to do. But Mary said persuasively:

'Please, Tom—that's a good boy.'

So he got into his shoes, snarling. Mary was soon ready, and the three children set out for Sunday-school, a place that Tom hated with his whole heart; but Sid and Mary were fond of it.

Sabbath-school hours were from nine to half-past ten; and then church service. Two of the children always remained for the sermon voluntarily; and the other always remained, too—for stronger reasons. The church's high-backed uncushioned pews would seat about three hundred persons; the edifice was but a small, plain affair, with a sort of pine-board tree-box on top of it for a steeple. At the door Tom dropped back a step and accosted a Sunday-dressed comrade:

'Say, Bill, got a yaller ticket?'

'Yes.'

'What'll you take for her?'

'What'll you give?'

'Piece of lickrish and a fish-hook.'

'Less see 'em.'

Tom exhibited. They were satisfactory, and the property changed hands. Then Tom traded a couple of white alleys for three red tickets, and some small trifle or other for a couple of blue ones. He waylaid other boys as they came, and went on buying tickets of various colours ten or fifteen minutes longer. He entered the church, now, with a swarm of clean and noisy boys and girls, proceeded to his seat and started a quarrel with the first boy that came handy. The teacher, a grave, elderly man, interfered; then turned his back a moment, and Tom pulled a boy's hair in the next bench, and was absorbed in his book when the boy turned around; stuck a pin in another boy, presently, in order to hear him say 'Ouch!' and got a new reprimand from his teacher. Tom's whole class were of a pattern—restless, noisy, and troublesome. When they came to recite their lessons, not one of them knew his verses perfectly, but had to be prompted all along. However, they worried through, and each got his reward in small blue tickets, each with a passage of Scripture on it; each blue ticket was pay for two verses of the recitation. Ten blue tickets equalled a red one, and could be exchanged for it; ten red tickets equalled a yellow one; for ten yellow tickets the Superintendent gave a very plainly bound Bible (worth forty cents in those easy times) to the pupil. How many of my readers would have the industry and application to memorise two thousand verses, even for a Doré Bible?*And yet Mary had acquired two Bibles in this way; it was the patient work of two years: and a boy of German parentage had won four or five. He once recited three thousand verses without stopping; but the strain upon his mental faculties was too great, and he was little better than an idiot from that day forth—a grievous misfortune for the school, for on great occasions before company, the Superintendent (as Tom expressed it) had always made this boy come out and 'spread himself'. Only the older pupils managed to keep their tickets and stick to their tedious work long enough to get a Bible, and so the delivery of one of these prizes was a rare and noteworthy circumstance; the successful pupil was so great and conspicuous for that day that on the spot every scholar's heart was fired with a fresh ambition that often lasted a couple of weeks. It is possible that Tom's mental stomach had never really hungered for one of those prizes, but unquestionably his entire being had for many a day longed for the glory and the *éclat* that came with it.

In due course the Superintendent stood up in front of the pulpit, with a closed hymn-book in his hand and his forefinger inserted between its leaves, and commanded attention. When a Sunday-school superintendent makes his customary little speech, a hymn-book in the hand is as necessary as is the inevitable sheet of music in the hand of a singer who stands forward on the platform and sings a solo at a concert—though why is a mystery;

for neither the hymn-book nor the sheet of music is ever referred to by the sufferer. This superintendent was a slim creature of thirty-five, with a sandy goatee, and short sandy hair; he wore a stiff standing-collar whose upper edge almost reached his ears, and whose sharp points curved forward abreast the corners of his mouth—a fence that compelled a straight look-out ahead, and a turning of the whole body when a side view was required. His chin was propped on a spreading cravat, which was as broad and as long as a bank-note, and had fringed ends; his boot toes were turned sharply up, in the fashion of the day, like sleigh-runners—an effect patiently and laboriously produced by the young men by sitting with their toes pressed against a wall for hours together. Mr. Walters was very earnest of mien, and very sincere and honest at heart; and he held sacred things and places in such reverence, and so separated them from worldly matters, that unconsciously to himself his Sunday-school voice had acquired a peculiar intonation which was wholly absent on weekdays. He began after this fashion:

'Now, children, I want you all to sit up just as straight and pretty as you can, and give me all your attention for a minute or two. There, that is it. That is the way good little boys and girls should do. I see one little girl who is looking out of the window—I am afraid she thinks I am out there somewhere—perhaps up in one of the trees making a speech to the little birds. [Applausive titter.] I want to tell you how good it makes me feel to see so many bright, clean little faces assembled in a place like this, learning to do right and be good.'

And so forth, and so on. It is not necessary to set down the rest of the oration. It was of a pattern which does not vary, and so it is familiar to us all.

The latter third of the speech was marred by the resumption of fights and other recreations among certain of the bad boys, and by fidgetings and whisperings that extended far and wide, washing even to the bases of isolated and incorruptible rocks like

Sid and Mary. But now every sound ceased suddenly with the subsidence of Mr. Walters' voice, and the conclusion of the speech was received with a burst of silent gratitude.

A good part of the whispering had been occasioned by an event which was more or less rare—the entrance of visitors; Lawyer Thatcher, accompanied by a very feeble and aged man, a fine, portly, middle-aged gentleman with iron-grey hair, and a dignified lady who was doubtless the latter's wife. The lady was leading a child. Tom had been restless and full of chafings and repinings, conscience-smitten, too—he could not meet Amy Lawrence's eye, he could not brook her loving gaze. But when he saw this small new-comer his soul was all ablaze with bliss in a moment. The next moment he was 'showing off' with all his might—cuffing boys, pulling hair, making faces, in a word, using every art that seemed likely to fascinate a girl, and win her applause. His exultation had but one alloy—the memory of his humiliation in this angel's garden; and that record in sand was fast washing out under the waves of happiness that were sweeping over it now. The visitors were given the highest seat of honour, and as soon as Mr. Walters' speech was finished, he introduced them to the school. The middle-aged man turned out to be a prodigious personage: no less an one than the county judge—altogether the most august creation these children had ever looked upon; and they wondered what kind of material he was made of; and they half wanted to hear him roar, and were half afraid he might, too. He was from Constantinople, twelve miles away—so he had travelled and seen the world—these very eyes had looked upon the County Court House, which was said to have a tin roof. The awe which these reflections inspired was attested by the impressive silence and the ranks of staring eyes. This was the great Judge Thatcher, brother of their own lawyer. Jeff Thatcher immediately went forward to be familiar with the great man, and be envied by the school. It would have been music to his soul to hear the whisperings.

'Look at him, Jim! he's going up there. Say look! he's a going to shake hands with him; he *is* shaking hands with him. By jinks, don't you wish you was Jeff?'

Mr. Walters fell to 'showing off' with all sorts of official bustlings and activities, giving orders, delivering judgments, discharging directions here, there, everywhere that he could find a target. The librarian 'showed off', running hither and thither with his arms full of books and making a deal of the splutter and fuss that insect authority delights in. The young lady teachers 'showed off'—bending sweetly over pupils that were lately being boxed, lifting pretty warning fingers at bad little boys and patting good ones lovingly. The young gentleman teachers 'showed off' with small scoldings and other little displays of authority and fine attention to discipline; and most of the teachers, of both sexes, found business up at the library by the pulpit; and it was business that frequently had to be done over again two or three times (with much seeming vexation). The little girls 'showed off' in various ways, and the little boys 'showed off' with such diligence that the air was thick with paper wads and the murmur of scufflings. And above it all the great man sat and beamed a majestic judicial smile upon all the house, and warmed himself in the sun of his own grandeur, for he was 'showing off' too. There was only one thing wanting to make Mr. Walters' ecstasy complete, and that was a chance to deliver a Bible prize and exhibit a prodigy. Several pupils had a few yellow tickets, but none had enough—he had been around among the star pupils inquiring. He would have given worlds, now, to have that German lad back again with a sound mind.

And now at this moment, when hope was dead, Tom Sawyer came forward with nine yellow tickets, nine red tickets, and ten blue ones, and demanded a Bible! This was a thunderbolt out of a clear sky. Walters was not expecting an application from this source for the next ten years. But there was no getting around it —here were the certified checks, and they were good for their face. Tom was therefore elevated to a place with the Judge and the other elect, and the great news was announced from headquarters. It was the most stunning surprise of the decade; and so profound was the sensation that it lifted the new hero up to the judicial one's altitude, and the school had two marvels to gaze upon in place of one. The boys were all eaten up with envy; but those that suffered the bitterest pangs were those who perceived too late that they themselves had contributed to this hated splendour by trading tickets to Tom for the wealth he had amassed in selling whitewashing privileges. These despised themselves, as being the dupes of a wily fraud, a guileful snake in the grass.

The prize was delivered to Tom with as much effusion as the Superintendent could pump up under the circumstances; but it lacked somewhat of the true gush, for the poor fellow's instinct taught him that there was a mystery here that could not well bear the light, perhaps; it was simply preposterous that *this* boy had warehoused two thousand sheaves of Scriptural wisdom on his premises—a dozen would strain his capacity, without a doubt. Amy Lawrence was proud and glad, and she tried to make Tom see it in her face; but he wouldn't look. She wondered; then she was just a grain troubled; next a dim suspicion came and went—came again; she watched; a furtive glance told her worlds—and then her heart broke, and she was jealous, and angry, and the tears came and she hated everybody; Tom most of all, she thought.

Tom was introduced to the Judge; but his tongue was tied, his breath would hardly come, his heart quaked—partly because of the awful greatness of the man, but mainly because he was *her* parent. He would have liked to fall down and worship him, if it were in the dark. The Judge put his hand on Tom's head and called him a fine little man, and asked him what his name was. The boy stammered, gasped, and got it out.

'Tom.'

39

'Oh, no, not Tom—it is——'

'Thomas.'

'Ah, that's it. I thought there was more to it, maybe. That's very well. But you've another one I dare say, and you'll tell it to me, won't you?'

'Tell the gentleman your other name, Thomas,' said Walters, 'and say *sir*. You mustn't forget your manners.'

'Thomas Sawyer—sir.'

'That's it! that's a good boy. Fine boy. Fine, manly little fellow. Two thousand verses is a great many—very, very great many. And you never can be sorry for the trouble you took to learn them; for knowledge is worth more than anything there is in the world; it's what makes great men and good men; you'll be a great man and a good man yourself some day, Thomas, and then you'll look back and say, "It's all owing to the precious Sunday-school privileges of my boyhood; it's all owing to my dear teachers that taught me to learn; it's all owing to the good Superintendent, who encouraged me and watched over me, and gave me a beautiful Bible, a splendid, elegant Bible, to keep and have it all for my own, always; it's all owing to right bringing up!" That is what you will say, Thomas; and you wouldn't have any money for those two thousand verses—no, indeed you wouldn't. And now you wouldn't mind telling me and this lady some of the things you've learned—no, I know you wouldn't —for we are proud of little boys that learn. Now no doubt you know the names of all the twelve disciples. Won't you tell us the names of the first two that were appointed?'

Tom was tugging at a button and looking sheepish. He blushed now, and his eyes fell. Mr. Walters's heart sank within him. He said to himself, It is not possible that the boy can answer the simplest question—why *did* the Judge ask him? Yet he felt obliged to speak up and say:

'Answer the gentleman, Thomas—don't be afraid.'

Tom still hung fire.

'Now, I know you'll tell *me*,' said the lady. 'The names of the first two disciples were——'

'*David and Goliath!*'

Let us draw the curtain of charity over the rest of the scene.

CHAPTER V

A Useful Minister—In Church—The Climax

ABOUT half-past ten the cracked bell of the small church began to ring, and presently the people began to gather for the morning sermon. The Sunday-school children distributed themselves about the house, and occupied pews with their parents, so as to be under supervision. Aunt Polly came, and Tom and Sid, and Mary sat with her—Tom being placed next the aisle, in order that he might be as far away from the open window and the seductive outside summer scenes as possible. The crowd filed up the aisles: the aged and needy postmaster, who had seen better days; the mayor and his wife—for they had a mayor there, among other unnecessaries; the justice of the peace; the widow Douglas, fair, smart, and forty, a generous, good-hearted soul and well-to-do, her hill mansion the only palace in the town, and the most hospitable and much the most lavish in the matter of festivities that St. Petersburg could boast; the bent and venerable Major and Mrs. Ward; Lawyer Riverson, the new notable from a distance; next the belle of the village, followed by a troop of lawn-clad and ribbon-decked young heart breakers; then all the young clerks in town in a body—for they had stood in the vestibule sucking their cane heads, a circling wall of oiled and simpering admirers, till the last girl had run their gauntlet; and last of all came the Model Boy, Will Mufferson, taking as heedful care of his mother as if she were cut glass. He always brought his mother to church, and was the pride of all the matrons. The boys all hated him, he was so good; and besides, he had been 'thrown up to them' so much. His white handkerchief was hanging out of his pocket behind,

42

as usual on Sundays—accidentally. Tom had no handkerchief, and he looked upon boys who had as snobs. The congregation being fully assembled now, the bell rang once more, to warn laggards and stragglers, and then a solemn hush fell upon the church, which was only broken by the tittering and whispering of the choir in the gallery. The choir always tittered and whispered all through service. There was once a church choir that was not ill-bred, but I have forgotten where it was now. It was a great many years ago, and I can scarcely remember anything about it, but I think it was in some foreign country.

The minister gave out the hymn, and read it through with a relish, in a peculiar style which was much admired in that part of the country. His voice began on a medium key, and climbed steadily up till it reached a certain point, where it bore with strong emphasis upon the topmost word, and then plunged down as if from a spring-board—

Shall I be car-ri-ed to the skies, on flow'ry beds

of ease,

Whilst others fight to win the prize, and sail thro' blood-

y seas?

He was regarded as a wonderful reader. At church 'sociables' he was always called upon to read poetry; and when he was through, the ladies would lift up their hands and let them fall helplessly in their laps, and 'wall' their eyes, and shake their heads, as much as to say, 'Words cannot express it; it is too beautiful, *too* beautiful for this mortal earth.'

After the hymn had been sung, the Rev. Mr. Sprague turned himself into a bulletin board, and read off 'notices' of meetings and societies and things till it seemed that the list would stretch out to the crack of doom—a queer custom which is still kept up in America, even in cities, away here in this age of abundant newspapers. Often the less there is to justify a traditional custom, the harder it is to get rid of it.

And now the minister prayed. A good, generous prayer it was, and went into details. It pleaded for the Church, and the little children of the Church; for the other churches of the village; for the village itself; for the county; for the State; for the State officers; for the United States; for the churches of the United States; for Congress; for the President; for the officers of the Government; for poor sailors, tossed by stormy seas; for the oppressed millions groaning under the heel of European monarchies and Oriental despotisms; for such as have the light and the good tidings, and yet have not eyes to see nor ears to hear withal; for the heathen in the far islands of the sea; and closed with a supplication that the words he was about to speak might find grace and favour, and be as seed sown in fertile ground, yielding in time a grateful harvest of good. Amen.

There was a rustling of dresses, and the standing congregation sat down. The boy whose history this book relates did not enjoy the prayer, he only endured it—if he even did that much. He was restive all through it; he kept tally of the details of the prayer, unconsciously—for he was not listening, but he knew the ground of old, and the clergyman's regular route over it—and when a little trifle of new matter was interlarded, his ear detected it and his whole nature resented it; he considered additions unfair, and scoundrelly. In the midst of the prayer a fly had lit on the back of the pew in front of him, and tortured his spirit by calmly rubbing its hands together; embracing its head with its arms and polishing it so vigorously that it seemed to almost part company with the body, and the slender thread of a neck was exposed to view; scraping its wings with its hind legs and smoothing them to its body as if they had been coat-tails; going through its whole toilet as tranquilly as if it knew it was perfectly safe. As indeed it was; for as sorely as Tom's hands itched to grab for it they did not dare—he believed his soul would be instantly destroyed if he did such a thing while prayer was going on. But with the closing sentence his hand began to curve and steal forward; and the instant the 'Amen' was out, the fly was a prisoner of war. His aunt detected the act, and made him let it go.

The minister gave out his text and droned along monotonously through an argument that was so prosy that many a head by and by began to nod—and yet it was an argument that dealt in limitless fire and brimstone, and thinned the predestined elect down to a company so small as to be hardly worth the saving. Tom counted the pages of the sermon; after church he always knew how many pages there had been, but he seldom knew anything else about the discourse. However, this time he was really interested for a little while. The minister made a grand and moving picture of the assembling together of the world's hosts at the millennium, when the lion and the lamb should lie down together and a little child should lead them. But the pathos, the lesson, the moral of the great spectacle were lost upon the boy; he only thought of the conspicuousness of the principal character before the onlooking nations; his face lit with the thought, and he said to himself that he wished he could be that child, if it was a tame lion.

Now he lapsed into suffering again as the dry argument was resumed. Presently he bethought himself of a treasure he had, and got it out. It was a large black-beetle with formidable jaws —a 'pinch-bug' he called it. It was in a percussion-cap box.* The first thing the beetle did was to take him by the finger.

45

A natural fillip followed, the beetle went floundering into the aisle, and lit on its back, and the hurt finger went into the boy's mouth. The beetle lay there working its helpless legs, unable to turn over. Tom eyed it, and longed for it, but it was safe out of his reach. Other people, uninterested in the sermon, found relief in the beetle, and they eyed it too.

Presently a vagrant poodle dog came idling along, sad at heart, lazy with the summer softness and the quiet, weary of captivity, sighing for change. He spied the beetle; the drooping tail lifted and wagged. He surveyed the prize; walked around it; smelt at it from a safe distance; walked around it again; grew bolder, and took a closer smell; then lifted his lip, and made a gingerly snap at it, just missing it; made another, and another; began to enjoy the diversion; subsided to his stomach with the beetle between his paws, and continued his experiments; grew weary at last, and then indifferent and absent-minded. His head nodded, and little by little his chin descended and touched the enemy, who seized it. There was a sharp yelp, a flirt of the poodle's head, and the beetle fell a couple of yards away, and lit on its back once more. The neighbouring spectators shook with a gentle inward joy, several faces went behind fans and handkerchiefs, and Tom was entirely happy. The dog looked foolish, and probably felt so; but there was resentment in his heart, too, and a craving for revenge. So he went to the beetle, and began a wary attack on it again; jumping at it from every point of a circle, lighting with his fore-paws within an inch of the creature, making even closer snatches at it with his teeth, and jerking his head till his ears flapped again. But he grew tired once more, after a while; tried to amuse himself with a fly, but found no relief; followed an ant around, with his nose close to the floor, and quickly wearied of that; yawned, sighed, forgot the beetle entirely, and sat down on it! Then there was a wild yelp of agony, and the poodle went sailing up the aisle; the yelps continued, and so did the dog; he crossed the house in front of the altar; he flew down the other aisle; he crossed before the doors; he clamoured up the home-stretch; his anguish grew with his progress, till presently he was but a woolly comet moving in its orbit with the gleam and the speed of light. At last the frantic sufferer sheered from its course and sprang into its master's lap: he flung it out of the window, and the voice of distress quickly thinned away and died in the distance.

By this time the whole church was red-faced and suffocating with suppressed laughter, and the sermon had come to a dead standstill. The discourse was resumed presently, but it went lame and halting, all possibility of impressiveness being at an end; for even the gravest sentiments were constantly being received with a smothered burst of unholy mirth, under cover of some remote pewback, as if the poor parson had said a rarely facetious thing. It was a genuine relief to the whole congregation when the ordeal was over and the benediction pronounced.

Tom Sawyer went home quite cheerful, thinking to himself that there was some satisfaction about divine service when there was a bit of variety in it. He had but one marring thought; he was willing that the dog should play with his pinch-bug, but he did not think it was upright in him to carry it off.

CHAPTER VI

*Self-Examination— Dentistry—The Midnight
Charm—Witches and Devils—Cautious
Approaches—Happy Hours*

MONDAY morning found Tom Sawyer miserable. Monday morning always found him so, because it began another week's slow suffering in school. He generally began that day with wishing he had had no intervening holiday, it made the going into captivity and fetters again so much more odious.

Tom lay thinking. Presently it occurred to him that he wished he was sick; then he could stay home from school. Here was a vague possibility. He canvassed his system. No ailment was found, and he investigated again. This time he thought he could detect colicky symptoms, and he began to encourage them with considerable hope. But they soon grew feeble, and presently died wholly away. He reflected further. Suddenly he discovered something. One of his upper front teeth was loose. This was lucky; he was about to begin to groan, as a 'starter', as he called it, when it occurred to him that if he came into court with that argument his aunt would pull it out, and that would hurt. So he thought he would hold the tooth in reserve for the present, and seek further. Nothing offered for some little time, and then he remembered hearing the doctor tell about a certain thing that laid up a patient for two or three weeks and threatened to make him lose a finger. So the boy eagerly drew his sore toe from under the sheet and held it up for inspection. But now he did not know the necessary symptoms. However, it seemed well worth while to chance it, so he fell to groaning with considerable spirit.

But Sid slept on, unconscious.

Tom groaned louder, and fancied that he began to feel pain in the toe.

No result from Sid.

Tom was panting with his exertions by this time. He took a rest and then swelled himself up and fetched a succession of admirable groans.

Sid snored on.

Tom was aggravated. He said, 'Sid, Sid!' and shook him. This course worked well, and Tom began to groan again. Sid yawned stretched, then brought himself up on his elbow with a snort, and began to stare at Tom. Tom went on groaning. Sid said:

'Tom! say Tom!'

No response.

'Here, Tom! *Tom!* What is the matter, Tom?' And he shook him, and looked in his face anxiously.

Tom moaned out:

'Oh, don't, Sid. Don't joggle me.'

'Why, what's the matter, Tom? I must call auntie.'

'No, never mind. It'll be over by and by, maybe. Don't call anybody.'

'But I must! *Don't* groan so, Tom, it's awful. How long you been this way?'

'Hours. Ouch! Oh, don't stir so, Sid. You'll kill me.'

'Tom, why didn't you wake me sooner? Oh, Tom, *don't!* It makes my flesh crawl to hear you. Tom, what *is* the matter?'

'I forgive you everything, Sid. (Groan.) Everything you've ever done to me. When I'm gone——'

'Oh, Tom, you ain't dying, are you? Don't, Tom. Oh, don't. Maybe——'

'I forgive everybody, Sid. (Groan.) Tell 'em so, Sid. And, Sid, you give my window-sash and my cat with one eye to that new girl that's come to town, and tell her——'

But Sid had snatched his clothes and gone. Tom was suffering

49

in reality now, so handsomely was his imagination working, and so his groans had gathered quite a genuine tone.

Sid flew downstairs and said:

'Oh, Aunt Polly, come! Tom's dying!'

'Dying!'

'Yes'm. Don't wait, come quick!'

'Rubbage! I don't believe it!'

But she fled upstairs nevertheless, with Sid and Mary at her heels. And her face grew white, too, and her lips trembled. When she reached the bed she gasped out:

'You Tom! Tom, what's the matter with you?'

'Oh, auntie, I'm——'

'What's the matter with you—what *is* the matter with you, child?'

'Oh, auntie, my sore toe's mortified!'

The old lady sank down into a chair, and laughed a little, then cried a little, then did both together. This restored her, and she said:

'Tom, what a turn you did give me. Now you shut up that nonsense and climb out of this.'

The groans ceased, and the pain vanished from the toe. The boy felt a little foolish, and he said:

'Aunt Polly, it *seemed* mortified, and it hurt so; I never minded my tooth at all.'

'Your tooth, indeed! What's the matter with your tooth?'

'One of them's loose, and it aches perfectly awful.'

'There, there now, don't begin that groaning again. Open your mouth. Well, your tooth *is* loose, but you're not going to die about that. Mary, get me a silk thread, and a chunk of fire out of the kitchen.'

Tom said:

'Oh, please auntie, don't pull it out, it don't hurt any more. I wish I may never stir if it does. Please don't, auntie; *I* don't want to stay home from school.'

'Oh, you don't, don't you? So all this row was because you thought you'd get to stay home from school and go a fishing? Tom, Tom, I love you so, and you seem to try every way you can to break my old heart with your outrageousness.'

By this time the dental instruments were ready. The old lady made one end of the silk thread fast to Tom's tooth with a loop and tied the other to the bed-post. Then she seized the chunk of fire and suddenly thrust it almost into the boy's face. The tooth hung dangling by the bed-post, now.

But all trials bring their compensations. As Tom wended to school after breakfast, he was the envy of every boy he met because the gap in his upper row of teeth enabled him to expectorate in a new and admirable way. He gathered quite a following of lads interested in the exhibition; and one that had cut his finger and had been a centre of fascination and homage up to this time, now found himself suddenly without an adherent, and shorn of his glory. His heart was heavy, and he said with a disdain which he did not feel, that it wasn't anything to spit like Tom Sawyer; but another boy said 'Sour grapes!' and he wandered away a dismantled hero.

Shortly Tom came upon the juvenile pariah of the village, Huckleberry Finn, son of the town drunkard. Huckleberry was cordially hated and dreaded by all the mothers of the town, because he was idle, and lawless, and vulgar, and bad—and because all their children admired him so, and delighted in his forbidden society and wished they dared to be like him. Tom was like the rest of the respectable boys, in that he envied Huckleberry his gaudy outcast condition, and was under strict orders not to play with him. So he played with him every time he got a chance. Huckleberry was always dressed in the cast-off clothes of full-grown men, and they were in perennial bloom and fluttering with rags. His hat was a vast ruin with a wide crescent lopped out of its brim; his coat, when he wore one, hung nearly to his heels, and had the rearward buttons far down the back; but one suspender supported his trousers; the seat of the trousers bagged low and contained nothing; the fringed legs dragged in the dirt when not rolled up. Huckleberry came and went at his own free will. He slept on door-steps in fine weather, and in empty hogs-heads in wet; he did not have to go to school or to church, or call any being master, or obey anybody: he could go fishing or swimming when and where he chose, and stay as long as it suited him; nobody forbade him to fight; he could sit up as late as he pleased; he was always the first boy that went barefoot in the spring and the last to resume leather in the fall; he never had to wash, nor put on clean clothes; he could swear wonderfully. In a word, everything that goes to make life precious, that boy had. So thought every harassed, hampered, respectable boy in St. Petersburg. Tom hailed the romantic outcast:

'Hello, Huckleberry!'

'Hello, yourself, and see how you like it.'

'What's that you got?'

'Dead cat.'

'Lemme see him, Huck. My, he's pretty stiff. Where'd you get him?'

'Bought him off'n a boy.'

'What did you give?'

'I give a blue ticket and a bladder that I got at the slaughter-house.'

'Where'd you get the blue ticket?'

'Bought it off'n Ben Rogers two weeks ago for a hoop-stick.'

'Say—what is dead cats good for, Huck?'

'Good for? Cure warts with.'

'No? Is that so? I know something that's better.'

'I bet you don't. What is it?'

'Why, spunk water.'

'Spunk water! I wouldn't give a dern for spunk water.'

'You wouldn't, wouldn't you? D'you ever try it?'

'No, I hain't. But Bob Tanner did.'

'Who told you so?'

'Why, he told Jeff Thatcher, and Jeff told Johnny Baker, and Johnny told Jim Hollis, and Jim told Ben Rogers, and Ben told a nigger, and the nigger told me. There, now!'

'Well, what of it? They'll all lie. Leastways all but the nigger. I don't know *him*. But I never see a nigger that *would'nt* lie. Shucks! Now you tell me how Bob Tanner done it, Huck.'

'Why, he took and dipped his hand in a rotten stump where the rain-water was.'

'In the daytime?'

'Certainly.'

'With his face to the stump?'

'Yes. Least I reckon so.'

'Did he *say* anything?'

'I don't reckon he did, I don't know.'

'Aha! Talk about trying to cure warts with spunk water such a blame fool way as that! Why, that ain't a going to do any good. You got to go all by yourself to the middle of the woods, where you know there's a spunk water stump, and just as it's midnight you back up against the stump and jam your hand in and say:

> *Barley-corn, barley-corn, injun-meal shorts,*
> *Spunk water, spunk water, swaller these warts,*

and then walk away quick, eleven steps, with your eyes shut, and then turn around three times and walk home without speaking to anybody. Because if you speak, the charm's busted.'

'Well, that sounds like a good way; but that ain't the way Bob Tanner done.'

'No, sir, you can bet he didn't; becuz he's the wartiest boy in this town; and he wouldn't have a wart on him if he'd knowed how to work spunk water. I've took off thousands of warts off of my hands that way, Huck. I play with frogs so much that I've always got considerable many warts. Sometimes I take 'em off with a bean.'

'Yes, bean's good. I've done that.'

'Have you? What's your way?'

'You take and split the bean, and cut the wart so as to get some blood, and then you put the blood on one piece of the bean, and take and dig a hole and bury it 'bout midnight at the cross-roads in the dark of the moon, and then you burn up the rest of the bean. You see that piece that's got the blood on it will keep drawing and drawing, trying to fetch the other piece to it, and so that helps the blood to draw the wart, and pretty soon off she comes.'

'Yes, that's it, Huck—that's it; though, when you're burying it, if you say, "Down bean, off wart; come no more to bother me!" it's better. That's the way Joe Harper does, and he's been nearly to Coonville, and most everywheres. But say—how do you cure 'em with dead cats?'

'Why, you take your cat and go and get in the graveyard 'long about midnight, when somebody that was wicked has been buried; and when it's midnight a devil will come, or maybe two or three, but you can't see 'em, you can only hear something like the wind, or maybe hear 'em talk; and when they're taking that feller away, you heave your cat after 'em and say, "Devil follow corpse, cat follow devil, warts follow cat, *I'm* done with ye!" That'll fetch *any* wart.'

'Sounds right. D'you ever try it, Huck?'

'No, but old Mother Hopkins told me.'

'Well, I reckon it's so, then, becuz they say she's a witch.'

'*Say*! Why, Tom, I *know* she is. She witched pap. Pap says so his own self. He come along one day, and he see she was a witching him, so he took up a rock, and if she hadn't dodged he'd a got her. Well, that very night he rolled off'n a shed wher' he was a layin' drunk, and broke his arm.'

'Why, that's awful. How did he know she was a witching him?'

'Lord, pap can tell, easy. Pap says when they keep looking at you right stiddy, they're a witching you, specially if they mumble. Becuz when they mumble they're saying the Lord's Prayer back'ards.'

'Say, Hucky, when you going to try the cat?'

'To-night. I reckon they'll come after old Hoss Williams to-night.'

'But they buried him Saturday. Didn't they get him Saturday night?'

'Why, how you talk! How could their charms work till midnight? and *then* it's Sunday. Devils don't slosh around much of a Sunday, I don't reckon.'

'I never thought of that. That's so. Lemme go with you?'

'Of course—if you ain't afeard.'

'Afeard! 'Tain't likely. Will you meow?'

'Yes, and you meow back if you get a chance. Last time you kep' me a meowing around till old Hays went to throwing rocks at me, and says, "Dern that cat!" and so I hove a brick through his window—but don't you tell.'

'I won't. I couldn't meow that night becuz auntie was watching me; but I'll meow this time. Say—what's that?'

'Nothing but a tick.'

'Where'd you get him?'

'Out in the woods.'

'What'll you take for him?'

'I don't know. I don't want to sell him.'

'All right. It's a mighty small tick, anyway.'

'Oh, anybody can run a tick down that don't belong to them. I'm satisfied with it. It's a good enough tick for me.'

'Sho, there's ticks a plenty. I could have a thousand of 'em if I wanted to.'

'Well, why don't you? Becuz you know mighty well you can't. This is a pretty early tick, I reckon. It's the first one I've seen this year.'

'Say, Huck, I'll give you my tooth for him.'

'Less see it.'

Tom got out a bit of paper and carefully unrolled it. Huckleberry viewed it wistfully. The temptation was very strong. At last he said:

'Is it genuwyne?'

Tom lifted his lip and showed the vacancy.

'Well, all right,' said Huckleberry; 'it's a trade.'

Tom enclosed the tick in the percussion-cap box that had lately been the pinch-bug's prison, and the boys separated, each feeling wealthier than before.

When Tom reached the little isolated frame schoolhouse, he strode in briskly, with the manner of one who had come with all honest speed. He hung his hat on a peg, and flung himself into his seat with business-like alacrity. The master, throned on high in his great splint-bottom arm-chair, was dozing, lulled by the drowsy hum of study. The interruption roused him:

'Thomas Sawyer!'

Tom knew that when his name was pronounced in full it meant trouble.

'Sir!'

'Come up here. Now, sir, why are you late again, as usual?'

Tom was about to take refuge in a lie, when he saw two long tails of yellow hair hanging down a back that he recognized by the electric sympathy of love; and by that form was *the only vacant place* on the girls' side of the school-house. He instantly said:

'*I stopped to talk with Huckleberry Finn!*'

The master's pulse stood still, and he stared helplessly. The buzz of study ceased; the pupils wondered if this foolhardy boy had lost his mind. The master said:

'You—you did what?'

'Stopped to talk with Huckleberry Finn.'

There was no mistaking the words.

'Thomas Sawyer, this is the most astounding confession I have ever listened to; no mere ferule will answer for this offence. Take off your jacket.'

The master's arm performed until it was tired, and the stock of switches notably diminished. Then the order followed:

'Now, sir, go and sit with the *girls*! And let this be a warning to you.'

The titter that rippled around the room appeared to abash the boy, but in reality that result was caused rather more by his worshipful awe of his unknown idol and the dread pleasure that lay in his high good fortune. He sat down upon the end of the pine bench, and the girl hitched herself away from him with a toss of her head. Nudges and winks and whispers traversed the room, but Tom sat still, with his arms upon the long, low desk before him, and seemed to study his book. By and by attention ceased from him, and the accustomed school murmur rose upon the dull air once more. Presently the boy began to steal furtive glances at the girl. She observed it, 'made a mouth' at him, and gave him the back of her head for the space of a minute. When she cautiously faced around again, a peach lay before her. She thrust it away. Tom gently put it back; she thrust it away again, but with less animosity. Tom patiently returned it to its place; then she let it remain. Tom scrawled on his slate, 'Please take it —I got more.' The girl glanced at the words, but made no sign. Now the boy began to draw something on the slate, hiding his work with his left hand. For a time the girl refused to notice; but her human curiosity presently began to manifest itself by hardly perceptible signs. The boy worked on, apparently unconscious. The girl made a sort of non-committal attempt to see, but the boy did not betray that he was aware of it. At last she gave in, and hesitatingly whispered:

'Let me see it.'

Tom partly uncovered a dismal caricature of a house with two gable ends to it and a cork-screw of smoke issuing from the chimney. Then the girl's interest began to fasten itself upon the work, and she forgot everything else. When it was finished, she gazed a moment, then whispered:

'It's nice—make a man.'

The artist erected a man in the front yard, that resembled a derrick. He could have stepped over the house; but the girl was not hypercritical; she was satisfied with the monster, and whispered:

'It's a beautiful man—now make me coming along.'

Tom drew an hourglass, with a full moon and straw limbs to it, and armed the spreading fingers with a portentous fan. The girl said:

'It's ever so nice—I wish I could draw.'

'It's easy,' whispered Tom. 'I'll learn you.'

'Oh, will you? When?'

'At noon. Do you go home to dinner?'

'I'll stay if you will.'

'Good—that's a whack. What's your name?'

'Becky Thatcher. What's yours? Oh, I know. It's Thomas Sawyer.'

'That's the name they lick me by. I'm Tom when I'm good. You call me Tom, will you?'

'Yes.'

Now Tom began to scrawl something on the slate, hiding the words from the girl. But she was not backward this time. She begged to see. Tom said:

'Oh, it ain't anything.'

'Yes it is.'

'No it ain't; you don't want to see.'

'Yes, I do, indeed I do. Please let me.'

'You'll tell.'

'No I won't—deed and deed and double deed I won't.'

'You won't tell anybody at all? Ever, as long as you live?'

'No, I won't ever tell *any*body. Now let me.'

'Oh, *you* don't want to see!'

58

'Now that you treat me so I *will* see.' And she put her small hand upon his, and a little scuffle ensued, Tom pretending to resist in earnest, but letting his hand slip by degrees till these words were revealed: '*I love you.*'

'Oh, you bad thing!' And she hit his hand a smart rap, but reddened and looked pleased nevertheless.

Just at this juncture the boy felt a slow, fateful grip closing on his ear, and a steady lifting impulse. In that vice he was borne across the house and deposited in his own seat, under a peppering fire of giggles from the whole school. Then the master stood over him during a few awful moments, and finally moved away to his throne without saying a word. But although Tom's ear tingled, his heart was jubilant.

As the school quieted down, Tom made an honest effort to study, but the turmoil within him was too great. In turn he took his place in the reading class and made a botch of it, then in the geography class and turned lakes into mountains, mountains into rivers, and rivers into continents, till chaos was come again; then in the spelling class, and got 'turned down' by a succession of mere baby words till he brought up at the foot and yielded up the pewter medal which he had worn with ostentation for months.

CHAPTER VII

A Treaty entered into—Early Lessons—A Mistake made

THE harder Tom tried to fasten his mind on his book, the more his ideas wandered. So at last, with a sigh and a yawn, he gave it up. It seemed to him that the noon recess would never come. The air was utterly dead. There was not a breath stirring. It was the sleepiest of sleepy days. The drowsing murmur of the five-and-twenty studying scholars soothed the soul like the spell that is in the murmur of bees. Away off in the flaming sunshine Cardiff Hill lifted its soft green sides through a shimmering veil of heat, tinted with the purple of distance; a few birds floated on lazy wing high in the air; no other living thing was visible but some cows, and they were asleep.

Tom's heart ached to be free, or else to have something of interest to do to pass the dreary time. His hand wandered into his pocket, and his face lit up with a glow of gratitude that was prayer, though he did not know it. Then furtively the percussion-cap box came out. He released the tick, and put him on the long flat desk. The creature probably glowed with a gratitude that amounted to prayer, too, at this moment, but it was premature; for when he started thankfully to travel off, Tom turned him aside with a pin, and made him take a new direction.

Tom's bosom friend sat next him, suffering just as Tom had been, and now he was deeply and gratefully interested in this entertainment in an instant. This bosom friend was Joe Harper. The two boys were sworn friends all the week, and embattled enemies on Saturdays. Joe took a pin out of his lappel, and began to assist in exercising the prisoner. The sport grew in interest momently. Soon Tom said that they were interfering with each other, and neither getting the fullest benefit of the tick. So he put Joe's slate on the desk and drew a line down the middle of it from top to bottom.

'Now,' said he, 'as long as he is on your side you can stir him up and I'll let him alone; but if you let him get away and get on my side, you're to leave him alone as long as I can keep him from crossing over.'

'All right, go ahead—start him up.'

The tick escaped from Tom, presently, and crossed the equator. Joe harassed him a while, and then he got away and crossed back again. This change of base occured often. While one boy was worrying the tick with absorbing interest, the other would look on with interest as strong, the two heads bowed together over the slate, and the two souls dead to all things else. At last luck seemed to settle and abide with Joe. The tick tried this, that, and the other course, and got as excited and as anxious as the boys themselves, but time and again, just as he would have victory in his very grasp, so to speak, and Tom's fingers would be twitching to begin, Joe's pin would deftly head him off and keep possession. At last Tom could stand it no longer. The temptation was too strong. So he reached out and lent a hand with his pin. Joe was angry in a moment. Said he:

'Tom, you let him alone.'

'I only just want to stir him up a little, Joe.'

'No, sir, it ain't fair; you just let him alone.'

'Blame it, I ain't going to stir him much.'

'Let him alone, I tell you!'

'I won't!'

'You shall—he's on my side of the line.'

'Look here, Joe Harper, whose is that tick?'

'*I* don't care whose tick he is—he's on my side of the line, and you shan't touch him.'

'Well, I'll just bet I will, though. He's my tick, and I'll do what I blame please with him, or die!'

A tremendous whack came down on Tom's shoulders and its duplicate on Joe's, and for the space of two minutes the dust continued to fly from the two jackets and the whole school to enjoy it. The boys had been too absorbed to notice the hush that had stolen upon the school a while before when the master came tiptoeing down the room and stood over them. He had contemplated a good part of the performance before he contributed his bit of variety to it. When school broke up at noon, Tom flew to Becky Thatcher, and whispered in her ear:

'Put on your bonnet and let on you're going home; and when you get to the corner, give the rest of 'em the slip, and turn down through the lane and come back. I'll go the other way, and come it over 'em the same way.'

So the one went off with one group of scholars, and the other with another. In a little while the two met at the bottom of the lane, and when they reached the school they had it all to themselves. Then they sat together, with a slate before them and Tom gave Becky the pencil and held her hand in his, guiding it, and so created another surprising house. When the interest in art began to wane, the two fell to talking. Tom was swimming in bliss. He said:

'Do you love rats?'

'No, I hate them!'

'Well, I do too—*live* ones. But I mean dead ones, to swing round your head with a string.'

'No, I don't care for rats much, anyway. What *I* like is chewing-gum!'

'Oh, I should say so! I wish I had some now!'

'Do you? I've got some. I'll let you chew it a while, but you must give it back to me.'

That was agreeable, so they chewed it turn about, and dangled their legs against the bench in excess of contentment.

'Was you ever at a circus?' said Tom.

'Yes, and my pa's going to take me again some time, if I'm good.'

'I been to the circus three or four times—lots of times. Church ain't shucks to a circus. There's things going on at a circus all the time. I'm going to be a clown in a circus when I grow up.'

'Oh, are you! That will be nice. They're so lovely, all spotted up.'

'Yes, that's so. And they get slathers of money—most a dollar a day, Ben Rogers says. Say, Becky, was you ever engaged?'

'What's that?'

'Why, engaged to be married.'

'No.'

'Would you like to?'

'I reckon so. I don't know. What is it like?'

'Like? Why, it ain't like anything. You only just tell a boy you won't ever have anybody but him, ever ever *ever*, and then you kiss, and that's all. Anybody can do it.'

'Kiss? What do you kiss for?'

'Why that, you know, is to—well, they always do that.'

'Everybody?'

'Why, yes, everybody that's in love with each other. Do you remember what I wrote on the slate?'

'Ye—yes.'

'What was it?'

'I shan't tell you.'

'Shall I tell *you*?'

'Ye—yes—but some other time.'

'No, now.'

'No, not now—to-morrow.'

'Oh, no, *now*, please, Becky. I'll whisper it, I'll whisper it ever so easy.'

63

Becky hesitating, Tom took silence for consent, and passed his arm about her waist and whispered the tale ever so softly, with his mouth close to her ear. And then he added:

'Now you whisper it to me—just the same.'

She resisted for a while, and then said:

'You turn your face away, so you can't see, and then I will. But you mustn't ever tell anybody—*will* you, Tom? Now you won't—*will* you?'

'No, indeed indeed I won't. Now, Becky.'

He turned his face away. She bent timidly around till her breath stirred his curls, and whispered, 'I—love—you!'

Then she sprang away and ran around and around the desks and benches, with Tom after her, and took refuge in a corner at last, with her little white apron to her face. Tom clasped her about her neck and pleaded:

'Now Becky, it's all done—all over but the kiss. Don't you be afraid of that—it ain't anything at all. Please, Becky.'

And he tugged at her apron and her hands.

By and by she gave up and let her hands drop; her face, all glowing with the struggle, came up and submitted. Tom kissed the red lips and said:

'Now it's all done, Becky. And always after this, you know, you ain't ever to love anybody but me, and you ain't ever to marry anybody but me, never never and for ever. Will you?'

'No, I'll never love anybody but you, Tom, and I'll never marry anybody but you, and you ain't to ever marry anybody but me, either.'

'Certainly. Of course. That's *part* of it. And always, coming to school, or when we're going home, you're to walk with me, when there ain't anybody looking—and you choose me and I choose you at parties, because that's the way you do when you're engaged.'

'It's so nice. I never heard of it before.'

'Oh, it's ever so gay! Why me and Amy Lawrence——'

The big eyes told Tom his blunder, and he stopped, confused.

'Oh, Tom! Then I ain't the first you've ever been engaged to!'

The child began to cry. Tom said:

'Oh, don't cry, Becky. I don't care for her any more.'

'Yes, you do, Tom—you know you do.'

Tom tried to put his arm about her neck, but she pushed him away and turned her face to the wall, and went on crying. Tom tried again, with soothing words in his mouth, and was repulsed again. Then his pride was up, and he strode away and went outside. He stood about, restless and uneasy, for a while, glancing at the door every now and then, hoping she would repent and come to find him. But she did not. Then he began to feel badly, and fear that he was in the wrong. It was a hard struggle with him to make new advances now, but he nerved himself to it and entered. She was still standing back there in the corner, sobbing with her face to the wall. Tom's heart smote him. He went to her and stood a moment, not knowing exactly how to proceed. Then he said, hesitantly:

'Becky, I—I don't care for anybody but you.'

No reply—but sobs.

'Becky?' pleadingly. 'Becky, won't you say something?'

More sobs.

Tom got out his chiefest jewel, a brass knob from the top of an andiron, and passed it around her so that she could see it, and said:

'Please, Becky, won't you take it?'

She struck it to the floor. Then Tom marched out of the house and over the hills and far away, to return to school no more that day. Presently Becky began to suspect. She ran to the door; he was not in sight; she flew around to the play-yard; he was not there. Then she called:

'Tom! Come back, Tom!'

She listened intently, but there was no answer. She had no

companions but silence and loneliness. So she sat down to cry again and upbraid herself; and by this time the scholars began to gather again, and she had to hide her griefs and still her broken heart, and take up the cross of a long dreary, aching afternoon, with none among the strangers about her to exchange sorrows with.

CHAPTER VIII

Tom decides on His Course—Old Scenes re-enacted

TOM dodged hither and thither through lanes until he was well out of the track of returning scholars, and then fell into a moody jog. He crossed a small 'branch' two or three times, because of a prevailing juvenile superstition that to cross water baffled pursuit. Half an hour later he was disappearing behind the Douglas mansion on the summit of Cardiff Hill, and the school-house was hardly distinguishable away off in the valley behind him. He entered a dense wood, picked his pathless way to the centre of it, and sat down on a mossy spot under a spreading oak. There was not even a zephyr stirring; the dead noon-day heat had even stilled the songs of the birds; nature lay in a trance that was broken by no sound but the occasional far-off hammering of a woodpecker, and this seemed to render the pervading silence and sense of loneliness the more profound. The boy's soul was steeped in melancholy; his feelings were in happy accord with his surroundings. He sat long with his elbows on his knees and his chin in his hands, meditating. It seemed to him that life was but a trouble at best, and he more than half envied Jimmy Hodges, so lately released. It must be very peaceful, he thought, to lie and slumber and dream for ever and ever, with the wind whispering through the trees and caressing the grass and the flowers of the grave, and nothing to bother and grieve about, ever any more. If he only had a clean Sunday-school record he could be willing to go, and be done with it all. Now as to this girl. What had he done? Nothing. He had meant the best in the world, and

67

been treated like a dog—like a very dog. She would be sorry some day—maybe when it was too late. Ah, if he could only die *temporarily*!

But the elastic heart of youth cannot be kept compressed into one constrained shape long at a time. Tom presently began to drift insensibly back into the concerns of this life again. What if he turned his back, now, and disappeared mysteriously? What if he went away—ever so far away, into unknown countries beyond the seas—and never come back any more! How would she feel then! The idea of being a clown recurred to him now, only to fill him with disgust. For frivolity and jokes, and spotted tights, were an offence when they intruded themselves upon a spirit that was exalted into the vague, august realm of the romantic. No, he would be a soldier, and return after long years, all war-worn and illustrious. No, better still, he would join the Indians and hunt buffaloes, and go on the war-path in the mountain ranges and the trackless great plains of the Far West, and away in the future come back a great chief, bristling with feathers, hideous with paint, and prance into Sunday-school, some drowsy summer morning, with a blood-curdling war-whoop, and sear the eye-balls of all his companions with unappeasable envy. But no, there was something gaudier even than this. He would be a pirate! That was it! *Now* his future lay plain before him, and glowing with unimaginable splendour. How his name would fill the world, and make people shudder! How gloriously he would go ploughing the dancing seas, in his long, low, black-hulled racer, the 'Spirit of the Storm', with his grisly flag flying at the fore! And, at the zenith of his fame, how he would suddenly appear at the old village and stalk into church, brown and weather-beaten, in his black velvet doublet and trunks, his great jack-boots, his crimson sash, his belt bristling with horse-pistols, his crime-rusted cutlass at his side, his slouch hat with waving plumes, his black flag unfurled, with the skull and crossbones on it, and hear with swelling ecstasy the whisperings: 'It's Tom Sawyer, the Pirate!—the Black Avenger of the Spanish Main!'*

Yes, it was settled; his career was determined. He would run away from home and enter upon it. He would start the very next morning. Therefore he must now begin to get ready. He would collect his resources together. He went to a rotten log near at hand, and began to dig under one end of it with his Barlow knife. He soon struck wood that sounded hollow. He put his hand there, and uttered this incantation, impressively:

'What hasn't come here, *come*! What's here, *stay* here!'

Then he scraped away the dirt, and exposed a pine shingle. He took it up and disclosed a shapely little treasure-house, whose bottom and sides were of shingles. In it lay a marble. Tom's astonishment was boundless! He scratched his head with a perplexed air, and said:

'Well, that beats anything!'

Then he tossed the marble away pettishly, and stood cogitating. The truth was, that a superstition of his had failed here, which he and all his comrades had always looked upon as infallible. If you buried a marble with certain necessary incantations, and left it alone a fortnight, and then opened the place with the incantation he had just used, you would find that all the marbles you had ever lost had gathered themselves together there, meantime, no matter how widely they had been separated. But now this thing had actually and unquestionably failed. Tom's whole structure of faith was shaken to its foundations. He had many a time heard of this thing succeeding, but never of its failing before. It did not occur to him that he had tried it several times before himself, but could never find the hiding-places afterwards. He puzzled over the matter some time, and finally decided that some witch had interfered and broken the charm. He thought he would satisfy himself on that point, so he searched around till he found a small sandy spot with a little funnel-shaped depression in it. He laid himself down and put his mouth close to this depression and called:

Doodle-bug, doodle-bug, tell me what I want to know!
Doodle-bug, doodle-bug, tell me what I want to know!

The sand began to work, and presently a small black bug appeared for a second, and then darted under again in a fright. 'He dasn't tell! So it *was* a witch that done it. I just knowed it.'

He well knew the futility of trying to contend against witches, so he gave up, discouraged. But it occurred to him that he might as well have the marble he had just thrown away, and therefore he went and made a patient search for it. But he could not find at. Now he went back to his treasure-house, and carefully placed himself just as he had been standing when he tossed the marble away; then he took another marble from his pocket, and tossed it in the same way, saying: 'Brother, go find your brother!'

He watched where it stopped, and went there and looked. But it must have fallen short or gone too far, so he tried twice more. The last repetition was successful. The two marbles lay within a foot of each other.

Just here the blast of a toy tin trumpet came faintly down the green aisles of the forest. Tom flung off his jacket and trousers, turned a suspender into a belt, raked away some brush behind the rotten log, disclosing a rude bow and arrow, a lath sword, and a tin trumpet, and in a moment had seized these things, and bounded away, bare-legged, with fluttering shirt. He presently halted under a great elm, blew an answering blast, and then began to tip-toe and look warily out, this way and that. He said cautiously—to an imaginary company:

'Hold, my merry men! Keep hid till I blow.'

Now appeared Joe Harper, as airily clad and elaborately armed as Tom. Tom called:

'Hold! Who comes here into Sherwood Forest without my pass?'

'Guy of Guisborne wants no man's pass! Who art thou that —that——'

'Dares to hold such language,' said Tom, prompting, for they talked 'by the book' from memory.

'Who art thou that dares to hold such language?'

'I, indeed! I am Robin Hood, as thy caitiff carcass soon shall know.'

'Then art thou indeed that famous outlaw? Right gladly will I dispute with thee the passes of the merry wood. Have at thee!'

They took their lath swords, dumped their other traps on the ground, struck a fencing attitude, foot to foot, and began a grave, careful combat, 'two up and two down'. Presently Tom said:

'Now if you've got the hang, go it lively!'

So they 'went it lively', panting and perspiring with the work. By and by Tom shouted:

'Fall! fall! Why don't you fall?'

'I shan't! Why don't you fall yourself? You're getting the worst of it.'

'Why, that ain't anything. *I* can't fall. That ain't the way it is in the book. The book says, 'Then with one back-handed stroke he slew poor Guy of Guisborne!' You're to turn around and let me hit you in the back.'

There was no getting around the authorities, so Joe turned, received the whack, and fell.

'Now,' said Joe, getting up, 'you got to let me kill *you*. That's fair.'

'Why, I can't do that. It ain't in the book.'

'Well, it's blamed mean. That's all.'

'Well, say Joe, you can be Friar Tuck or Much the Miller's son, and lam me with a quarter-staff; or I'll be the Sheriff of Nottingham, and you be Robin Hood a little while, and kill me.'

This was satisfactory, and so these adventures were carried out. Then Tom became Robin Hood again, and was allowed by the treacherous nun to bleed his strength away through his neglected wound. And at last Joe, representing a whole tribe of weeping outlaws, dragged him sadly forth, gave his bow into his feeble hands, and Tom said, 'Where this arrow falls there bury poor Robin Hood under the greenwood tree.' Then he shot the arrow, and fell back, and would have died; but he lit on a nettle, and sprang up too gaily for a corpse.

The boys dressed themselves, hid their accoutrements and went off grieving that there were no outlaws any more, and wondering what modern civilization could claim to have done to compensate for their loss. They said they would rather be outlaws a year in Sherwood Forest than President of the United States for ever.

CHAPTER IX

A Solemn Situation—Grave Subjects introduced— Injun Joe explains

A<small>T</small> half-past nine that night Tom and Sid were sent to bed as usual. They said their prayers, and Sid was soon asleep. Tom lay awake and waited in restless impatience. When it seemed to him that it must be nearly daylight, he heard the clock strike ten! This was despair. He would have tossed and fidgeted, as his nerves demanded, but he was afraid he might wake Sid. So he lay still and stared up into the dark. Everything was dismally still. By and by, out of the stillness little, scarcely perceptible noises began to emphasize themselves. The ticking of the clock began to bring itself into notice. Old beams began to crack mysteriously. The stairs creaked faintly. Evidently spirits were abroad. A measured, muffled snore issued from Aunt Polly's chamber. And now the tiresome chirping of a cricket that no human ingenuity could locate began. Next the ghastly ticking of a death-watch in the wall at the bed's head made Tom shudder—it meant that somebody's days were numbered. Then the howl of a far-off dog rose on the night air, and was answered by a fainter howl from a remoter distance. Tom was in an agony. At last he was satisfied that time had ceased and eternity begun; he began to doze in spite of himself; the clock chimed eleven, but he did not hear it. And then there came, mingling with his half-formed dreams, a most melancholy caterwauling. The raising of a neighbouring window disturbed him. A cry of 'Scat! you devil!' and the crash of an empty bottle against the back of his aunt's wood-shed brought him wide awake, and a single minute later he was dressed and out of the window and creeping along the roof of the 'ell' on all fours. He 'meow'd' with caution once or twice as he went; then jumped to the roof of the wood-shed, and thence to the ground. Huckleberry Finn was there, with his dead cat. The boys moved off and disappeared in the gloom. At the end of half an hour they were wading through the tall grass of the graveyard.

It was a graveyard of the old-fashioned western kind. It was on a hill, about a mile and a half from the village. It had a crazy board fence around it, which leaned inwards in places, and outward the rest of the time, but stood upright nowhere. Grass and weeds grew rank over the whole cemetery. All the old graves were sunken in. There was not a tombstone on the place; round-topped, worm-eaten boards staggered over the graves, leaning for support and finding none. 'Sacred to the memory of So-and-So' had been painted on them once, but it could no longer have been read, on the most of them, now, even if there had been light.

A faint wind moaned through the trees, and Tom feared it might be the spirits of the dead complaining at being disturbed. The boys talked little, and only under their breath, for the time and the place and the pervading solemnity and silence oppressed their spirits. They found the sharp new heap they were seeking, and ensconced themselves within the protection of three great elms that grew in a bunch within a few feet of the grave.

Then they waited in silence for what seemed a long time. The hooting of a distant owl was all the sound that troubled the dead stillness. Tom's reflections grew oppressive. He must force some talk. So he said in a whisper:

'Hucky, do you believe the dead people like it for us to be here?'

Huckleberry whispered:

'I wisht I knowed. It's awful solemn like, *ain't* it?'

'I bet it is.'

There was a considerable pause, while the boys canvassed this matter inwardly. Then Tom whispered:

'Say, Hucky—do you reckon Hoss Williams hears us talking?'

'O' course he does. Least his sperrit does.'

Tom, after a pause:

'I wish I'd said *Mister* Williams. But I never meant any harm. Everybody calls him Hoss.'

'A body can't be too partic'lar how they talk 'bout these yer dead people, Tom.'

This was a damper, and conversation died again. Presently Tom seized his comrade's arm and said:

'*Sh!*'

'What is it, Tom?' And the two clung together with beating hearts.

'*Sh!* There 'tis again! Didn't you hear it?'

'I——'

'There! Now you hear it!'

'Lord, Tom, they're coming! They're coming, sure. What'll we do?'

'I dono. Think they'll see us?'

'Oh, Tom, they can see in the dark, same as cats. I wisht I hadn't come.'

'Oh, don't be afeard. *I* don't believe they'll bother us. We ain't doing any harm. If we keep perfectly still, maybe they won't notice us at all.'

'I'll try to, Tom, but, Lord! I'm all of a shiver.'

'Listen!'

The boys bent their heads together and scarcely breathed. A muffled sound of voices floated up from the far end of the graveyard.

'Look! see there!' whispered Tom. 'What is it?'

'It's devil-fire.* Oh, Tom, this is awful.'

Some vague figures approached through the gloom, swinging an old-fashioned tin lantern that freckled the ground with innumerable little spangles of light. Presently Huckleberry whispered with a shudder:

'It's the devils, sure enough. Three of 'em! Lordy, Tom, we're goners! Can you pray?'

'I'll try, but don't you be afeard. They ain't going to hurt us. "Now I lay me down to sleep, I——".'

'*Sh!*'

'What is it, Huck?'

'They're *humans*! One of 'em is, anyway. One of 'em's old Muff Potter's voice.'

'No—'tain't so, is it?'

'I bet I know it. Don't you stir nor budge. *He* ain't sharp enough to notice us. Drunk, same as usual, likely—blamed old rip!'

'All right, I'll keep still. Now they're stuck. Can't find it. Here they come again. Now they're hot. Cold again. Hot again. Red hot! They're p'inted right, this time. Say, Huck, I know another o' them voices; it's Injun Joe.'

'That's so—that murderin' half-breed! I'd druther they was devils a dern sight. What kin they be up to?'

The whispers died wholly out now, for the three men had reached the grave, and stood within a few feet of the boys' hiding-place.

'Here it is,' said the third voice; and the owner of it held the lantern up and revealed the face of young Dr. Robinson.

Potter and Injun Joe were carrying a handbarrow with a rope and a couple of shovels on it. They cast down their load and began to open the grave. The doctor put the lantern at the head of the grave, and came and sat down with his back against one of the elm trees. He was so close the boys could have touched him.

'Hurry, men!' he said in a low voice. 'The moon might come out at any moment.'

They growled a response and went on digging. For some time

76

there was no noise but the grating sound of the spades discharging their freight of mould and gravel. It was very monotonous. Finally a spade struck upon the coffin with a dull, woody accent, and within another minute or two the men had hoisted it out on the ground. They prised off the lid with their shovels, got out the body and dumped it rudely on the ground. The moon drifted from behind the clouds and exposed the pallid face. The barrow was got ready and the corpse placed on it, covered with a blanket, and bound to its place with the rope. Potter took out a large spring-knife and cut off the dangling end of the rope, and then said:

'Now the cussed thing's ready, Sawbones, and you'll just out with another five, or here she stays.'

'That's the talk!' said Injun Joe.

'Look here; what does this mean?' said the doctor 'You required your pay in advance, and I've paid you.'

'Yes, and you done more than that,' said Injun Joe, approaching the doctor, who was now standing. 'Five years ago you drove me away from your father's kitchen one night, when I come to ask for something to eat, and you said I warn't there for any good; and when I swore I'd get even with you if it took a hundred years, your father had me jailed for a vagrant. Did you think I'd forget? The Injun blood ain't in me for nothing. And now I've *got* you, and you got to *settle*, you know!'

He was threatening the doctor with his fist in his face by this time. The doctor struck out suddenly, and stretched the ruffian on the ground. Potter dropped his knife and exclaimed:

'Here, now, don't you hit my pard!' and the next moment he had grappled with the doctor, and the two were struggling with might and main, trampling the grass and tearing the ground with their heels. Injun Joe sprang to his feet, his eyes flaming with passion, snatched up Potter's knife, and went creeping, cat-like and stooping, round and round about the combatants, seeking an opportunity. All at once the doctor flung himself free, seized the heavy headboard of Williams's grave and felled Potter to the earth with it; and in the same instance the half-breed saw his chance, and drove the knife to the hilt in the young man's breast. He reeled and fell partly upon Potter, flooding him with his blood, and in the same moment the clouds blotted out the dreadful spectacle, and the two frightened boys went speeding away in the dark.

Presently, when the moon emerged again, Injun Joe was standing over the two forms, contemplating them. The doctor murmured inarticulately, gave a long gasp or two, and was still. The half-breed muttered:

'*That* score is settled, damn you.'

Then he robbed the body. After which he put the fatal knife in Potter's open right hand, and sat down on the dismantled coffin. Three—four—five minutes passed, and then Potter began to stir and moan. His hand closed upon the knife, he raised it, glanced at it, and let it fall with a shudder. Then he sat up, pushing the body from him, and gazed at it, and then around him confusedly. His eyes met Joe's.

'Lord, how is this, Joe?' he said.

'It's a dirty business,' said Joe, without moving. 'What did you do it for?'

'I! I never done it!'

'Look here! that kind of talk won't wash.'

Potter trembled and grew white.

'I thought I'd got sober. I'd no business to drink to-night. But it's in my head yet—worse'n when we started here. I'm all in a muddle; can't recollect anything of it hardly. Tell me, Joe—*honest*, now, old feller—did I do it? Joe, I never meant to; 'pon my soul and honour I never meant to, Joe. Tell me how it was, Joe. Oh, it's awful—and him so young and promising.'

'Why you two was scuffling, and he fetched you one with the headboard, and you fell flat; and then up you come, all reeling and staggering like, and snatched the knife and jammed it into him just as he fetched you another awful clip, and here you've laid, as dead as a wedge till now.'

'Oh, I didn't know what I was a-doing. I wish I may die this minute if I did. It was all on account of the whisky and the excitement, I reckon. I never used a weapon in my life before, Joe. I've fought, but never with weapons. They'll all say that. Joe, don't tell! Say you won't tell, Joe; that's a good feller. I always liked you, Joe, and stood up for you too. Don't you remember? You *won't* tell, *will* you, Joe?' And the poor creature dropped on his knees before the stolid murderer, and clasped his appealing hands.

'No, you've always been fair and square with me, Muff Potter, and I won't go back on you. There, now, that's as fair as a man can say.'

'Oh, Joe, you're an angel. I'll bless you for this the longest day I live.' And Potter began to cry.

'Come, now, that's enough of that. This ain't any time for blubbering. You be off yonder way and I'll go this. Move, now, and don't leave any tracks behind you.'

Potter started on a trot that quickly increased to a run. The half-breed stood looking after him. He muttered:

'If he's as much stunned with the lick and fuddled with the rum as he had the look of being, he won't think of the knife till he's gone so far he'll be afraid to come back after it to such a place by himself—chicken heart!'

Two or three minutes later the murdered man, the blanketed corpse, the lidless coffin, and the open grave, were under no inspection but the moon's. The stillness was complete again, too.

CHAPTER X

The Solemn Oath—Terror brings Repentance—
Mental Punishment

THE two boys flew on and on toward the village, speechless with horror. They glanced backward over their shoulders from time to time apprehensively, as if they feared they might be followed. Every stump that started up in their path seemed a man and an enemy, and made them catch their breath; and as they sped by some outlying cottages that lay near the village, the barking of the aroused watch-dogs seemed to give wings to their feet.

'If we can only get to the old tannery before we break down!' whispered Tom, in short catches between breaths. 'I can't stand it much longer.'

Huckleberry's hard pantings were his only reply, and the boys fixed their eyes on the goal of their hopes, and bent to their work to win it. They gained steadily on it, and at last, breast to breast, they burst through the open door, and fell, grateful and exhausted, in the sheltering shadows beyond. By and by their pulses slowed down, and Tom whispered:

'Huckleberry, what do you reckon 'll come of this?'

'If Dr. Robinson dies, I reckon hanging'll come of it.'

'Do you, though?'

'Why, I *know* it, Tom.'

Tom thought a while; then he said:

'Who'll tell? We?'

'What are you talking about? S'pose something happened and Injun Joe *didn't* hang? Why he'd kill us some time or other, just as dead sure as we're a-laying here.'

'That's just what I was thinking to myself, Huck.'

'If anybody tells, let Muff Potter do it, if he's fool enough. He's generally drunk enough.'

Tom said nothing—went on thinking. Presently he whispered:

'Huck, Muff Potter don't *know* it. How can he tell?'

'What's the reason he don't know it?'

'Because he'd just got that whack when Injun Joe done it. D'you reckon he could see anything? D'you reckon he knowed anything?'

'By hokey, that's so, Tom!'

'And besides, look-a-here—maybe that whack done for *him*!'

'No, 'tain't likely, Tom. He had liquor in him; I could see that; and besides, he always has. Well, when pap's full, you might take and belt him over the head with a church and you couldn't phase him. He says so his own self. So it's the same with Muff Potter, of course. But if a man was dead sober, I reckon maybe that whack might fetch him; I dono.'

After another reflective silence, Tom said:

'Hucky, you sure you can keep mum?'

'Tom, we *got* to keep mum. *You* know that. That Injun devil wouldn't make any more of drowning us than a couple of cats, if we was to squeak 'bout this and they didn't hang him. Now look-a-here, Tom, less take and swear to one another— that's what we got to do—swear to keep mum.'

'I'm agreed. It's the best thing. Would you just hold hands and swear that we——'

'Oh, no, that wouldn't do for this. That's good enough for little rubbishy common things—specially with gals, cuz *they* go back on you anyway, and blab if they get in a huff—but there orter be writing 'bout a big thing like this. And blood.'

Tom's whole being applauded this idea. It was deep, and dark, and awful; the hour, the circumstances, the surroundings, were in keeping with it. He picked up a clean pine shingle that lay in

81

the moonlight, took a little fragment of 'red keel' out of his pocket, got the moon on his work, and painfully scrawled these lines, emphasizing each slow down-stroke by clamping his tongue between his teeth, and letting up the pressure on the upstrokes:

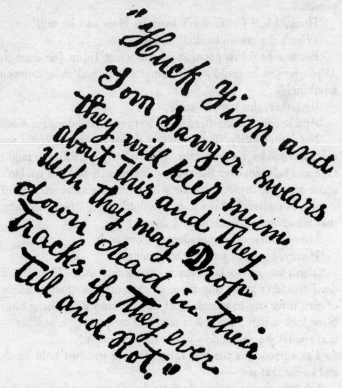

"Huck Finn and Tom Sawyer swears they will keep mum about this and They wish they may Drop down dead in their tracks if they ever Tell and Rot."

Huckleberry was filled with admiration of Tom's facility in writing and the sublimity of his language. He at once took a pin from his lappel and was going to prick his flesh, but Tom said:

'Hold on! Don't do that. A pin's brass. It might have verdigrease on it.'

'What's verdigrease?'

82

'It's p'ison. That's what it is. You just swaller some of it once—you'll see.'

So Tom unwound the thread from one of his needles, and each boy pricked the ball of his thumb and squeezed out a drop of blood.

In time, after many squeezes, Tom managed to sign his initials, using the ball of his little finger for a pen. Then he showed Huckleberry how to make an H and an F, and the oath was complete. They buried the shingle close to the wall, with some dismal ceremonies and incantations, and the fetters that bound their tongues were considered to be locked and the key thrown away.

A figure crept stealthily through a break in the other end of the ruined building now, but they did not notice it.

'Tom,' whispered Huckleberry, 'does this keep us from *ever* telling—*always?*'

'Of course it does. It don't make any difference *what* happens, we got to keep mum. We'd drop down dead—don't *you* know that?'

'Yes, I reckon that's so.'

They continued to whisper for some little time. Presently a dog set up a long, lugubrious howl just outside—within ten feet of them. The boys clasped each other suddenly, in an agony of fright.

'Which of us does he mean?' gasped Huckleberry.

'I dono—peep through the crack. Quick!'

'No, *you*, Tom!'

'I can't—I can't *do* it, Huck!'

'Please, Tom. There 'tis again!'

'Oh, lordy, I'm thankful!' whispered Tom. 'I know his voice. It's Bull Harbison.' [1]

[1] If Mr. Harbison had owned a slave named Bull, Tom would have spoken of him as 'Harbison's Bull'; but a son or dog of that name was 'Bull Harbison'.

'Oh, that's good—I tell you, Tom, I was most scared to death; I'd a bet anything it was a *stray* dog.'

The dog howled again. The boys' hearts sank once more.

'Oh, my! that ain't no Bull Harbison!' whispered Huckleberry. '*Do*, Tom!'

Tom, quaking with fear, yielded, and put his eye to the crack. His whisper was hardly audible when he said:

'Oh, Huck, *it's a stray dog*!'

'Quick, Tom, quick! Who does he mean?'

'Huck, he must mean us both—we're right together.'

'Oh, Tom, I reckon we're goners. I reckon there ain't no mistake 'bout where *I'll* go to. I been so wicked.'

'Dad fetch it! This comes of playing hookey and doing everything a feller's told *not* to do. I might a been good, like Sid, if I'd a tried—but no, I wouldn't, of course. But if ever I get off this time, I lay I'll just *waller* in Sunday-schools!' And Tom began to snuffle a little.

'*You* bad!' And Huckleberry began to snuffle too. 'Confound it, Tom Sawyer, you're just old pie 'longside o' what *I* am. Oh, *lordy*, lordy, lordy, I wisht I only had half your chance.'

Tom choked off and whispered:

'Look, Hucky, look! He's got his *back* to us!'

Hucky looked with joy in his heart.

'Well he has, by jingoes! Did he before?'

'Yes, he did. But I, like a fool, never thought. Oh, this is bully, you know. *Now*, who can he mean?'

The howling stopped. Tom pricked up his ears.

'*Sh!* What's that?' he whispered.

'Sounds like—like hogs grunting. No—it's somebody snoring, Tom.'

'That *is* it. Where'bouts is it, Huck?'

'I b'leeve it's down at t'other end. Sounds so, anyway. Pap used to sleep there sometimes, 'long with the hogs, but laws bless you, he just lifts things when *he* snores. Besides, I reckon he ain't ever coming back to this town any more.'

The spirit of adventure rose in the boys' souls once more.

'Hucky, do you das't to go if I lead?'

'I don't like to, much. Tom, s'pose its' Injun Joe!'

Tom quailed. But presently the temptation rose up strong again and the boys agreed to try, with the understanding that they would take to their heels if the snoring stopped. So they went tip-toeing stealthily down, the one behind the other. When they had got to within five steps of the snorer, Tom stepped on a stick, and it broke with a sharp snap. The man moaned, writhed a little, and his face came into the moonlight. It was Muff Potter. The boys' hearts had stood still, and their hopes too, when the man moved, but their fears passed away now. They tip-toed out, through the broken weather-boarding, and stopped at a little distance to exchange a parting word. That loud, lugubrious howl rose on the night air again! They turned and saw the strange dog standing within a few feet of where Potter was lying, and *facing* Potter, with his nose pointing heavenward.

"Oh, geeminy, it's *him*!" exclaimed both boys in a breath.

'Say, Tom, they say a stray dog come howling around Johnny Miller's house, 'bout midnight, as much as two weeks ago; and a whippoorwill come in and lit on the bannisters and sung, the very same evening; and there ain't anybody dead there yet.'

'Well, I know that. And suppose there ain't. Didn't Gracie Miller fall in the kitchen fire and burn herself terrible the very next Saturday?'

'Yes, but she ain't *dead*. And what's more, she's getting better, too.'

'All right; you wait and see. She's a goner, just as dead sure as Muff Potter's a goner. That's what the niggers say, and they know all about these kind of things, Huck.'

Then they separated, cogitating.

85

When Tom crept in at his bedroom window, the night was almost spent. He undressed with excessive caution, and fell asleep congratulating himself that nobody knew of his escapade. He was not aware that the gentle snoring Sid was awake, and had been so for an hour.

When Tom woke Sid was dressed and gone. There was a late look in the light, a late sense in the atmosphere. He was startled. Why had he not been called—persecuted till he was up as usual? The thought filled him with bodings. Within five minutes he was dressed and downstairs, feeling sore and drowsy. The family were still at table, but they had finished breakfast. There was no voice of rebuke; but there were averted eyes; there was a silence and an air of solemnity that struck a chill to the culprit's heart. He sat down and tried to seem gay, but it was up-hill work; it roused no smile, no response, and he lapsed into silence and let his heart sink down to the depths.

After breakfast his aunt took him aside, and Tom almost brightened in the hope that he was going to be flogged; but it was not so. His aunt wept over him and asked him how he could go and break her old heart so; and finally told him to go on, and ruin himself and bring her grey hairs with sorrow to the grave, for it was no use for her to try any more. This was worse than a thousand whippings, and Tom's heart was sorer now than his body. He cried, he pleaded for forgiveness, promised reform over and over again, and then received his dismissal, feeling that he had won but an imperfect forgiveness and established but a feeble confidence.

He left the presence too miserable to even feel revengeful toward Sid; and so the latter's prompt retreat through the back gate was unnecessary. He moped to school gloomy and sad, and took his flogging, along with Joe Harper, for playing hookey the day before, with the air of one whose heart was busy with heavier woes and wholly dead to trifles. Then he betook himself to his seat, rested his elbows on his desk and his jaws in his hands, and stared at the wall with the stony stare of suffering that has reached the limit and can no further go. His elbow was pressing against some hard substance. After a long time he slowly and sadly changed his position, and took up this object with a sigh. It was in a paper. He unrolled it. A long, lingering, colossal sigh followed, and his heart broke. It was his brass andiron knob! This final feather broke the camel's back.

CHAPTER XI

Muff Potter comes Himself—Tom's Conscience at Work

CLOSE upon the hour of noon the whole village was suddenly electrified with the ghastly news. No need of the as yet undreamed-of telegraph: the tale flew from man to man, from group to group, from house to house, with little less than telegraphic speed. Of course the schoolmaster gave holiday for that afternoon; the town would have thought strangely of him if he had not. A gory knife had been found close to the murdered man, and it had been recognized by somebody as belonging to Muff Potter—so the story ran. And it was said that a belated citizen had come upon Potter washing himself in the 'branch' about one or two o'clock in the morning, and that Potter had at once sneaked off—suspicious circumstances, especially the washing, which was not a habit with Potter. It was also said that the town had been ransacked for this 'murderer' (the public are not slow in the matter of sifting evidence and arriving at a verdict), but that he could not be found. Horsemen had departed down all the roads in every direction, and the Sheriff 'was confident' that he would be captured before night.

All the town was drifting toward the graveyard. Tom's heartbreak vanished, and he joined the procession, not because he would not a thousand times rather go anywhere else, but because an awful, unaccountable fascination drew him on. Arrived at the dreadful place, he wormed his small body through the crowd and saw the dismal spectacle. It seemed to him an age since he was there before. Somebody pinched his arm. He turned, and his eyes met Huckleberry's. Then both looked elsewhere at once, and wondered if anybody had noticed anything in their mutual glance. But everybody was talking, and intent upon the grisly spectacle before them.

'Poor fellow!' 'Poor young fellow!' 'This ought to be a lesson to grave-robbers!' 'Muff Potter'll hang for this if they catch him!' This was the drift of remark; and the minister said, 'It was a judgment; His hand is here.'

Now Tom shivered from head to heel; for his eye fell upon the stolid face of Injun Joe. At this moment the crowd began to sway and struggle, and voices shouted, 'It's him! it's him! he's coming himself!'

'Who? who?' from twenty voices.

'Muff Potter!'

'Hallo, he's stopped! Look out, he's turning! Don't let him get away!'

People in the branches of the trees over Tom's head said he wasn't trying to get away—he only looked doubtful and perplexed.

'Infernal impudence!' said a bystander; 'wanted to come and take a quiet look at his work, I reckon—didn't expect any company.'

The crowd fell apart now, and the Sheriff came through, ostentatiously, leading Potter by the arm. The poor fellow's face was haggard, and his eyes showed the fear that was upon him. When he stood before the murdered man he shook as with a palsy, and he put his face in his hands and burst into tears.

'I didn't do it, friends,' he sobbed; ''pon my word and honour I never done it.'

'Who's accused you!' shouted a voice.

This shot seemed to carry home. Potter lifted his face and looked around him with a pathetic hopelessness in his eyes. He saw Injun Joe, and exclaimed:

'Oh, Injun Joe, you promised me you'd never——'

'Is that your knife?' and it was thrust before him by the Sheriff.

Potter would have fallen if they had not caught him and eased him to the ground. Then he said:

'Something told me 't if I didn't come back and get——'
He shuddered; then waved his nerveless hand with a vanquished gesture, and said, 'Tell 'em, Joe, tell 'em—it ain't any use any more.'

Then Huckleberry and Tom stood dumb and staring, and heard the stony-hearted liar reel off his serene statement, they expecting every moment that the clear sky would deliver God's lightnings upon his head, and wondering to see how long the stroke was delayed. And when he had finished and still stood alive and whole, their wavering impulse to break their oath and save the poor betrayed prisoner's life faded and vanished away, for plainly this miscreant had sold himself to Satan, and it would be fatal to meddle with the property of such a power as that.

'Why didn't you leave? What did you want to come here for?' somebody said.

'I couldn't help it—I couldn't help it,' Potter moaned. 'I wanted to run away, but I couldn't seem to come anywhere but here.' And he fell to sobbing again.

Injun Joe repeated his statement, just as calmly, a few minutes afterward on the inquest, under oath; and the boys, seeing that the lightnings were still withheld, were confirmed in their belief that Joe had sold himself to the devil. He was now become, to them, the most balefully interesting object they had ever looked upon, and they could not take their fascinated eyes from his face. They inwardly resolved to watch him, nights, when opportunity should offer, in the hope of getting a glimpse of his dread master.

Injun Joe helped to raise the body of the murdered man, and put it in a waggon for removal; and it was whispered through the shuddering crowd that the wound bled a little!*The boys thought that this happy circumstance would turn suspicion in the right direction; but they were disappointed, for more than one villager remarked:

'It was within three feet of Muff Potter when it done it.'

Tom's fearful secret and gnawing conscience disturbed his sleep for as much as a week after this; and at breakfast one morning, Sid said:

'Tom, you pitch around and talk in your sleep so much that you keep me awake about half the time.'

Tom blanched and dropped his eyes.

'It's a bad sign,' said Aunt Polly gravely. 'What you got on your mind, Tom?'

'Nothing. Nothing 't I know of.' But the boy's hand shook so that he spilled his coffee.

'And you do talk such stuff,' Sid said. 'Last night you said, "It's blood, it's blood, that's what it is!" You said that over and over. And you said, "Don't torment me so—I'll tell." Tell *what*? What is it you'll tell?'

Everything was swimming before Tom. There is no telling what might have happened now, but luckily the concern passed out of Aunt Polly's face, and she came to Tom's relief without knowing it. She said:

'Sho! It's that dreadful murder. I dream about it most every night myself. Sometimes I dream it's me that done it.'

Mary said she had been affected much the same way. Sid seemed satisfied. Tom got out of the presence as quick as he plausibly could, and after that he complained of toothache for a week, and tied up his jaws every night. He never knew that Sid lay nightly watching, and frequently slipped the bandage free, and then leaned on his elbow listening a good while at a time, and afterwards slipped the bandage back to its place again. Tom's distress of mind wore off gradually, and the toothache grew irksome and was discarded. If Sid really managed to make anything out of Tom's disjointed mutterings, he kept it to himself.

It seemed to Tom that his schoolmates never would get done

holding inquests on dead cats, and thus keeping his trouble present to his mind. Sid noticed that Tom never was coroner at one of these inquiries, though it had been his habit to take the lead in all new enterprises; he noticed, too, that Tom never acted as a witness—and that was strange; and Sid did not overlook the fact that Tom even showed a marked aversion to these inquests, and always avoided them when he could. Sid marvelled, but said nothing. However, even inquests went out of vogue at last, and ceased to torture Tom's conscience.

Every day or two during this time of sorrow Tom watched his opportunity, and went to the little grated jail window and smuggled such small comforts through to the 'murderer' as he could get hold of. The jail was a trifling little brick den that stood in a marsh at the edge of the village, and no guards were afforded for it; indeed, it was seldom occupied. These offerings greatly helped to ease Tom's conscience.

The villagers had a strong desire to tar-and-feather Injun Joe and ride him on a rail for body-snatching, but so formidable was his character that nobody could be found who was willing to take the lead in the matter, so it was dropped. He had been careful to begin both of his inquest-statements with the fight, without confessing the grave-robbery that preceded it; therefore it was deemed wisest not to try the case in the courts at present.

CHAPTER XII

Tom shows his Generosity—Aunt Polly weakens

ONE of the reasons why Tom's mind had drifted away
from its secret troubles was that it had found a new and
weighty matter to interest itself about. Becky Thatcher
had stopped coming to school. Tom had struggled with his pride
a few days, and tried to 'whistle her down the wind',* but failed.
He began to find himself hanging around her father's house,
nights, and feeling very miserable. She was ill. What if she should
die! There was distraction in the thought. He no longer took an
interest in war, nor even in piracy. The charm of life was gone,
there was nothing but dreariness left. He put his hoop away,
and his bat; there was no joy in them any more. His aunt was
concerned; she began to try all manner of remedies on him. She
was one of those people who are infatuated with patent medicines
and all new-fangled methods of producing health or mending it.
She was an inveterate experimenter in these things. When something fresh in this line came out she was in a fever right away
to try it; not on herself, for she was never ailing; but on anybody
else that came handy. She was a subscriber for all the 'Health'
periodicals and phrenological frauds; and the solemn ignorance
they were inflated with was breath to her nostrils. All the 'rot'
they contained about ventilation, and how to go to bed, and how
to get up, and what to eat, and what to drink, and how much
exercise to take, and what frame of mind to keep oneself in,
and what sort of clothing to wear, was all gospel to her, and she
never observed that her health journals of the current month
customarily upset everything they had recommended the month
before. She was as simple-hearted and honest as the day was long,

and so she was an easy victim. She gathered together her quack periodicals and her quack medicines, and thus armed with death, went about on her pale horse, metaphorically speaking, with 'hell following after'. But she never suspected that she was not an angel of healing, and the balm of Gilead in disguise, to the suffering neighbours.

The water treatment was new, now, and Tom's low condition was a windfall to her. She had him out at daylight every morning, stood him up in the wood-shed and drowned him with a deluge of cold water; then she scrubbed him down with a towel like a file, and so brought him to; then she rolled him up in a wet sheet and put him away under blankets till she sweated his soul clean and 'the yellow stains of it came through his pores', as Tom said.

Yet notwithstanding all this the boy grew more and more melancholy and pale and dejected. She added hot baths, sitz baths, shower baths, and plunges. The boy remained as dismal as a hearse. She began to assist the water with a slim oatmeal diet and blister plasters. She calculated his capacity as she would a jug's, and filled him up every day with quack cure-alls.

Tom had become indifferent to persecution by this time. This phase filled the old lady's heart with consternation. This indifference must be broken up at any cost. Now she heard of Pain-killer for the first time. She ordered a lot at once. She tasted it and was filled with gratitude. It was simply fire in a liquid form. She dropped the water treatment and everything else, and pinned her faith to Pain-killer. She gave Tom a tea-spoonful and watched with the deepest anxiety for the result. Her troubles were instantly at rest, her soul at peace again; for the 'indifference' was broken up. The boy could not have shown a wilder, heartier interest, if she had built a fire under him.

Tom felt that it was time to wake up; this sort of life might be romantic enough in his blighted condition, but it was getting to have too little sentiment and too much distracting variety about it. So he thought over various plans for relief, and finally hit upon that of professing to be fond of Pain-killer. He asked for it so often that he became a nuisance, and his aunt ended by telling him to help himself and quit bothering her. If it had been Sid she would have had no misgivings to alloy her delight; but since it was Tom she watched the bottle clandestinely. She found that the medicine did really diminish, but it did not occur to her that the boy was mending the health of a crack in the sitting-room floor with it.

One day Tom was in the act of dosing the crack when his aunt's yellow cat came along, purring, eyeing the teaspoon avariciously, and begging for a taste. Tom said:

'Don't ask for it unless you want it, Peter.'

But Peter signified that he did want it.

'You better make sure.'

Peter was sure.

'Now you've asked for it, and I'll give it to you, because there ain't anything mean about *me*; but if you find you don't like it you mustn't blame anybody but your own self.'

Peter was agreeable, so Tom prised his mouth open and poured down the Pain-killer. Peter sprang a couple of yards in the air, and then delivered a war-whoop and set off round and round the room, banging against furniture, upsetting flower pots, and making general havoc. Next he rose on his hind feet and pranced around, in a frenzy of enjoyment, with his head over his shoulder and his voice proclaiming his unappeasable happiness. Then he went tearing around the house, again spreading chaos and destruction in his path. Aunt Polly entered in time to see him throw a few double summersets, deliver a final mighty hurrah, and sail through the open window, carrying the rest of the flower-pots with him. The old lady stood petrified with astonishment, peering over her glasses; Tom lay on the floor, expiring with laughter.

'Tom, what on earth ails that cat?'

'*I* don't know, aunt,' gasped the boy.

'Why I never see anything like it. What *did* make him act so?'

''Deed I don't know, Aunt Polly; cats always act so when they're having a good time.'

'They do, do they?' There was something in the tone that made Tom apprehensive.

'Yes'm. That is, I believe they do.'

'You *do*?'

'Yes'm.'

The old lady was bending down, Tom watching with interest emphasized by anxiety. Too late he divined her 'drift'. The handle of the tell-tale teaspoon was visible under the bed-valance. Aunt Polly took it, held it up. Tom winced, and dropped his eyes. Aunt Polly raised him by the usual handle—his ear—and cracked his head soundly with her thimble.

'Now, sir, what did you want to treat that poor dumb beast so for?'

'I done it out of pity for him—because he hadn't any aunt.'

'Hadn't any aunt!—you numskull. What has that got to do with it?'

'Heaps. Because if he'd a had one she'd a burnt him out herself! She'd a roasted his bowels out of him 'thout any more feeling than if he was a human!'

Aunt Polly felt a sudden pang of remorse. This was putting the thing in a new light; what was cruelty to a cat *might* be cruelty to a boy too. She began to soften: she felt sorry. Her eyes watered a little, and she put her hand on Tom's head and said gently:

'I was meaning for the best, Tom. And Tom, it *did* do you good.'

Tom looked up in her face with just a perceptible twinkle peeping through his gravity:

'I know you was meaning for the best, aunty, and so was I with Peter. It done *him* good, too. I never see him get around so since——'

'Oh, go 'long with you, Tom, before you aggravate me again. And you try and see if you can't be a good boy for once, and you needn't take any more medicine.'

Tom reached school ahead of time. It was noticed that this strange thing had been occurring every day latterly. And now, as usual of late, he hung about the gate of the school-yard instead of playing with his comrades. He was sick, he said; and he looked it. He tried to seem to be looking everywhere but whither he was really looking—down the road. Presently Jeff Thatcher hove in sight, and Tom's face lighted; he gazed a moment, and then turned sorrowfully away. When Jeff Thatcher arrived, Tom accosted him, and 'led up' warily to opportunities for remark about Becky, but the giddy lad never could see the bait. Tom watched and watched, hoping whenever a frisking frock came in sight, and hating the owner of it as soon as he saw she was not the right one. At last frocks ceased to appear, and he dropped hopelessly into the dumps; he entered the empty school-house and sat down to suffer. Then one more frock passed in at the gate, and Tom's heart gave a great bound. The next instant he was out, and 'going on' like an Indian; yelling, laughing, chasing boys, jumping over the fence at risk of life and limb, throwing handsprings, standing on his head—doing all the heroic things he could conceive of, and keeping a furtive eye out, all the while, to see if Becky Thatcher was noticing. But she seemed to be unconscious of it all; she never looked. Could it be possible that she was not aware that he was there? He carried his exploits to her immediate vicinity; came war-whooping around, snatched a boy's cap, hurled it to the roof of the school-house, broke through a group of boys, tumbling them in every direction, and fell sprawling himself under Becky's nose, almost upsetting her —and she turned, with her nose in the air, and he heard her say,

'Mf! some people think they're mighty smart—always showing off!'

Tom's cheeks burned. He gathered himself up and sneaked off, crushed and crestfallen.

CHAPTER XIII

The Young Pirates—Going to the Rendezvous—
The Camp-fire Talk

Tom's mind was made up now. He was gloomy and desperate. He was a forsaken, friendless boy, he said; nobody loved him: when they found out what they had driven him to, perhaps they would be sorry; he had tried to do right and get along, but they would not let him; since nothing would do them but to be rid of him, let it be so; and let them blame *him* for the consequences—why shouldn't they? what right had the friendless to complain? Yes, they had forced him to it at last: he would lead a life of crime. There was no choice. By this time he was far down Meadow Lane, and the bell for school to 'take up' tinkled faintly upon his ear. He sobbed, now, to think he should never, never hear that old familiar sound any more— it was very hard, but it was forced on him; since he was driven out into the cold world, he must submit—but he forgave them. Then the sobs came thick and fast.

Just at this point he met his soul's sworn comrade, Joe Harper —hard-eyed, and with evidently a great and dismal purpose in his heart. Plainly here were 'two souls with but a single thought'. Tom, wiping his eyes with his sleeve, began to blubber out something about a resolution to escape from hard usage and lack of sympathy at home by roaming abroad into the great world, never to return; and ended by hoping that Joe would not forget him.

But it transpired that this was a request which Joe had just been going to make of Tom, and had come to hunt him up for that purpose. His mother had whipped him for drinking some cream which he had never tasted and knew nothing about; it was plain that she was tired of him and wished him to go; if she felt that way, there was nothing for him to do but succumb; he hoped she would be happy, and never regret having driven her poor boy out into the unfeeling world to suffer and die.

As the two boys walked sorrowing along, they made a new compact to stand by each other and be brothers, and never separate till death relieved them of their troubles. Then they began to lay their plans. Joe was for being a hermit, and living on crusts in a remote cave, and dying, some time, of cold, and want, and grief; but after listening to Tom, he conceded that there were some conspicuous advantages about a life of crime, and so he consented to be a pirate.

Three miles below St. Petersburg, at a point where the Mississippi river was a trifle over a mile wide, there was a long, narrow, wooded island, with a shallow bar at the head of it, and this offered well as a rendezvous. It was not inhabited; it lay far over toward the further shore, abreast a dense and almost wholly unpeopled forest. So Jackson's Island was chosen. Who were to be the subjects of their piracies was a matter that did not occur to them. Then they hunted up Huckleberry Finn, and he joined them promptly, for all careers were one to him; he was indifferent. They presently separated, to meet at a lonely spot on the river bank two miles above the village, at the favourite hour, which was midnight. There was a small log raft there which they meant to capture. Each would bring hooks and lines, and such provision as he could steal in the most dark and mysterious way—as became outlaws; and before the afternoon was done, they had all managed to enjoy the sweet glory of spreading the fact that pretty soon the town would 'hear something'. All who got this vague hint were cautioned to 'be mum and wait'.

About midnight Tom arrived with a boiled ham and a few trifles, and stopped in a dense undergrowth on a small bluff overlooking the meeting-place. It was starlight, and very still.

The mighty river lay like an ocean at rest. Tom listened a moment, but no sound disturbed the quiet. Then he gave a low, distinct whistle. It was answered from under the bluff. Tom whistled twice more; these signals were answered in the same way. Then a guarded voice said:

'Who goes there?'

'Tom Sawyer, the Black Avenger of the Spanish Main. Name your names.'

'Huck Finn the Red-Handed, and Joe Harper the Terror of the Seas.' Tom had furnished these titles from his favourite literature.

''Tis well. Give the countersign.'

Two hoarse whispers delivered the same awful word simultaneously to the brooding night:

'*Blood!*'

Then Tom tumbled his ham over the bluff and let himself down after it, tearing both skin and clothes to some extent in the effort. There was an easy, comfortable path along the shore under the bluff, but it lacked the advantages of difficulty and danger so valued by a pirate.

The Terror of the Seas had brought a side of bacon, and had about worn himself out with getting it there. Finn the Red-Handed had stolen a skillet, and a quantity of half-cured leaf tobacco, and had also brought a few corn-cobs to make pipes with. But none of the pirates smoked or 'chewed' but himself. The Black Avenger of the Spanish Main said it would never do to start without some fire. That was a wise thought; matches were hardly known there in that day. They saw a fire smouldering upon a great raft a hundred yards above, and they went stealthily thither and helped themselves to a chunk. They made an imposing adventure of it, saying 'Hist!' every now and then, and suddenly halting with finger on lip; moving with hands on imaginary dagger-hilts; and giving orders in dismal whispers that if 'the foe' stirred, to 'let him have it to the hilt', because 'dead men tell no tales'. They knew well enough that the rafts-men were all down at the village laying in stores or having a spree, but still that was no excuse for their conducting this thing in an unpiratical way.

They shoved off presently, Tom in command, Huck at the after oar and Joe at the forward. Tom stood amidships, gloomy-browed, and with folded arms, and gave his orders in a low, stern whisper.

'Luff, and bring her to the wind!'

'Aye, aye, sir!'

'Steady, stead-y-y-y!'

'Steady it is, sir!'

'Let her go off a point!'

'Point it is, sir!'

As the boys steadily and monotonously drove the raft toward mid-stream, it was no doubt understood that these orders were given for 'style', and were not intended to mean anything in particular.

'What sail's she carrying?'

'Courses, tops'ls, and flying-jib, sir!'

'Send the r'yals up! Lay out aloft there, half a dozen of ye, foretopmast-stuns'l! Lively, now!'

'Aye, aye, sir!'

'Shake out that mainto-galans'l! Sheets and braces! *Now*, my hearties!'

'Aye, aye, sir!'

'Hellum-a-lee—hard a-port! Stand by to meet her when she comes! Port, port! *Now*, men! With a will! Stead-y-y-y!'

'Steady it is, sir!'

The raft drew beyond the middle of the river; the boys pointed her head right, and then lay on their oars. The river was not high, so there was not more than a two- or three-mile current. Hardly a word was said during the next three-quarters of an hour. Now the raft was passing before the distant town.

Two or three glimmering lights showed where it lay, peacefully sleeping, beyond the vague vast sweep of star-gemmed water, unconscious of the tremendous event that was happening. The Black Avenger stood still with folded arms, 'looking his last' upon the scene of his former joys and his later sufferings, and wishing 'she' could see him now, abroad on the wild sea, facing peril and death with dauntless heart, going to his doom with a grim smile on his lips. It was but a small strain on his imagination to remove Jackson's Island beyond eye-shot of the village, and so he 'looked his last' with a broken and satisfied heart. The other pirates were looking their last, too; and they all looked so long that they came near letting the current drift them out of the range of the island. But they discovered the danger in time, and made shift to avert it. About two o'clock in the morning the raft grounded on the bar two hundred yards above the head of the island, and they waded back and forth until they had landed their freight. Part of the little raft's belongings consisted of an old sail, and this they spread over a nook in the bushes for a tent to shelter their provisions; but they themselves would sleep in the open air in good weather, as became outlaws.

They built a fire against the side of a great log twenty or thirty steps within the sombre depths of the forest, and then cooked some bacon in the frying-pan for supper, and used up half of the corn 'pone' stock they had brought. It seemed glorious sport to be feasting in that wild free way in the virgin forest of an unexplored and uninhabited island, far from the haunts of men, and they said they would never return to civilization. The climbing fire lit up their faces and threw its ruddy glare upon the pillared tree-tunks of their forest temple, and upon the varnished foliage and festooning vines. When the last crisp slice of bacon was gone, and the last allowance of corn pone devoured, the boys stretched themselves out on the grass, filled with contentment. They could have found a cooler place, but they would not deny themselves such a romantic feature as the roasting campfire.

'*Ain't* it gay?' said Joe.

'It's *nuts*!' said Tom. 'What would the boys say if they could see us?'

'Say! Well they'd just die to be here—hey, Hucky?'

'I reckon so,' said Huckleberry; 'anyways *I'm* suited. I don't want nothing better'n this. I don't ever get enough to eat gen'ally —and here they can't come and pick at a feller and bullyrag him so.'

'It's just the life for me,' said Tom. 'You don't have to get up, mornings, and don't have to go to school, and wash, and all that blame foolishness. You see a pirate don't have to do *anything*, Joe, when he's ashore, but a hermit *he* has to be praying considerable, and then he don't have any fun, any way, all by himself that way.'

'Oh yes, that's so,' said Joe, 'but I hadn't thought much about it, you know. I'd a good deal rather be a pirate now that I've tried it.'

'You see,' said Tom, 'people don't go much on hermits, nowadays, like they used to in old times, but a pirate's always respected. And a hermit's got to sleep on the hardest place he can find, and put sackcloth and ashes on his head, and stand out in the rain, and——'

'What does he put sackcloth and ashes on his head for?' inquired Huck.

'*I* dunno. But they've *got* to do it. Hermits always do. You'd have to do that if you was a hermit.'

'Dern'd if I would,' said Huck.

'Well, what would you do?'

'I dunno. But I wouldn't do that.'

'Why, Huck, you'd *have* to. How'd you get around it?'

'Why I just wouldn't stand it. I'd run away.'

'Run away! Well, you *would* be a nice old slouch of a hermit. You'd be a disgrace.'

The Red-Handed made no response, being better employed.

He had finished gouging out a cob, and now he fitted a weed stem to it, loaded it with tobacco, and was pressing a coal to the charge and blowing a cloud of fragrant smoke; he was in the full bloom of luxurious contentment. The other pirates envied him this majestic vice, and secretly resolved to acquire it shortly. Presently Huck said:

'What does pirates have to do?'

Tom said:

'Oh, they have just a bully time—take ships, and burn them and get the money and bury it in awful places in their island where there's ghosts and things to watch it, and kill everybody in the ships—make 'em walk a plank.'

'And they carry the women to the island,' said Joe; 'they don't kill the women.'

'No,' assented Tom, 'they don't kill the women—they're too noble. And the women's always beautiful, too.'

'And don't they wear the bulliest clothes! Oh, no! All gold and silver and di'monds,' said Joe with enthusiasm.

'Who?' said Huck.

'Why, the pirates.'

Huck scanned his own clothing forlornly.

'I reckon I ain't dressed fitten for a pirate,' said he, with a regretful pathos in his voice; 'but I ain't got none but these.'

But the other boys told him the fine clothes would come fast enough after they should have begun their adventures. They made him understand that his poor rags would do to begin with, though it was customary for wealthy pirates to start with a proper wardrobe.

Gradually their talk died out and drowsiness began to steal upon the eyelids of the little waifs. The pipe dropped from the fingers of the Red-Handed, and he slept the sleep of the conscience free and the weary. The Terror of the Seas and the Black Avenger of the Spanish Main had more difficulty in getting to sleep. They said their prayers inwardly, and lying down, since there was nobody there with authority to make them kneel and recite aloud; in truth, they had a mind not to say them at all, but they were afraid to proceed to such lengths as that, lest they might call down a sudden and special thunderbolt from Heaven. Then at once they reached and hovered upon the imminent verge of sleep—but an intruder came now that would not 'down'. It was conscience. They began to feel a vague fear that they had been doing wrong to run away; and next they thought of the stolen meat, and then the real torture came. They tried to argue it away by reminding conscience that they had purloined sweetmeats and apples scores of times; but conscience was not to be appeased by such thin plausibilities. It seemed to them, in the end, that there was no getting around the stubborn fact that taking sweetmeats was only 'hooking', while taking bacon and ham and such valuables was plain, simple *stealing*—and there was a command against that in the Bible. So they inwardly resolved that so long as they remained in the business, their piracies should not again be sullied with the crime of stealing. Then conscience granted a truce, and these curiously inconsistent pirates fell peacefully to sleep.

CHAPTER XIV

*Camp Life—A Sensation—Tom steals away
from Camp*

WHEN Tom awoke in the morning, he wondered
where he was. He sat up and rubbed his eyes and
looked around; then he comprehended. It was the
cool grey dawn, and there was a delicious sense of repose and
peace in the deep pervading calm and silence of the woods. Not
a leaf stirred; not a sound obtruded upon great Nature's medi-
tation. Beaded dew-drops stood upon the leaves and grasses. A
white layer of ashes covered the fire, and a thin blue wreath of
smoke rose straight into the air. Joe and Huck still slept. Now,
far away in the woods, a bird called; another answered; presently
the hammering of a woodpecker was heard. Gradually the cool
dim grey of the morning whitened, and as gradually sounds multiplied and life manifested itself. The marvel of Nature shaking
off sleep and going to work unfolded itself to the musing boy. A
little green worm came crawling over a dewy leaf, lifting two-
thirds of his body into the air from time to time, 'sniffing around',
then proceeding again, for he was measuring, Tom said; and
when the worm approached him of its own accord he sat as
still as a stone, with his hopes rising and falling by turns as the
creature still came toward him or seemed inclined to go elsewhere; and when at last it considered a painful moment with its
curved body in the air and then came decisively down upon
Tom's leg and began a journey over him, his whole heart was
glad—for that meant that he was going to have a new suit
of clothes—without the shadow of a doubt, a gaudy piratical
uniform. Now a procession of ants appeared, from nowhere in

particular, and went about their labours; one struggled manfully by with a dead spider five times as big as itself in its arms, and lugged it straight up a tree-trunk. A brown spotted lady-bug climbed the dizzy height of a grass-blade, and Tom bent down close to it and said:

> Lady-bug, lady-bug, fly away home,
> Your house is on fire, your children's alone;

and she took wing and went off to see about it—which did not surprise the boy, for he knew of old that this insect was credulous about conflagrations, and he had practised upon its simplicity more than once. A tumble-bug came next, heaving sturdily at its ball, and Tom touched the creature, to see it shut its legs against its body and pretend to be dead. The birds were fairly rioting by this time. A cat-bird, the northern mocker, lit in a tree over Tom's head, and trilled out her imitations of her neighbours in a rapture of enjoyment; then a shrill jay swept down, a flash of blue flame, and stopped on a twig almost within the boy's reach, cocked his head to one side and eyed the strangers with a consuming curiosity; a grey squirrel and a big fellow of the 'fox' kind came scurrying along, sitting up at intervals to inspect and chatter at the boys, for the wild things had probably never seen a human being before, and scarcely knew whether to be afraid or not. All Nature was wide awake and stirring now; long lances of sunlight pierced down through the dense foliage far and near, and a few butterflies came fluttering upon the scene.

Tom stirred up the other pirates and they all clattered away with a shout, and in a minute or two were stripped and chasing after and tumbling over each other in the shallow limpid water of the white sand-bar. They felt no longing for the little village sleeping in the distance beyond the majestic waste of water. A vagrant current or a slight rise in the river had carried off their raft, but this only gratified them, since its going was something like burning the bridge between them and civilization.

They came back to camp wonderfully refreshed, glad-hearted, and ravenous; and they soon had the camp-fire blazing up again. Huck found a spring of clear cold water close by, and the boys made cups of broad oak or hickory leaves, and felt that water, sweetened with such a wild-wood charm as that, would be a good enough substitute for coffee. While Joe was slicing bacon for breakfast, Tom and Huck asked him to hold on a minute; they stepped to a promising nook in the river bank and threw in their lines; almost immediately they had reward. Joe had not had time to get impatient before they were back again with some handsome bass, a couple of sun-perch, and a small catfish—provisions enough for quite a family. They fried the fish with the bacon and were astonished; for no fish had ever seemed so delicious before. They did not know that the quicker a fresh-water fish is on the fire after he is caught the better he is; and they reflected little upon what a sauce open-air sleeping, open-air exercise, bathing, and a large ingredient of hunger make, too.

They lay around in the shade after breakfast, while Huck had a smoke, and then went off through the woods on an exploring expedition. They tramped gaily along, over decaying logs, through tangled underbrush, along solemn monarchs of the forest, hung from their crowns to the ground with a drooping regalia of grape-vines. Now and then they came upon snug nooks carpeted with grass and jewelled with flowers.

They found plenty of things to be delighted with, but nothing to be astonished at. They discovered that the island was about three miles long and a quarter of a mile wide, and that the shore it lay closest to was only separated from it by a narrow channel hardly two hundred yards wide. They took a swim about every hour, so it was close upon the middle of the afternoon when they got back to camp. They were too hungry to stop to fish, but they fared sumptuously upon cold ham, and then threw themselves down in the shade to talk. But the talk soon began to drag, and then died. The stillness, the solemnity that brooded in the woods, and the sense of loneliness, began to tell upon the spirits of the boys. They fell to thinking. A sort of undefined longing crept upon them. This took dim shape presently—it was budding home-sickness. Even Finn the Red-Headed was dreaming of his door-steps and empty hogsheads. But they were all ashamed of their weakness, and none was brave enough to speak his thought.

For some time now the boys had been dully conscious of a peculiar sound in the distance, just as one sometimes is of the ticking of a clock which he takes no distinct note of. But now this mysterious sound became more pronounced, and forced a recognition. The boys started, glanced at each other, and then each assumed a listening attitude. There was a long silence, profound and unbroken; then a deep, sullen boom came floating down out of the distance.

'What is it?' exclaimed Joe, under his breath.

'I wonder,' said Tom in a whisper.

''Tain't thunder,' said Huckleberry, in an awed tone, 'becuz thunder——'

'Hark!' said Tom; 'listen—don't talk.'

They waited a time that seemed an age, and then the same muffled boom troubled the solemn hush.

'Let's go and see.'

They sprang to their feet and hurried to the shore toward the town. They parted the bushes on the bank and peered out over the water. The little steam ferryboat was about a mile below the village, drifting with the current. Her broad deck seemed crowded with people. There were a great many skiffs rowing about or floating with the stream in the neighbourhood of the ferry-boat, but the boys could not determine what the men in them were doing. Presently a great jet of white smoke burst from the ferry-boat's side, and as it expanded and rose in a lazy cloud, that same dull throb of sound was borne to the listeners again.

'I know now!' exclaimed Tom; 'somebody's drownded!'

'That's it,' said Huck; 'they done that last summer when Bill Turner got drownded; they shoot a cannon over the water, and that makes him come up to the top. Yes, and they take loaves of bread and put quicksilver in 'em and set 'em afloat, and wherever there's anybody that's drownded, they'll float right there and stop.'

'Yes, I've heard about that,' said Joe. 'I wonder what makes the bread do that.'

'Oh, it ain't the bread so much,' said Tom; 'I reckon it's mostly what they *say* over it before they start it out.'

'But they don't say anything over it,' said Huck. 'I've seen 'em and they don't.'

'Well, that's funny,' said Tom. 'But maybe they say it to themselves. Of *course* they do. Anybody might know that.'

The other boys agreed that there was reason in what Tom said, because an ignorant lump of bread, uninstructed by an incantation, could not be expected to act very intelligently when sent upon an errand of such gravity.

'By jings! I wish I was over there now,' said Joe.

'I do too,' said Huck. 'I'd give heaps to know who it is.'

The boys still listened and watched. Presently a revealing thought flashed through Tom's mind, and he exclaimed:

'Boys, I know who's drownded; it's us!'

They felt like heroes in an instant. Here was a gorgeous triumph; they were missed; they were mourned; hearts were breaking on their account; tears were being shed; accusing memories of unkindnesses to these poor lost lads were rising up, and unavailing regrets and remorse were being indulged; and best of all, the departed were the talk of the whole town, and the envy of all the boys, as far as this dazzling notoriety was concerned. This was fine. It was worth while to be a pirate, after all.

As twilight drew on, the ferry-boat went back to her accustomed business and the skiffs disappeared. The pirates returned to camp. They were jubilant with vanity over their new grandeur and the illustrious trouble they were making. They caught fish, cooked supper and ate it, and then fell to guessing at what the village was thinking and saying about them; and the pictures they drew of the public distress on their account were gratifying to look upon—from their point of view. But when the shadows of night closed them in, they gradually ceased to talk, and sat gazing into the fire, with their minds evidently wandering elsewhere. The excitement was gone now, and Tom and Joe could not keep back thoughts of certain persons at home who were not enjoying this fine frolic as much as they were. Misgivings came; they grew troubled and unhappy; a sigh or two escaped unawares. By and by Joe timidly ventured upon a roundabout 'feeler' as to how the others might look upon a return to civilization—not right now, but——

Tom withered him with derision! Huck, being uncommitted as yet, joined in with Tom, and the waverer quickly 'explained', and was glad to get out of the scrape with as little taint of chicken-hearted home-sickness clinging to his garments as he could. Mutiny was effectually laid to rest for the moment.

As the night deepened Huck began to nod, and presently to snore; Joe followed next. Tom lay upon his elbow motionless for some time, watching the two intently. At last he got up cautiously on his knees, and went searching among the grass and the flickering reflections flung by the camp-fire. He picked up and inspected several large semi-cylinders of the thin white bark of a sycamore, and finally chose two which seemed to suit him. Then he knelt by the fire and painfully wrote something upon each of these with his 'red keel'; one he rolled up and put in his jacket pocket, and the other he put in Joe's hat and removed it to a little distance from the owner. And he also put into the hat certain schoolboy treasures of almost inestimable value—among them a lump of chalk, an india-rubber ball, three fish-hooks, and one of that kind of marbles known as a 'sure 'nough crystal'. Then he tip-toed his way cautiously among the trees till he felt that he was out of hearing, and straightway broke into a keen run in the direction of the sand-bar.

CHAPTER XV

Tom reconnoitres—Learns the Situation—
Reports at Camp

A FEW minutes later Tom was in the shoal water of the bar, wading toward the Illinois shore. Before the depth reached his middle he was half-way over: the current would permit no more wading now, so he struck out confidently to swim the remaining hundred yards. He swam quartering up stream, but still was swept downward rather faster than he had expected. However, he reached the shore finally, and drifted along till he found a low place and drew himself out. He put his hand on his jacket pocket, found his piece of bark safe, and then struck through the woods, following the shore, with streaming garments. Shortly before ten o'clock he came out into an open place opposite the village, and saw the ferry-boat lying in the shadow of the trees and the high bank. Everything was quiet under the blinking stars. He crept down the bank, watching with all his eyes, slipped into the water, swam three or four strokes and climbed into the skiff that did 'yawl' duty at the boat's stern. He laid himself down under the thwarts and waited, panting.

Presently the cracked bell tapped, and a voice gave the order to 'cast off'. A minute or two later the skiff's head was standing high up against the boat's swell, and the voyage was begun. Tom felt happy in his success, for he knew it was the boat's last trip for the night. At the end of a long twelve or fifteen minutes the wheels stopped, and Tom slipped overboard and swam ashore in the dusk, landing fifty yards down stream, out of danger of possible stragglers. He flew along unfrequented alleys, and shortly found himself at his aunt's back fence. He climbed over, approached the 'ell', and looked in at the sitting-room window, for a light was burning there. There sat Aunt Polly, Sid, Mary, and Joe Harper's mother, grouped together, talking. They were by the bed, and the bed was between them and the door. Tom went to the door and began to softly lift the latch; then he pressed gently and the door yielded a crack; he continued pushing cautiously, and quaking every time it creaked, till he judged he might squeeze through on his knees; and so he put his head through and began, warily.

'What makes the candle blow so?' said Aunt Polly. Tom hurried up. 'Why that door's open, I believe. Why, of course it is. No end of strange things now. Go 'long and shut it, Sid.'

Tom disappeared under the bed, just in time. He lay and 'breathed' himself for a time, and then crept to where he could almost touch his aunt's foot.

'But as I was saying,' said Aunt Polly. 'he warn't *bad*, so to say—only misch*ee*vous. Only just giddy, and harum-scarum, you know. He warn't any more responsible than a colt. *He* never meant any harm, and he was the best-hearted boy that ever was' —and she began to cry.

'It was just so with my Joe—always full of his devilment, and up to every kind of mischief, but he was just as unselfish and kind as he could be—and laws bless me, to think I went and whipped him for taking that cream, never once recollecting that I throwed it out myself because it was sour, and I never to see him again in this world, never, never, never, poor abused boy!' And Mrs. Harper sobbed as if her heart would break.

'I hope Tom's better off where he is,' said Sid; 'but if he'd been better in some ways——'

'*Sid!*' Tom felt the glare of the old lady's eye, though he could not see it. 'Not a word against my Tom, now that he's gone! God'll take care of *him*—never you trouble *yourself*, sir. Oh, Mrs. Harper, I don't know how to give him up, I don't know how to give him up! He was such a comfort to me, although he tormented my old heart out of me, 'most.'

'The Lord giveth, and the Lord hath taken away. Blessed be the name of the Lord! But it's *so* hard—oh, it's so hard! Only last Saturday my Joe busted a firecracker right under my nose, and I knocked him sprawling. Little did I know then, how soon—oh, if it was to do over again, I'd hug him and bless him for it.'

'Yes, yes, yes, I know just how you feel, Mrs. Harper, I know just exactly how you feel. No longer ago than yesterday noon, my Tom took and filled the cat full of Pain-killer, and I did think the cretur would tear the house down. And God forgive me, I cracked Tom's head with my thimble, poor boy, poor dead boy. But he's out of all his troubles now. And the last words I ever heard him say was to reproach——'

But this memory was too much for the old lady, and she broke entirely down. Tom was snuffling now himself—and more in pity of himself than anybody else. He could hear Mary crying and putting in a kindly word for him from time to time. He began to have a nobler opinion of himself than ever before. Still he was sufficiently touched by his aunt's grief to long to rush out from under the bed and overwhelm her with joy—and the theatrical gorgeousness of the thing appealed strongly to his nature, too, but he resisted and lay still. He went on listening, and gathered by odds and ends that it was conjectured at first that the boys had got drowned while taking a swim; then the small raft had been missed; next, certain boys said the missing lads had promised that the village should 'hear something' soon; the wise heads had 'put this and that together', and decided that the lads had gone off on that raft, and would turn up at the next town below presently; but toward noon the raft had been found, lodged against the Missouri shore some five or six miles below the village—and then hope perished; they must be drowned, else hunger would have driven them home by nightfall if not sooner. It was believed that the search for the bodies had been a fruitless effort merely because the drowning must have occurred in midchannel, since the boys, being good swimmers, would otherwise have escaped to shore. This was Wednesday night. If the bodies continued missing until Sunday, all hope would be given over, and the funerals would be preached on that morning. Tom shuddered.

Mrs. Harper gave a sobbing good night and turned to go. Then with a mutual impulse the two bereaved women flung themselves into each other's arms and had a good consoling cry, and then parted. Aunt Polly was tender far beyond her wont in her good night to Sid and Mary. Sid snuffled a bit, and Mary went off crying with all her heart.

Aunt Polly knelt down and prayed for Tom so touchingly, so appealingly, and with such measureless love in her words and her old trembling voice, that he was weltering in tears again long before she was through.

He had to keep still long after she went to bed, for she kept making broken-hearted ejaculations from time to time, tossing unrestfully, and turning over. But at last she was still, only moaning a little in her sleep. Now the boy stole out, rose gradually by the bedside, shaded the candle-light with his hand, and stood regarding her. His heart was full of pity for her. He took out his sycamore scroll and placed it by the candle. But something occurred to him, and he lingered, considering. His face lighted with a happy solution of his thoughts; he put the bark hastily in his pocket, then he bent over and kissed the faded lips, and straightway made his stealthy exit, latching the door behind him.

He threaded his way back to the ferry landing, found nobody at large there, and walked boldly on board the boat, for he knew she was tenantless except that there was a watchman, who always turned in and slept like a graven image. He untied the skiff at the stern, slipped into it, and was soon rowing cautiously up stream.

When he had pulled a mile above the village, he started quartering across, and bent himself stoutly to his work. He hit the landing on the other side neatly, for this was a familiar bit of work to him. He was moved to capture the skiff, arguing that it might be considered a ship and therefore legitimate prey for a pirate; but he knew a thorough search would be made for it, and that might end in revelations. So he stepped ashore and entered the wood. He sat down and took a long rest, torturing himself meantime to keep awake, and then started wearily down the home-stretch. The night was far spent. It was broad daylight before he found himself fairly abreast the island-bar. He rested again until the sun was well up and gilding the great river with its splendour, and then he plunged into the stream. A little later he paused, dripping, upon the threshold of the camp, and heard Joe say:

'No, Tom's true-blue, Huck, and he'll come back. He won't desert. He knows that would be a disgrace to a pirate, and Tom's too proud for that sort of thing. He's up to something or other. Now I wonder what?'

'Well, the things is ours anyway, ain't they?'

'Pretty near, but not yet, Huck. The writing says they are if he ain't back here to breakfast.'

'Which he is!' exclaimed Tom, with fine dramatic effect, stepping grandly into camp.

A sumptuous breakfast of bacon and fish was shortly provided, and as the boys set to work upon it, Tom recounted (and adorned) his adventures. They were a vain and boastful company of heroes when the tale was done. Then Tom hid himself away in a shady nook to sleep till noon, and the other pirates got ready to fish and explore.

CHAPTER XVI

A Day's Amusements—Tom reveals a Secret—
The Pirates take a Lesson—A Night Surprise—
An Indian War

AFTER dinner all the gang turned out to hunt for turtle eggs on the bar. They went about poking sticks into the sand, and when they found a soft place they went down on their knees and dug with their hands. Sometimes they would take fifty or sixty eggs out of one hole. They were perfectly round, white things, a trifle smaller than an English walnut. They had a famous fried-egg feast that night, and another on Friday morning. After breakfast they went whooping and prancing out on the bar, and chased each other round and round, shedding clothes as they went, until they were naked, and then continued the frolic far away up the shoal water of the bar, against the stiff current, which latter tripped their legs from under them from time to time, and greatly increased the fun. And now and then they stooped in a group and splashed water in each other's faces with their palms, gradually approaching each other with averted faces, to avoid the strangling sprays, and finally gripping and struggling till the best man ducked his neighbour, and then they all went under in a tangle of white legs and arms, and came up blowing, sputtering, laughing, and gasping for breath at one and the same time.

When they were well exhausted, they would run out and sprawl on the dry, hot sand, and lie there and cover themselves up with it, and by and by break for the water again and go through the original performance once more. Finally it occurred to them that their naked skin represented flesh-coloured 'tights' very fairly; so they drew a ring in the sand and had a circus—with three clowns in it, for none would yield this proudest post to his neighbour.

Next they got their marbles, and played 'knucks' and 'ring-taw' and 'keeps',* till that amusement grew stale. Then Joe and Huck had another swim, but Tom would not venture, because he found that in kicking off his trousers he had kicked his string of rattlesnake rattles off his ankles, and he wondered how he had escaped cramp so long without the protection of this mysterious charm. He did not venture again until he had found it, and by that time the other boys were tired and ready to rest. They gradually wandered apart, dropped into the 'dumps', and fell to gazing longingly across the wide river to where the village lay drowsing in the sun. Tom found himself writing *Becky* in the sand with his big toe; he scratched it out, and was angry with himself for his weakness. But he wrote it again, nevertheless; he could not help it. He erased it once more, and then took himself out of temptation by driving the other boys together and joining them.

But Joe's spirits had gone down almost beyond resurrection. He was so home-sick that he could hardly endure the misery of it. The tears lay very near the surface. Huck was melancholy too. Tom was down-hearted, but tried hard not to show it. He had a secret which he was not ready to tell yet, but if this mutinous depression was not broken up soon, he would have to bring it out. He said, with a great show of cheerfulness:

'I bet there's been pirates on this island before, boys. We'll explore it again. They've hid treasures here somewhere. How'd you feel to light on a rotten chest full of gold and silver—hey?'

But it roused only a faint enthusiasm, which faded out, with no reply. Tom tried one or two other seductions; but they failed too. It was discouraging work. Joe sat poking up the sand with a stick, and looking very gloomy. Finally he said:

'Oh, boys, let's give it up. I want to go home. It's so lonesome.'

'Oh, no, Joe, you'll feel better by and by,' said Tom. 'Just think of the fishing that's here.'

'I don't care for the fishing. I want to go home.'

'But Joe, there ain't such another swimming place anywhere.'

'Swimming's no good; I don't seem to care for it, somehow, when there ain't anybody to say I shan't go in. I mean to go home.'

'Oh, shucks! baby! You want to see your mother, I reckon.'

'Yes, I *do* want to see my mother, and you would too, if you had one. I ain't any more baby than you are.' And Joe snuffled a little.

'Well, we'll let the cry-baby go home to his mother, *won't* we, Huck? Poor thing—does it want to see its mother? And so it shall. *You* like it here, *don't* you, Huck? We'll stay, won't we?'

Huck said 'Y-e-s'—without any heart in it.

'I'll never speak to you again as long as I live,' said Joe, rising. 'There now!' And he moved moodily away and began to dress himself.

'Who cares?' said Tom. 'Nobody wants you to. Go 'long home and get laughed at. Oh, you're a nice pirate! Huck and me ain't cry-babies. We'll stay, won't we, Huck? Let him go if he wants to. I reckon we can get along without him, per'aps.'

But Tom was uneasy nevertheless, and was alarmed to see Joe go sullenly on with his dressing. And then it was discomforting to see Huck eyeing Joe's preparations so wistfully, and keeping up such an ominous silence. Presently, without a parting word, Joe began to wade off toward the Illinois shore. Tom's heart began to sink. He glanced at Huck. Huck could not bear the look, and dropped his eyes. Then he said:

'I want to go too, Tom; it was getting so lonesome anyway, and now it'll be worse. Let's us go too, Tom.'

'I won't; you can all go if you want to. I mean to stay.'

'Tom, I better go.'

'Well, go 'long—who's hindering you?'

Huck began to pick up his scattered clothes. He said:

'Tom, I wisht you'd come too. Now you think it over. We'll wait for you when we get to shore.'

'Well, you'll wait a blame long time, that's all.'

Huck started sorrowfully away, and Tom stood looking after him, with a strong desire tugging at his heart to yield his pride and go along too. He hoped the boys would stop, but they still waded slowly on. It suddenly dawned on Tom that it was become very lonely and still. He made one final struggle with his pride, and then darted after his comrades, yelling:

'Wait! wait! I want to tell you something!'

They presently stopped and turned around. When he got to where they were, he began unfolding his secret, and they listened moodily till at last they saw the 'point' he was driving at, and then they set up a war-whoop of applause and said it was 'splendid'; and said if he had told them that at first, they wouldn't have started away. He made a plausible excuse; but his real reason had been the fear that not even the secret would keep them with him any very great length of time, and so he had meant to hold it in reserve as a last seduction.

The lads came gaily back and went at their sports again with a will, chattering all the time about Tom's stupendous plan and admiring the genius of it. After a dainty egg and fish dinner, Tom said he wanted to learn to smoke now. Joe caught at the idea, and said he would like to try too. So Huck made pipes and filled them. These novices had never smoked anything before but cigars made of grape-vine, and they 'bit' the tongue, and were not considered manly, anyway.

Now they stretched themselves out on their elbows and began to puff charily, and with slender confidence. The smoke had an unpleasant taste, and they gagged a little, but Tom said:

'Why, it's just as easy! If I'd a know'd *this* was all, I'd a learnt long ago.'

'So would I,' said Joe. 'It's just nothing.'

'Why, many a time I've looked at people smoking and thought, Well, I wish I could do that; but I never thought I could,' said Tom. 'That's just the way with me, ain't it, Huck? You've heard me talk just that way, haven't you, Huck? I'll leave it to Huck if I haven't.'

'Yes, heaps of times,' said Huck.

'Well, I have too,' said Tom, 'oh, hundreds of times. Once down by the slaughter-house. Don't you remember, Huck? Bob Tanner was there, and Johnny Miller, and Jeff Thatcher, when I said it. Don't you remember, Huck, 'bout me saying that?'

'Yes, that's so,' said Huck. 'That was the day after I lost a white alley—no, 'twas the day before!'

'There, I told you so,' said Tom. 'Huck recollects it.'

'I b'leeve I could smoke this pipe all day,' said Joe. '*I* don't feel sick.'

'Neither do I,' said Tom. '*I* could smoke it all day, but I bet Jeff Thatcher couldn't.'

'Jeff Thatcher! Why, he'd keel over just with two draws. Just let him try it once; *he'd* see!'

'I bet he would, and Johnny Miller—I wish I could see Johnny Miller tackle it once.'

'Oh, don't *I*?' said Joe. 'Why, I bet you Johnny Miller couldn't any more do this than nothing. Just one little snifter would fetch *him*.'

''Deed it would, Joe. Say—I wish the boys could see us now.'

'So do I!'

'Say—boys, don't say anything about it, and some time when they're around I'll come up to you and say, "Joe, got a pipe? I want a smoke!" And you'll say, kind of careless like, as if it warn't anything, you'll say, "Yes. I got my *old* pipe, and another one, but my tobacker ain't very good!" And I'll say, "Oh, that's all right, if it's *strong* enough." And then you'll out with the pipes, and we'll light up just as ca'm, and then just see 'em look!'

'By jings that'll be gay, Tom! I wish it was *now*!'

'So do I! And when we tell 'em we learned when we was off pirating, won't they wish they'd been along!'

'Oh, I reckon not. I'll just *bet* they will!'

So the talk ran on; but presently it began to flag a trifle, and grow disjointed. The silences widened; the expectoration marvellously increased. Every pore inside the boys' cheeks became a spouting fountain; they could scarcely bale out the cellars under their tongues fast enough to prevent an inundation; little overflowings down their throats occurred in spite of all they could do, and sudden retchings followed every time. Both boys were looking very pale and miserable now. Joe's pipe dropped from his nerveless fingers. Tom's followed. Both fountains were going furiously, and both pumps baling with might and main. Joe said feebly:

'I've lost my knife. I reckon I better go and find it.'

Tom said, with quivering lips and halting utterance: 'I'll help you. You go over that way, and I'll hunt around by the spring. No, you needn't come, Huck—we can find it.'

So Huck sat down again, and waited an hour. Then he found it lonesome, and went to find his comrades. They were wide apart in the woods, both very pale, both fast asleep. But something informed him that if they had had any trouble they had got rid of it.

They were not talkative at supper that night; they had a humble look; and when Huck prepared his pipe after the meal, and was going to prepare theirs, they said no, they were not feeling very well—something they ate at dinner had disagreed with them.

About midnight Joe awoke, and called the boys. There was a brooding oppressiveness in the air that seemed to bode something. The boys huddled themselves together, and sought the friendly companionship of the fire, though the dull dead heat of the breathless atmosphere was stifling. They sat still, intent and waiting. The solemn hush continued. Beyond the light of the fire everything was swallowed up in the blackness of darkness. Presently there came a quivering glow that vaguely revealed the foliage for a moment and then vanished. By and by another came, a little stronger. Then another. Then a faint moan came sighing through the branches of the forest, and the boys felt a fleeting breath upon their cheeks, and shuddered with the fancy that the Spirit of the Night had gone by. There was a pause. Now a weird flash turned night into day, and showed every little grass-blade, separate and distinct, that grew about their feet. And it showed three white startled faces, too. A deep peal of thunder went rolling and tumbling down the heavens, and lost itself in sullen rumblings in the distance. A sweep of chilly air passed by, rustling all the leaves and snowing the flaky ashes broadcast about the fire. Another fierce glare lit up the forest, and an instant crash followed that seemed to rend the tree-tops right over the boys' heads. They clung together in terror, in the thick gloom that followed. A few big rain-drops fell pattering upon the leaves.

'Quick, boys, go for the tent!' exclaimed Tom.

They sprang away, stumbling over roots and among vines in the dark, no two plunging in the same direction. A furious blast roared through the trees, making everything sing as it went. One blinding flash after another came, and peal on peal of deafening thunder. And now a drenching rain poured down, and the rising hurricane drove it in sheets along the ground. The boys cried out to each other, but the roaring wind and the booming thunder-blasts drowned their voices utterly. However, one by one they straggled in at last, and took shelter under the tent, cold, scared, and streaming with water; but to have company in misery seemed something to be grateful for. They could not talk, the old sail flapped so furiously, even if the other noises would have allowed them. The tempest rose higher and higher, and presently the sail tore loose from its fastenings, and went winging away on the blast. The boys seized each other's hands, and fled, with many tumblings and bruises, to the shelter of a great oak that stood upon the river bank. Now the battle was at its highest. Under the ceaseless conflagration of lightning that flamed in the skies, everything below stood out in clean-cut and shadowless distinctness; the bending trees, the billowy river, white with foam, the driving spray of spume-flakes, the dim outlines of the high bluffs on the other side, glimpsed through the drifting cloud-rack and the slanting veil of rain. Every little while some giant tree yielded the fight and fell crashing through the younger growth; and the unflagging thunder-peals came now in ear-splitting explosive bursts, keen and sharp, and unspeakably appalling. The storm culminated in one matchless effort that seemed likely to tear the island to pieces, burn it up, drown it to the tree-tops, blow it away, and deafen every creature in it, all at one and the same moment. It was a wild night for homeless young heads to be out in.

But at last the battle was done, and the forces retired, with weaker and weaker threatenings and grumblings, and peace resumed her sway. The boys went back to camp a good deal awed; but they found there was still something to be thankful for, because the great sycamore, the shelter of their beds, was a ruin now, blasted by the lightning, and they were not under it when the catastrophe happened.

Everything in camp was drenched, the campfire as well; for they were but heedless lads, like their generation, and had made no provision against rain. Here was matter for dismay, for they were soaked through and chilled. They were eloquent in their distress; but they presently discovered that the fire had eaten so far up under the great log it had been built against (where it curved upward and separated itself from the ground), that a hand-breadth or so of it had escaped wetting; so they patiently wrought until, with shreds and bark gathered from the under sides of sheltered logs, they coaxed the fire to burn again. They then piled on great dead boughs till they had a roaring furnace and were glad hearted once more. They dried their boiled ham and had a feast, and after that they sat by the fire and expanded and glorified their midnight adventure until morning, for there was not a dry spot to sleep on, anywhere around.

As the sun began to steal in upon the boys, drowsiness came over them and they went out on the sand-bar and lay down to sleep. They got scorched out by and by, and drearily set about getting breakfast. After the meal they felt rusty, and stiff-jointed, and a little home-sick once more. Tom saw the signs, and fell to cheering up the pirates as well as he could. But they cared nothing for marbles, or circus, or swimming, or anything. He reminded them of the imposing secret, and raised a ray of cheer. While it lasted he got them interested in a new device. This was to knock off being pirates for a while, and be Indians for a change. They were attracted by this idea; so it was not long before they were stripped, and striped from head to heel with black mud, like so many zebras—all of them chiefs, of course—and they went tearing through the woods to attack an English settlement.

By and by they separated into three hostile tribes, and darted upon each other from ambush with dreadful war-whoops, and killed and scalped each other by thousands. It was a gory day. Consequently it was an extremely satisfactory one.

They assembled in camp towards supper-time, hungry and happy. But now a difficulty arose—hostile Indians could not break the bread of hospitality together without first making peace, and this was a simple impossibility without smoking a pipe of peace. There was no other process that ever they had heard of. Two of the savages almost wished they had remained pirates. However, there was no other way, so with such show of cheerfulness as they could muster they called for the pipe and took their whiff, as it passed, in due form.

And behold, they were glad they had gone into savagery, for they had gained something; they found that they could now smoke a little without having to go and hunt for a lost knife; they did not get sick enough to be seriously uncomfortable. They were not likely to fool away this high promise for lack of effort. No, they practised cautiously after supper with right fair success, and so they spent a jubilant evening. They were prouder and happier in their new acquirement than they would have been in the scalping and skinning of the Six nations. We will leave them to smoke and chatter and brag, since we have no further use for them at present.

CHAPTER XVII

Memories of the Lost Heroes—The Point in Tom's Secret

BUT there was no hilarity in the little town that same tranquil Saturday afternoon. The Harpers and Aunt Polly's family were being put into mourning with great grief and many tears. An unusual quiet possessed the village, although it was ordinarily quiet enough, in all conscience. The villagers conducted their concerns with an absent air, and talked little; but they sighed often. The Saturday holiday seemed a burden to the children. They had no heart in their sports, and gradually gave them up.

In the afternoon Becky Thatcher found herself moping about the deserted school-house yard, and feeling very melancholy. But she found nothing there to comfort her. She soliloquized:

'Oh, if I only had his brass andiron-knob again! But I haven't got anything now to remember him by;' and she choked back a little sob.

Presently she stopped, and said to herself:

'It was right here. Oh, if it was to do over again, I wouldn't say that—I wouldn't say it for the whole world. But he's gone now; I'll never, never, never see him any more.'

This thought broke her down, and she wandered away with the tears rolling down her cheeks. Then quite a group of boys and girls—playmates of Tom's and Joe's—came by, and stood looking over the paling fence and talking in reverent tones of how Tom did so-and-so the last time they saw him, and how Joe said this and that small trifle (pregnant with awful prophecy, as they could easily see now!)—and each speaker pointed out the exact spot where the lost lads stood at the time, and then added something like, 'and I was a-standing just so—just as I am now, and as if you was him—I was as close as that—and he smiled, just this way—and then something seemed to go all over me, like—awful, you know—and I never thought what it meant, of course, but I can see now!'

Then there was a dispute about who saw the dead boys last in life, and many claimed that dismal distinction, and offered evidences more or less tampered with by the witness; and when it was ultimately decided who *did* see the departed last, and exchanged the last words with them, the lucky parties took upon themselves a sort of sacred importance, and were gaped at and envied by all the rest. One poor chap, who had no other grandeur to offer, said, with tolerably manifest pride in the remembrance:

'Well, Tom Sawyer he licked me once.'

But that bid for glory was a failure. Most of the boys could say that, and so that cheapened the distinction too much. The group loitered away, still recalling memories of the lost heroes in awed voices.

When the Sunday-school hour was finished the next morning, the bell began to toll, instead of ringing in the usual way. It was a very still Sabbath, and the mournful sound seemed in keeping with the musing hush that lay upon nature. The villagers began to gather, loitering a moment in the vestibule to converse in whispers about the sad event. But there was no whispering in the house; only the funereal rustling of dresses, as the women gathered to their seats, disturbed the silence there. None could remember when the little church had been so full before. There was finally a waiting pause, an expectant dumbness, and then Aunt Polly entered, followed by Sid and Mary, and then by the Harper family, all in deep black, and the whole congregation, the old minister as well, rose reverently and stood, until the mourners were seated in the front pew. There was another communing silence, broken at intervals by muffled sobs, and then the minister spread his hands abroad and prayed. A moving hymn was sung, and the text followed: 'I am the Resurrection and the Life.'

As the service proceeded, the clergyman drew such pictures of the graces, the winning ways, and the rare promise of the lost lads, that every soul there, thinking he recognized these pictures, felt a pang in remembering that he had persistently blinded himself to them always before, and had as persistently seen only faults and flaws in the poor boys. The minister related many a touching incident in the lives of the departed, too, which illustrated their sweet, generous natures, and the people could easily see, now, how noble and beautiful those episodes were, and remembered with grief that at the time they occurred they had seemed rank rascalities, well deserving of the cowhide. The congregation became more and more moved as the pathetic tale went on, till at last the whole company broke down and joined the weeping mourners in a chorus of anguished sobs, the preacher himself giving way to his feelings, and crying in the pulpit.

There was a rustle in the gallery which nobody noticed; a moment later the church door creaked; the minister raised his streaming eyes above his handkerchief, and stood transfixed! First one and then another pair of eyes followed the minister's, and then, almost with one impulse, the congregation rose and stared while the three dead boys came marching up the aisle, Tom in the lead, Joe next, and Huck, a ruin of drooping rags, sneaking sheepishly in the rear. They had been hid in the unused gallery, listening to their own funeral sermon!

Aunt Polly, Mary, and the Harpers threw themselves upon their restored ones, smothered them with kisses, and poured out thanksgivings, while poor Huck stood abashed and uncomfortable, not knowing exactly what to do or where to hide from so many unwelcoming eyes. He wavered, and started to slink away, but Tom seized him and said:

'Aunt Polly, it ain't fair. Somebody's got to be glad to see Huck.'

'And so they shall! *I*'m glad to see him, poor motherless thing!' And the loving attentions Aunt Polly lavished upon him were the one thing capable of making him more uncomfortable than he was before.

Suddenly the minister shouted at the top of his voice:

' "Praise God from whom all blessings flow"—*sing!*—and put your hearts in it!'

And they did. Old Hundred swelled up with a triumphant burst, and while it shook the rafters Tom Sawyer the Pirate looked round upon the envying juveniles about him, and confessed in his heart that this was the proudest moment of his life.

As the 'sold' congregation trooped out, they said they would almost be willing to be made ridiculous again to hear old Hundred sung like that once more.

Tom got more cuffs and kisses that day—according to Aunt Polly's varying moods—than he had earned before in a year; and he hardly knew which expressed the most gratefulness to God and affection for himself.

CHAPTER XVIII

*Tom's Feelings investigated—Wonderful Dream
—Becky Thatcher overshadowed—Tom becomes
Jealous—Black Revenge*

THAT was Tom's great secret—the scheme to return home
with his brother pirates and attend their own funerals.
They had paddled over to the Missouri shore on a log, at
dusk on Saturday, landing five or six miles below the village;
they had slept in the woods at the edge of the town till nearly
daylight, and had then crept through back lanes and alleys and
finished their sleep in the gallery of the church among a chaos
of invalided benches.

At breakfast, Monday morning, Aunt Polly and Mary were
very loving to Tom, and very attentive to his wants. There
was an unusual amount of talk. In the course of it Aunt Polly
said:

'Well, I don't say it wasn't a fine joke, Tom, to keep everybody suffering most a week so you boys had a good time, but it is
a pity you could be so hard-hearted as to let *me* suffer so. If you
could come over on a log to go to your funeral, you could have
come over and give me a hint some way that you warn't *dead*
but only run off.'

'Yes, you could have done that, Tom,' said Mary; 'and I
believe you would if you had thought of it.'

'Would you, Tom?' said Aunt Polly, her face lighting wistfully. 'Say, now, would you, if you'd thought of it?'

'I—well, I don't know. 'Twould a spoiled everything.'

'Tom, I hoped you loved me that much,' said Aunt Polly,
with a grieved tone that discomforted the boy. 'It would been

133

something if you'd cared enough to *think* of it, even if you didn't *do* it.'

'Now, auntie, that ain't any harm,' pleaded Mary; 'it's only Tom's giddy way—he is always in such a rush that he never thinks of anything.'

'More's the pity. Sid would have thought. And Sid would have come and *done* it, too. Tom, you'll look back, some day, when it's too late, and wish you'd cared a little more for me when it would have cost you so little.'

'Now, auntie, you know I do care for you,' said Tom.

'I'd know it better if you acted more like it.'

'I wish now I'd thought,' said Tom, with a repentant tone; 'but I dreamed about you, anyway. That's something, ain't it?'

'It ain't much—a cat does that much—but it's better than nothing. What did you dream?'

'Why, Wednesday night I dreamt that you was sitting over there by the bed, and Sid was sitting by the wood-box, and Mary next to him.'

'Well, so we did. So we always do. I'm glad your dreams could take even that much trouble about us.'

'And I dreamt that Joe Harper's mother was here.'

'Why, she *was* here! Did you dream any more?'

'Oh, lots. But it's so dim now.'

'Well, *try* to recollect—can't you?'

'Somehow it seems to me that the wind—the wind blowed the—the——'

'Try harder, Tom! The wind did blow something. Come!'

Tom pressed his fingers on his forehead an anxious minute, and then said:

'I've got it now! I've got it now! It blowed the candle!'

'Mercy on us! Go on, Tom—go on!'

'And it seems to me that you said, 'Why, I believe that that door——' "

'Go *on*, Tom!'

'Just let me study a moment—just a moment. Oh, yes—you said you believed the door was open.'

'As I'm a sitting here, I did! Didn't I, Mary? Go on!'

'And then—and then—well I won't be certain, but it seems like as if you made Sid go and—and——'

'Well? Well? What did I make him do, Tom? What did I make him do?'

'You made him—you——. Oh, you made him shut it!'

'Well, for the land's sake! I never heard the beat of that in all my days! Don't tell *me* there ain't anything in dreams any more. Sereny Harper shall know of this before I'm an hour older. I'd like to see her get around *this* with her rubbage 'bout superstition. Go on, Tom!'

'Oh, it's all getting just as bright as day, now. Next you said I warn't *bad*, only mischeevous and harum-scarum, and not any more responsible than—than—I think it was a colt or something.'

'And so it was! Well, goodness gracious! Go on, Tom!'

'And then you began to cry.'

'So I did. So I did. Not the first time, neither. And then——'

'Then Mrs. Harper, she began to cry, and said Joe was just the same, and she wished she hadn't whipped him for taking cream when she'd throwed it out her own self——'

'Tom! The sperrit was upon you! You was a prophesying—that's what you was doing! Land alive!—go on, Tom!'

'Then Sid he said—he said——'

'I don't think I said anything,' said Sid.

'Yes, you did, Sid,' said Mary.

'Shut your heads and let Tom go on! What did he say, Tom?'

'He said—I *think* he said he hoped I was better off where I was gone to, but if I'd been better sometimes——'

'*There*, d'you hear that? It was his very words!'

'And you shut him up sharp.'

'I lay I did! There must a been an angel there. There *was* an angel there, somewheres!'

'And Mrs. Harper told about Joe scaring her with a fire-cracker, and you told about Peter and the Pain-killer——'

'Just as true as I live!'

'And then there was a whole lot of talk 'bout dragging the river for us, and 'bout having the funeral Sunday, and then you and old Mrs. Harper hugged and cried, and she went.'

'It happened just so! It happened just so, as sure as I'm a sitting on these very tracks. Tom, you couldn't told it more like if you'd seen it! And *then* what? Go on, Tom!'

'Then I thought you prayed for me—and I could see you and hear every word you said. And you went to bed, and I was so sorry, that I took and wrote on a piece of sycamore bark, "*We ain't dead—we are only off being pirates*," and put it on the table by the candle; and then you looked so good, laying there asleep, that I thought I went and leaned over and kissed you on the lips.'

'Did you, Tom, *did* you? I just forgive you everything for that!' And she seized the boy in a crushing embrace that made him feel like the guiltiest of villains.

'It was very kind, even though it was only a dream.' Sid soliloquized just audibly.

'Shut up, Sid! A body does just the same in a dream as he'd do if he was awake. Here's a big Milum apple*I've been saving for you, Tom, if you was ever found again—now go 'long to school. I'm thankful to the good God and Father of us all I've got you back, that's long-suffering and merciful to them that believe on Him and keep His word, though goodness knows I'm unworthy of it, but if only the worthy ones got His blessings and had His hands to help them over the rough places, there's few enough would smile here or ever enter into His rest when the long night comes. Go 'long, Sid, Mary, Tom—take yourselves off— you've hendered me long enough.'

136

The children left for school, and the old lady to call on Mrs. Harper, and vanquish her realism with Tom's marvellous dream. Sid had better judgment than to utter the thought that was in his mind as he left the house. It was this:

'Pretty thin—as long a dream as that, without any mistakes in it!'

What a hero Tom was become now! He did not go skipping and prancing, but moved with a dignified swagger, as became a pirate who felt that the public eye was on him. And indeed it was; he tried not to seem to see the looks or hear the remarks as he passed along, but they were food and drink to him. Smaller boys than himself flocked at his heels, as proud to be seen with him and tolerated by him as if he had been the drummer at the head of a procession or the elephant leading a menagerie into town. Boys of his own size pretended not to know he had been away at all; but they were consuming with envy, nevertheless. They would have given anything to have that swarthy, sun-tanned skin of his, and his glittering notoriety; and Tom would not have parted with either for a circus.

At school the children made so much of him and of Joe, and delivered such eloquent admiration from their eyes, that the two heroes were not long in becoming insufferably 'stuck up'. They began to tell their adventures to hungry listeners—but they only began; it was not a thing likely to have an end, with imaginations like theirs to furnish material. And finally, when they got out their pipes and went serenely puffing around, the very summit of glory was reached.

Tom decided that he could be independent of Becky Thatcher now. Glory was sufficient. He would live for glory. Now that he was distinguished, maybe she would be wanting to 'make up'. Well, let her—she should see that he could be as indifferent as some other people. Presently she arrived. Tom pretended not to see her. He moved away and joined a group of boys and girls and began to talk. Soon he observed that she was tripping gaily back and forth with flushed face and dancing eyes, pretending to be busy chasing school-mates, and screaming with laughter when she made a capture; but he noticed that she always made her captures in his vicinity, and that she seemed to cast a conscious eye in his direction at such times, too. It gratified all the vicious vanity that was in him; and so, instead of winning him it only 'set him up' the more and made him the more diligent to avoid betraying that he knew she was about. Presently she gave over skylarking, and moved irresolutely about, sighing once or twice and glancing furtively and wistfully toward Tom. Then she observed that now Tom was talking more particularly to Amy Lawrence than to anyone else. She felt a sharp pang, and grew disturbed and uneasy at once. She tried to go away, but her feet were treacherous, and carried her to the group instead. She said to a girl almost at Tom's elbow—with sham vivacity:

'Why, Mary Austin! you bad girl, why didn't you come to Sunday-school?'

'I did come—didn't you see me?'

'Why, no! Did you? Where did you sit?'

'I was in Miss Peter's class, where I always go. I saw *you*.'

'Did you? Why, it's funny I didn't see you. I wanted to tell you about the picnic.'

'Oh, that's jolly. Who's going to give it?'

'My ma's going to let me have one.'

'Oh, goody; I hope she'll let *me* come.'

'Well, she will. The picnic's for me. She'll let anybody come that I want, and I want you.'

'That's ever so nice. When is it going to be?'

'By and by. Maybe about vacation.'

'Oh, won't it be fun! You going to have all the girls and boys?'

'Yes, everyone that's friends to me—or wants to be;' and she glanced ever so furtively at Tom, but he talked right along to Amy Lawrence about the terrible storm on the island, and

how the lightning tore the great sycamore tree 'all to flinders'
while he was 'standing within three feet of it.'

'Oh, may I come?' said Gracie Miller.

'Yes.'

'And me?' said Sally Rogers.

'Yes?'

'And me, too?' said Susy Harper. 'And Joe?'

'Yes.'

And so on, with clapping of joyful hands, till all the group
had begged for invitations but Tom and Amy. Then Tom
turned coolly away, still talking, and took Amy with him.
Becky's lips trembled and the tears came to her eyes; she hid
these signs with a forced gaiety and went on chattering, but the
life had gone out of the picnic now, and out of everything else;
she got away as soon as she could and hid herself, and had what
her sex call 'a good cry.' Then she sat moody, with wounded
pride till the bell rang. She roused up now, with a vindictive cast
in her eye, and gave her plaited tails a shake, and said she knew
what *she'd* do.

At recess Tom continued his flirtation with Amy with
jubilant self-satisfaction. And he kept drifting about to find
Becky and lacerate her with the performance. At last he spied
her, but there was a sudden falling of his mercury. She was sitting
cosily on a little bench behind the school-house, looking at a
picture-book with Alfred Temple; and so absorbed were they,
and their heads so close together over the book, that they did not
seem to be conscious of anything in the world besides. Jealousy
ran red-hot through Tom's veins. He began to hate himself for
throwing away the chance Becky had offered for a reconcilia-
tion. He called himself a fool, and all the hard names he could
think of. He wanted to cry with vexation. Amy chatted happily
along as they walked, for her heart was singing, but Tom's
tongue had lost its function. He did not hear what Amy was
saying, and whenever she paused expectantly he could only

stammer an awkward assent, which was as often misplaced as otherwise. He kept drifting to the rear of the school-house again and again, to sear his eye-balls with the hateful spectacle there. He could not help it. And it maddened him to see, as he thought he saw, that Becky Thatcher never once suspected that he was even in the land of the living. But she did see, nevertheless; and she knew she was winning her fight, too, and was glad to see him suffer as she had suffered.

Amy's happy prattle became intolerable. Tom hinted at things he had to attend to; things that must be done; and time was fleeting. But in vain—the girl chirped on. Tom thought, 'Oh, hang her, ain't I ever going to get rid of her?' At last he *must* be attending to those things; and she said artlessly that she would be 'around' when school let out. And he hastened away, hating her for it.

'Any other boy!' Tom thought, grating his teeth. 'Any boy in the whole town but that Saint Louis smarty, that thinks he dresses so fine and is aristocracy! Oh, all right, I licked you the first day you ever saw this town, mister, and I'll lick you again! You just wait till I catch you out! I'll just take and——'

And he went through the motions of thrashing an imaginary boy—pummelling the air, and kicking and gouging.

'Oh, you do, do you? you holler 'nough, do you? Now, then, let that learn you!'

And so the imaginary flogging was finished to his satisfaction.

Tom fled home at noon. His conscience could not endure any more of Amy's grateful happiness, and his jealousy could bear no more of the other distress. Becky resumed her picture-inspections with Alfred, but as the minutes dragged along and no Tom came to suffer, her triumph began to cloud and she lost interest; gravity and absent-mindedness followed, and then melancholy; two or three times she pricked up her ear at a footstep, but it was a false hope; no Tom came. At last she grew entirely miserable, and wished she hadn't carried it so far. When poor

Alfred, seeing that he was losing her, he did not know how, and kept exclaiming: 'Oh, here's a jolly one! look at this!' she lost patience at last and said, 'Oh, don't bother me! I don't care for them!' and burst into tears, and got up and walked away.

Alfred dropped alongside and was going to try to comfort her, but she said:

'Go away and leave me alone, can't you. I hate you!'

So the boy halted, wondering what he could have done—for she had said she would look at pictures all through the nooning —and she walked on, crying. Then Alfred went musing into the deserted school-house. He was humiliated and angry. He easily guessed his way to the truth—the girl had simply made a convenience of him to vent her spite upon Tom Sawyer. He was far from hating Tom the less when this thought occurred to him. He wished there was some way to get that boy into trouble without much risk to himself. Tom's spelling-book fell under his eye. Here was his opportunity. He gratefully opened to the lesson for the afternoon, and poured ink upon the page. Becky, glancing in at a window behind him at the moment, saw the act and moved on, without discovering herself. She started homeward, now, intending to find Tom and tell him: Tom would be thankful, and their troubles would be healed. Before she was halfway home, however, she had changed her mind. The thought of Tom's treatment of her when she was talking about her picnic came scorching back, and filled her with shame. She resolved to let him get whipped on the damaged spelling-book's account and to hate him for ever into the bargain.

CHAPTER XIX

Tom tells the Truth

TOM arrived at home in a dreary mood, and the first thing his aunt said to him showed him that he had brought his sorrows to an unpromising market:

'Tom, I've a notion to skin you alive.'

'Auntie, what have I done?'

'Well, you've done enough. Here I go over to Sereny Harper, like an old softy, expecting I'm going to make her believe all that rubbage about that dream, when, lo and behold you, she'd found out from Joe that you was over here and heard all the talk we had that night. Tom, I don't know what is to become of a boy that will act like that. It makes me feel so bad to think you could let me go to Sereny Harper, and make such a fool of myself, and never say a word.'

This was a new aspect of the thing. His smartness of the morning had seemed to Tom a good joke before, and very ingenious. It merely looked mean and shabby now. He hung his head and could not think of anything to say for a moment; then he said:

'Auntie, I wish I hadn't done it—but I didn't think.'

'Oh, child, you never think. You never think of anything but your own selfishness. You could think to come all the way over here from Jackson's Island in the night to laugh at our troubles, and you could think to fool me with a lie about a dream; but you couldn't ever think to pity us and save us from sorrow.'

'Auntie, I know now it was mean, but I didn't mean to be mean; I didn't, honest. And besides, I didn't come over here to laugh at you that night.'

'What did you come for, then?'

'It was to tell you not to be uneasy about us, because we hadn't got drowned.'

'Tom, Tom, I would be the thankfullest soul in this world if I could believe you ever had as good a thought as that, but you know you never did—and I know it, Tom.'

'Indeed and 'deed I did, auntie—I wish I may never stir if I didn't.'

'Oh, Tom, don't lie—don't do it. It only makes things a hundred times worse.'

'It ain't a lie, auntie; it's the truth. I wanted to keep you from grieving—that was all that made me come.'

'I'd give the whole world to believe that—it would cover up a power of sins, Tom. I'd 'most be glad you'd run off and acted so bad. But it ain't reasonable; because, why didn't you tell me, child?'

'Why, you see, auntie, when you got to talking about the funeral, I just got all full of the idea of our coming and hiding in the church, and I couldn't, somehow, bear to spoil it. So I just put the bark back in my pocket and kept mum.'

'What bark?'

'The bark I had wrote on to tell you we'd gone pirating. I wish, now, you'd waked up when I kissed you—I do, honest.'

The hard lines in his aunt's face relaxed, and sudden tenderness dawned in her eyes.

'*Did* you kiss me, Tom?'

'Why, yes, I did.'

'Are you sure you did, Tom?'

'Why, yes, I did, auntie—certain sure.'

'What did you kiss me for, Tom?'

'Because I loved you so, and you laid there moaning, and I was so sorry.'

The words sounded like truth. The old lady could not hide a tremor in her voice when she said:

'Kiss me again, Tom!—and be off with you to school, now, and don't bother me any more.'

The moment he was gone, she ran to a closet and got out the ruin of a jacket which Tom had gone pirating in. Then she stopped with it in her hand, and said to herself:

'No, I don't dare. Poor boy, I reckon he's lied about it—but it's a blessed, blessed lie, there's such comfort come from it. I hope the Lord—I *know* the Lord will forgive him, because it was such good-heartedness in him to tell it. But I don't want to find out it's a lie. I won't look.'

She put the jacket away, and stood by musing a minute. Twice she put out her hand to take the garment again, and twice she refrained. Once more she ventured, and this time she fortified herself with the thought: 'It's a good lie—it's a good lie—I won't let it grieve me.' So she sought the jacket pocket. A moment later she was reading Tom's piece of bark through flowing tears, and saying:

'I could forgive the boy, now, if he'd committed a million sins!'

CHAPTER XX

Becky in a Dilemma—Tom's Nobility asserts Itself

THERE was something about Aunt Polly's manner, when she kissed Tom, that swept away his low spirits and made him light-hearted and happy again. He started to school, and had the luck of coming upon Becky Thatcher at the head of Meadow Land. His mood always determined his manner. Without a moment's hesitation he ran to her and said:

'I acted mighty mean to-day, Becky, and I'm so sorry. I won't ever, ever do that way again, as long as I live—please make up, won't you?'

The girl stopped and looked him scornfully in the face:

'I'll thank you to keep yourself *to* yourself, Mr. Thomas Sawyer. I'll never speak to you again.'

She tossed her head and passed on. Tom was so stunned that he had not even presence of mind enough to say 'Who cares, Miss Smarty?' until the right time to say it had gone by. So he said nothing. But he was in a fine rage, nevertheless. He moped into the schoolyard wishing she were a boy, and imagining how he would trounce her if she were. He presently encountered her and delivered a stinging remark as he passed. She hurled one in return, and the angry breach was complete. It seemed to Becky, in her hot resentment, that she could hardly wait for school to 'take in', she was so impatient to see Tom flogged for the injured spelling-book. If she had had any lingering notion of exposing Alfred Temple, Tom's offensive fling had driven it entirely away.

Poor girl, she did not know how fast she was nearing trouble herself. The master, Mr. Dobbins, had reached middle age with an unsatisfied ambition. The darling of his desires was to be a doctor, but poverty had decreed that he should be nothing higher than a village schoolmaster. Every day he took a mysterious book out of his desk, and absorbed himself in it at times when no classes were reciting. He kept that book under lock and key. There was not an urchin in school but was perishing to have a glimpse of it, but the chance never came. Every boy and girl had a theory about the nature of that book; but no two theories were alike, and there was no way of getting at the facts in the case. Now as Becky was passing by the desk, which stood near the door, she noticed that the key was in the lock! It was a precious moment. She glanced around; found herself alone, and the next instant she had the book in her hands. The title-page—Professor somebody's *Anatomy*—carried no information to her mind; so she began to turn the leaves. She came at once upon a handsomely engraved and coloured frontispiece—a human figure, stark naked. At that moment a shadow fell on the page, and Tom Sawyer stepped in at the door, and caught a glimpse of the picture. Becky snatched at the book to close it, and had the hard luck to tear the pictured page half down the middle. She thrust the volume into the desk, turned the key, and burst out crying with shame and vexation:

'Tom Sawyer, you are just as mean as you can be, to sneak up on a person and look at what they're looking at.'

'How could *I* know you was looking at anything?'

'You ought to be ashamed of yourself, Tom Sawyer; you know you're going to tell on me; and, oh, what shall I do, what shall I do! I'll be whipped, and I never was whipped in school.'

Then she stamped her little foot and said:

'*Be* so mean if you want to! I know something that's going to happen. You just wait, and you'll see! Hateful, hateful,

hateful!'—and she flung out of the house with a new explosion of crying.

Tom stood still, rather flustered by this onslaught. Presently he said to himself:

'What a curious kind of a fool a girl is. Never been licked in school! Shucks, what's a licking! That's just like a girl—they're so thin-skinned and chicken-hearted. Well, of course *I* ain't going to tell old Dobbins on this little fool, because there's other ways of getting even on her that ain't so mean; but what of it? Old Dobbins will ask who it was tore his book. Nobody'll answer. Then he'll do just the way he always does—ask first one and then t'other, and when he comes to the right girl he'll know it, without any telling. Girls' faces always tell on them. They ain't got any backbone. She'll get licked. Well, it's a kind of a tight place for Becky Thatcher, because there ain't any way out of it.' Tom conned the thing a moment longer, and then added: 'All right, though; she'd like to see me in just such a fix—let her sweat it out!'

Tom joined the mob of skylarking scholars outside. In a few moments the master arrived and school 'took in'. Tom did not feel a strong interest in his studies. Every time he stole a glance at the girls' side of the room Becky's face troubled him. Considering all things, he did not want to pity her, and yet was it all he could do to help it. He could get up no exultation that was really worthy the name. Presently the spelling-book discovery was made, and Tom's mind was entirely full of his own matters for a while after that. Becky roused up from her lethargy of distress, and showed good interest in the proceedings. She did not expect that Tom could get out of his trouble by denying that he spilt the ink on the book himself; and she was right. The denial only seemed to make the thing worse for Tom. Becky supposed she would be glad of that, and she tried to believe she was glad of it, but she found she was not certain. When the worst came to the worst, she had an impulse to get up and tell on Alfred Temple, but she made an effort and forced herself to keep still, because, said she to herself, 'he'll tell about me tearing the picture, sure. I wouldn't say a word, not to save his life!'

Tom took his whipping and went back to his seat not at all broken-hearted, for he thought it was possible that he had unknowingly upset the ink on the spelling-book himself, in some skylarking bout—he had denied it for form's sake and because it was custom, and had stuck to the denial from principle.

A whole hour drifted by; the master sat nodding in his throne, the air was drowsy with the hum of study. By and by Mr. Dobbins straightened himself up, yawned, then unlocked his desk, and reached for his book, but seemed undecided whether to take it out or leave it. Most of the pupils glanced up languidly, but there were two among them that watched his movements with intent eyes. Mr. Dobbins fingered his book absently for a while, then took it out, and settled himself in his chair to read.

Tom shot a glance at Becky. He had seen a hunted and help-less rabbit look as she did, with a gun levelled at its head. Instantly he forgot his quarrel with her. Quick! something must be done! done in a flash, too! But the very imminence of the emergency paralysed his invention. Good! he had an inspiration! He would run and snatch the book, spring through the door and fly! but his resolution shook for one little instant, and the chance was lost—the master opened the volume. If Tom only had the wasted opportunity back again! Too late; there was no help for Becky now, he said. The next moment the master faced the school. Every eye sunk under his gaze; there was that in it which smote even the innocent with fear; there was silence while one might count ten. The master was gathering his wrath. Then he spoke:

'Who tore this book?'

There was not a sound. One could have heard a pin drop. The stillness continued; the master searched face after face for signs of guilt.

'Benjamin Rogers, did you tear this book?'

A denial. Another pause.

'Joseph Harper, did you?'

Another denial. Tom's uneasiness grew more and more intense under the slow torture of these proceedings. The master scanned the rank of boys, considered a while, then turned to the girls:

'Amy Lawrence?'

A shake of the head.

'Gracie Miller?'

The same sign.

'Susan Harper, did you do this?'

Another negative. The next girl was Becky Thatcher. Tom was trembling from head to foot with excitement, and a sense of the hopelessness of the situation.

'Rebecca Thatcher'—(Tom glanced at her face; it was white with terror)—'did you tear—no, look me in the face'—(her hands rose in appeal)—'did you tear this book?'

A thought shot like lightning through Tom's brain. He sprang to his feet and shouted:

'*I* done it!'

The school stared in perplexity at this incredible folly. Tom stood a moment to gather his dismembered faculties; and when he stepped forward to go to his punishment, the surprise, the gratitude, the adoration that shone upon him out of poor Becky's eyes seemed pay enough for a hundred floggings. Inspired by the splendour of his own act, he took without an outcry the most merciless flaying that even Mr. Dobbins had ever administered; and also received with indifference the added cruelty of a command to remain two hours after school should be dismissed—for he knew who would wait for him outside till his captivity was done, and not count the tedious time as loss either.

Tom went to bed that night planning vengeance against Alfred Temple; for with shame and repentance Becky had told him all, not forgetting her own treachery; but even the longing for vengeance had to give way soon to pleasanter musings, and he fell asleep at last, with Becky's latest words lingering dreamily in his ear:

'Tom, how *could* you be so noble!'

CHAPTER XXI

*Youthful Eloquence—Compositions by the Young
Ladies—A Lengthy Vision—The Boy's
Vengeance satisfied*

VACATION was approaching. The schoolmaster, always
severe, grew severer and more exacting than ever, for he
wanted the school to make a good showing on 'Examination' day. His rod and the ferrule were seldom idle now—at least
among the smaller pupils. Only the biggest boys, and young
ladies of eighteen and twenty, escaped lashing. Mr. Dobbins's
lashings were very vigorous ones too; for although he carried,
under his wig, a perfectly bald and shiny head, he had only
reached middle age, and there was no sign of feebleness in his
muscle. As the great day approached, all the tyranny that was in
him came to the surface; he seemed to take a vindictive pleasure
in punishing the least shortcomings. The consequence was that
the smaller boys spent their days in terror and suffering and their
nights in plotting revenge. They threw away no opportunity to
do the master a mischief. But he kept ahead all the time. The
retribution that followed every vengeful success was so sweeping
and majestic that the boys always retired from the field badly
worsted. At last they conspired together and hit upon a plan that
promised a dazzling victory. They swore-in the sign-painter's
boy, told him the scheme, and asked his help. He had his own
reasons for being delighted, for the master boarded in his father's
family and had given the boy ample cause to hate him. The
master's wife would go on a visit to the country in a few days,
and there would be nothing to interfere with the plan; the master
always prepared himself for great occasions by getting pretty well

fuddled, and the sign-painter's boy said that when the dominie had reached the proper condition on Examination Evening he would 'manage the thing' while he napped in his chair; then he would have him awakened at the right time and hurried away to school.

In the fullness of time the interesting occasion arrived. At eight in the evening the school-house was brilliantly lighted and adorned with wreaths and festoons of foliage and flowers. The master sat throned in his great chair upon a raised platform, with his black-board behind him. He was looking tolerably mellow. Three rows of benches on each side and six rows in front of him were occupied by the dignitaries of the town and by the parents of the pupils. To his left, back of the rows of citizens, was a spacious temporary platform upon which were seated the scholars who were to take part in the exercises of the evening; rows of small boys, washed and dressed to an intolerable state of discomfort; rows of gawky big boys; snow-banks of girls and young ladies clad in lawn and muslin, and conspicuously conscious of their bare arms, their grandmothers' ancient trinkets, their bits of pink and blue ribbon, and the flowers in their hair. All the rest of the house was filled with non-participating scholars.

The exercises began. A very little boy stood up and sheepishly recited, 'You'd scarce expect one of my age, to speak in public on the stage,' etc., accompanying himself with the painfully exact and spasmodic gestures which a machine might have used—supposing the machine to be a trifle out of order. But he got through safely, though cruelly scared, and got a fine round of applause when he made his manufactured bow and retired.

A little shame-faced girl lisped 'Mary had a little lamb,' etc., performed a compassion-inspiring curtsey, got her meed of applause, and sat down flushed and happy.

Tom Sawyer stepped forward with conceited confidence, and soared into the unquenchable and indestructible 'Give me liberty or give me death' speech, with fine fury and frantic gesticulation, and broke down in the middle of it. A ghastly stage-fright seized him, his legs quaked under him, and he was like to choke. True, he had the manifest sympathy of the house—but he had the house's silence too, which was even worse than its sympathy. The master frowned, and this completed the disaster. Tom struggled a while and then retired, utterly defeated. There was a weak attempt at applause, but it died early.

'The Boy stood on the Burning Deck'*followed; also 'The Assyrian Came Down',*and other declamatory gems. Then there were reading exercises and a spelling fight. The meagre Latin class recited with honour. The prime feature of the evening was in order, now—original 'compositions' by the young ladies. Each in her turn stepped forward to the edge of the platform, cleared her throat, held up her manuscript (tied with dainty ribbon), and proceeded to read, with laboured attention to 'expression' and punctuation. The themes were the same that had been illuminated upon similar occasions by their mothers before them, their grandmothers, and doubtless all their ancestors in the female line clear back to the Crusades. 'Friendship' was one; 'Memories of other Days'; 'Religion in History'; 'Dream-land'; 'The Advantages of Culture'; 'Forms of Political Government Compared and Contrasted'; 'Melancholy'; 'Filial Love'; 'Heart Longings', etc., etc.

A prevalent feature in these compositions was a nursed and petted melancholy; another was a wasteful and opulent gush of 'fine language'; another was a tendency to lug in by the ears particularly prized words and phrases until they were worn entirely out; and a peculiarity that conspicuously marked and marred them was the inveterate and intolerable sermon that wagged its crippled tail at the end of each and every one of them. No matter what the subject might be, a brain-racking effort was made to squirm it into some aspect or other that the moral and religious mind could contemplate with edification. The glaring insincerity of these sermons was not sufficient to compass the banishment of the fashion from the schools, and it is not sufficient today; it never will be sufficient while the world stands, perhaps. There is no school in all our land where the young ladies do not feel obliged to close their compositions with a sermon; and you will find that the sermon of the most frivolous and least religious girl in the school is always the longest and the most relentlessly pious. But enough of this. Homely truth is unpalatable.

Let us return to the 'Examination'. The first composition that was read was one entitled 'Is this, then, Life?' Perhaps the reader can endure an extract from it:

'In the common walks of life,* with what delightful emotions does the youthful mind look forward to some anticipated scene of festivity! Imagination is busy sketching rose-tinted pictures of joy. In fancy, the voluptuous votary of fashion sees herself amid the festive throng, "the observed of all observers". Her graceful form, arrayed in snowy robes, is whirling through the mazes of the joyous dance; her eye is brightest, her step is lightest in the gay assembly.

'In such delicious fancies time quickly glides by, and the welcome hour arrives for her entrance into the Elysian world, of which she has had such bright dreams. How fairy-like does everything appear to her enchanted vision! Each new scene is more charming than the last. But after a while she finds that beneath this goodly exterior all is vanity; the flattery which once charmed her soul now grates harshly upon her ear; the ball-room has lost its charms; and with wasted health and embittered heart she turns away with the conviction that earthly pleasures cannot satisfy the longings of the soul!'

And so forth and so on. There was a buzz of gratification from time to time during the reading, accompanied by whispered ejaculations of 'How sweet!' 'How eloquent!' 'So true!' etc. and after the thing had closed with a peculiarly afflicting sermon, the applause was enthusiastic.

Then arose a slim, melancholy girl, whose face had the 'inter-

esting' paleness that comes of pills and indigestion, and read a
'poem'. Two stanzas of it will do:

A Missouri Maiden's Farewell to Alabama

Alabama, good-bye! I love thee well!
But yet for a while do I leave thee now!
Sad, yes, sad thoughts of thee my heart doth swell,
And burning recollections throng my brow!
For I have wandered through thy flowery woods;
Have roamed and read near Tallapoosa's stream;
Have listened to Tallassee's warring floods,
And wooed on Coosa's side Aurora's beam.

Yet shame I not to bear an o'er-full heart,
Nor blush to turn behind my tearful eyes;
'Tis from no stranger land I now must part,
'Tis to no strangers left I yield these sighs.
Welcome and home were mine within this State,
Whose vales I leave—whose spires fade fast from me,
And cold must be mine eyes, and heart, and tête,
When, dear Alabama! they turn cold on thee!

There were very few there who knew what 'tête' meant, but
the poem was very satisfactory nevertheless.

Next appeared a dark-complexioned, black-eyed, black-haired
young lady, who paused an impressive moment, assumed a tragic
expression, and began to read in a measured, solemn tone:

'A vision

'Dark and tempestuous was night. Around the throne on high
not a single star quivered; but the deep intonations of the heavy
thunder constantly vibrated upon the ear; whilst the terrific
lightning revelled in angry mood through the cloudy chambers of
heaven, seeming to scorn the power exerted over its terrors by the
illustrious Franklin! Even the boisterous winds unanimously

came forth from their mystic homes, and blustered about as if to enhance by their aid the wildness of the scene. At such a time, so dark, so dreary, for human sympathy my very spirit sighed; but instead thereof,

> *"My dearest friend, my counsellor, my comforter and guide—*
> *My joy in grief, my second bliss in joy," came to my side.*

She moved like one of those bright beings pictured in the sunny walks of fancy's Eden by the romantic and young, a queen of beauty unadorned save by her own transcendent loveliness. So soft was her step, it failed to make even a sound, and but for the magical thrill imparted by her genial touch, as other unobtrusive beauties, she would have glided away unperceived—unsought. A strange sadness rested upon her features, like icy tears upon the robe of December, as she pointed to the contending elements without, and bade me contemplate the two beings presented.'

This nightmare occupied some ten pages of manuscript, and wound up with a sermon so destructive of all hope to non-Presbyterians, that it took the first prize. This composition was considered to be the very finest effort of the evening. The mayor of the village, in delivering the prize to the author of it, made a warm speech, in which he said that it was by far the most 'eloquent' thing he had ever listened to, and that Daniel Webster himself might well be proud of it.

It may be remarked, in passing, that the number of compositions in which the word 'beauteous' was overfondled, and human experience referred to as 'life's page', was up to the usual average.

Now the master, mellow almost to the verge of geniality, put his chair aside, turned his back to the audience, and began to draw a map of America on the black-board, to exercise the geography class upon. But he made a sad business of it with his unsteady hand, and a smothered titter rippled over the house. He knew what the matter was, and set himself to right it. He sponged out lines and remade them; but he only distorted them more than ever, and the tittering was more pronounced. He threw his entire attention upon his work, now, as if determined not to be put down by the mirth. He felt that all eyes were fastened upon him; he imagined he was succeeding, and yet the tittering continued; it even manifestly increased. And well it might. There was a garret above, pierced with a scuttle over his head; and down through this scuttle came a cat, suspended around the haunches by a string; she had a rag tied about her head and jaws to keep her from mewing; as she slowly descended she curved upward and clawed at the string, she swung downward and clawed at the intangible air. The tittering rose higher and higher, the cat was within six inches of the absorbed teacher's head; down, down, a little lower, and she grabbed his wig with her desperate claws, clung to it, was snatched up into the garret in an instant with her trophy still in her possession! And how the light did blaze abroad from the master's bald pate, for the sign-painter's boy had *gilded* it!

That broke up the meeting. The boys were avenged. Vacation was come.

Note.—The pretended 'compositions' quoted in this chapter are taken without alteration from a volume entitled *Prose and Poetry, by a Western Lady*, but they are exactly and precisely after the schoolgirl pattern, and hence are much happier than any mere imitations could be.

CHAPTER XXII

Tom's Confidence betrayed—Expects Signal Punishment

TOM joined the new order of Cadets of Temperance, being attracted by the showy character of their 'regalia'. He promised to abstain from smoking, chewing, and profanity as long as he remained a member. Now he found out a new thing—namely, that to promise not to do a thing is the surest way in the world to make a body want to go and do that very thing. Tom soon found himself tormented with a desire to drink and swear; the desire grew to be so intense that nothing but the hope of a chance to display himself in his red sash kept him from withdrawing from the order. Fourth of July was coming: but he soon gave that up—gave it up before he had worn his shackles over forty-eight hours, and fixed his hopes upon old Judge Frazer, justice of the peace, who was apparently on his death-bed, and would have a big public funeral, since he was so high an official. During three days Tom was deeply concerned about the Judge's condition, and hungry for news of it. Sometimes his hopes ran high, so high that he would venture to get out his regalia and practise before the looking-glass. But the Judge had a most discouraging way of fluctuating. At last he was pronounced upon the mend, and then convalescent. Tom was disgusted; and felt a sense of injury, too. He handed in his resignation at once, and that night the Judge suffered a relapse and died. Tom resolved that he would never trust a man like that again. The funeral was a fine thing. The Cadets paraded in a style calculated to kill the late member with envy.

Tom was a free boy again, however; there was something in

that. He could drink and swear now, but found to his surprise that he did not want to. The simple fact that he could took the desire away, and the charm of it.

Tom presently wondered to find that his coveted vacation was beginning to hang a little heavily on his hands.

He attempted a diary, but nothing happened during three days, and so he abandoned it.

The first of all the negro minstrel shows came to town, and made a sensation. Tom and Joe Harper got up a band of performers, and were happy for two days.

Even the Glorious Fourth was in some sense a failure, for it rained hard; there was no procession in consequence, and the greatest man in the world (as Tom supposed), Mr. Benton,* an actual United States Senator, proved an overwhelming disappointment, for he was not twenty-five feet high, nor even anywhere in the neighbourhood of it.

A circus came. The boys played circus for three days afterwards in tents made of rag carpeting—admission, three pins for boys, two for girls—and then circusing was abandoned.

A phrenologist and a mesmerizer came—and went again and left the village duller and drearier than ever.

There were some boys' and girls' parties, but they were so few and so delightful that they only made the aching voids between ache the harder.

Becky Thatcher was gone to her Constantinople home to stay with her parents during vacation—so there was no bright side to life anywhere.

The dreadful secret of the murder was a chronic misery. It was a very cancer for permanency and pain.

Then came the measles.

During two long weeks Tom lay a prisoner, dead to the world and its happenings. He was very ill, he was interested in nothing. When he got upon his feet at last and moved feebly down town, a melancholy change had come over everything and every creature. There had been a 'revival', and everybody had 'got religion'; not only the adults, but even the boys and girls. Tom went about, hoping against hope for the sight of one blessed sinful face, but disappointment crossed him everywhere. He found Joe Harper studying a Testament, and turned sadly away from the depressing spectacle. He sought Ben Rogers, and found him visiting the poor with a basket of tracts. He hunted up Jim Hollis, who called his attention to the precious blessing of his late measles as a warning. Every boy he encountered added another ton to his depression; and when, in desperation, he flew for refuge at last to the bosom of Huckleberry Finn and was received with a Scriptural quotation, his heart broke; and he crept home and to bed, realizing that he alone of all the town was lost, for ever and for ever.

And that night there came on a terrific storm, with driving rain, awful claps of thunder, and blinding sheets of lightning. He covered his head with the bedclothes and waited in a horror of suspense for his doom; for he had not the shadow of a doubt that all this hubbub was about him. He believed he had taxed the forbearance of the powers above to the extremity of endurance, and that this was the result. It might have seemed to him a waste of pomp and ammunition to kill a bug with a battery of artillery but there seemed nothing incongruous about the getting up such an expensive thunderstorm as this to knock the turf from under an insect like himself.

By and by the tempest spent itself and died without accomplishing its object. The boy's first impulse was to be grateful, and reform. His second was to wait—for there might not be any more storms.

The next day the doctors were back; Tom had relapsed. The three weeks he spent on his back this time seemed an entire age. When he got abroad at last he was hardly grateful that he had been spared, remembering how lonely was his estate, how companionless and forlorn he was. He drifted listlessly down the street and found Jim Hollis acting as judge in a juvenile court that was trying a cat for murder, in the presence of her victim, a bird. He found Joe Harper and Huck Finn up an alley eating a stolen melon. Poor lads! they, like Tom, had suffered a relapse.

CHAPTER XXIII

Old Muff's Friends—Muff Potter in Court
—Muff Potter saved

At last the sleepy atmosphere was stirred, and vigorously. The murder trial came on in the court. It became the absorbing topic of village talk immediately. Tom could not get away from it. Every reference to the murder sent a shudder to his heart, for his troubled conscience and fears almost persuaded him that these remarks were put forth in his hearing as 'feelers'; he did not see how he could be suspected of knowing anything about the murder, but still he could not be comfortable in the midst of this gossip. He took Huck to a lonely place to have a talk with him. It would be some relief to unseal his tongue for a little while; to divide his burden of distress with another sufferer. Moreover, he wanted to assure himself that Huck had remained discreet:

'Huck, have you ever told anybody about that?'

''Bout what?'

'You know what.'

'Oh—'course I haven't.'

'Never a word?'

'Never a solitary word, so help me. What makes you ask?'

'Well, I was afeard.'

'Why, Tom Sawyer, we wouldn't be alive two days if that got found out. *You* know that.'

Tom felt more comfortable. After a pause:

'Huck, they couldn't anybody get you to tell, could they?'

'Get me to tell? Why, if I wanted that half-breed devil to drownd me they could get me to tell. They ain't no different way.'

'Well, that's all right then, I reckon we're safe as long as we keep mum. But let's swear again, anyway. It's more surer!'

'I'm agreed.'

So they swore again with dread solemnities.

'What is the talk around, Huck? I've heard a power of it.'

'Talk? Well, it's just Muff Potter, Muff Potter, Muff Potter all the time. It keeps me in a sweat, constant, so's I want to hide som'ers.'

'That's just the same way they go on round me. I reckon he's a goner. Don't you feel sorry for him sometimes?'

'Most always—most always. He ain't no account; but then he ain't ever done anything to hurt anybody. Just fishes a little to get money to get drunk on—and loafs around considerable; but, lord, we all do that—leastways most of us,—preachers and such like. But he's kind of good—he give me half a fish, once, when there warn't enough for two; and lots of times he's kind of stood by me when I was out of luck.'

'Well, he's mended kites for me, Huck, and knitted hooks on to my line. I wish we could get him out of there.'

'My! we couldn't get him out, Tom. And besides, 'twould'nt do any good; they'd ketch him again.'

'Yes—so they would. But I hate to hear 'em abuse him so like the dickens when he never done—that.'

'I do too, Tom. Lord, I hear 'em say he's the bloodiest-looking villain in this country, and they wonder he wasn't ever hung before.'

'Yes, they talk like that all the time. I've heard 'em say that if he was to get free they'd lynch him.'

'And they'd do it, too.'

The boys had a long talk, but it brought them little comfort. As the twilight drew on, they found themselves hanging about the neighbourhood of the little isolated jail, perhaps with an undefined hope that something would happen that might clear away their difficulties. But nothing happened; there seemed to be no angels or fairies interested in this luckless captive.

The boys did as they had often done before—went to the cell grating and gave Potter some tobacco and matches. He was on the ground floor, and there were no guards.

His gratitude for their gifts had always smote their consciences before—it cut deeper than ever, this time. They felt cowardly and treacherous to the last degree when Potter said:

'You've been mighty good to me, boys—better'n anybody else in this town. And I don't forget it, I don't. Often I says to myself, says I, "I used to mend all the boys' kites and things, and show 'em where the good fishin' places was, and befriend 'em what I could, and now they've all forgot old Muff when he's in trouble, but Tom don't, and Huck don't—*they* don't forget him," says I, "and I don't forget *them*." Well, boys, I done an awful thing—drunk and crazy at the time, that's the only way I account for it, and now I got to swing for it, and it's right. Right, and *best* too, I reckon; hope so, anyway. Well, we won't talk about that. I don't want to make *you* feel bad; you've befriended me. But what I want to say, is, don't *you* ever get drunk, then you won't ever get here. Stand a little furder west; so, that's it; it's a prime comfort to see faces that's friendly when a body's in such a muck of trouble, and there don't none come here but yourn. Good friendly faces—good friendly faces. Get up on one another's backs, and let me touch 'em. That's it. Shake hands—yourn'll come through the bars, but mine's too big. Little hands, and weak—but they've helped Muff Potter a power, and they'd help him more if they could.'

Tom went home miserable, and his dreams that night were full of horrors. The next day and the day after he hung about the court-room, drawn by an almost irresistible impulse to go in, but forcing himself to stay out. Huck was having the same experience. They studiously avoided each other. Each wandered away from time to time, but the same dismal fascination always brought them back presently. Tom kept his ears open when idlers sauntered out of the court-room, but invariably heard distressing news; the toils were closing more and more relentlessly around poor Potter. At the end of the second day the village talk was to the effect that Injun Joe's evidence stood firm and unshaken, and that there was not the slightest question as to what the jury's verdict would be.

Tom was out late that night, and came to bed through the window. He was in a tremendous state of excitement. It was hours before he got to sleep. All the village flocked to the court-house the next morning, for this was to be the great day. Both sexes were about equally represented in the packed audience. After a long wait the jury filed in and took their places; shortly afterwards, Potter, pale and haggard, timid and hopeless, was brought in with chains upon him, and seated where all the curious eyes could stare at him; no less conspicuous was Injun Joe, stolid as ever. There was another pause, and then the judge arrived, and the sheriff proclaimed the opening of the court. The usual whisperings among the lawyers and gathering together of papers followed. These details and accompanying delays worked up an atmosphere of preparation that was as impressive as it was fascinating.

Now a witness was called who testified that he found Muff Potter washing in the brook at an early hour of the morning that the murder was discovered, and that he immediately sneaked away. After some further questioning, counsel for the prosecution said:

'Take the witness.'

The prisoner raised his eyes for a moment, but dropped them again when his own counsel said:

'I have no questions to ask him.'

The next witness proved the finding of the knife near the corpse. Counsel for the prosecution said:

'Take the witness.'

'I have no questions to ask him,' Potter's lawyer replied.

A third witness swore he had often seen the knife in Potter's possession.

'Take the witness.'

Counsel for Potter declined to question him.

The faces of the audience began to betray annoyance. Did this attorney mean to throw away his client's life without an effort?

Several witnesses deposed concerning Potter's guilty behaviour when brought to the scene of the murder. They were allowed to leave the stand without being cross-questioned.

Every detail of the damaging circumstances that occurred in the graveyard upon that morning which all present remembered so well was brought out by credible witnesses, but none of them was cross-examined by Potter's lawyer. The perplexity and dissatisfaction of the house expressed itself in murmurs and provoked a reproof from the bench. Counsel for the prosecution now said:

'By the oaths of citizens whose simple word is above suspicion, we have fastened this awful crime beyond all possibility of question upon the unhappy prisoner at the bar. We rest our case here.'

A groan escaped from poor Potter, and he put his face in his hands, and rocked his body softly to and fro, while a painful silence reigned in the court-room. Many men were moved, and many women's compassion testified itself in tears. Counsel for the defence rose and said:

'Your Honour—In our remarks at the opening of this trial, we foreshadowed our purpose to prove that our client did this fearful deed while under the influence of a blind and irresponsible delirium produced by drink. We have changed our mind; we shall not offer that plea. [Then to the clerk:] Call Thomas Sawyer.'

A puzzled amazement awoke in every face in the house, not even excepting Potter's. Every eye fastened itself with wondering interest upon Tom as he rose and took his place upon the stand. The boy looked wild enough, for he was badly scared. The oath was administered.

'Thomas Sawyer, where were you on the seventeenth of June, about the hour of midnight?'

Tom glanced at Injun Joe's iron face, and his tongue failed him. The audience listened breathless, but the words refused to come. After a few moments, however, the boy got a little of his strength back, and managed to put enough of it into his voice to make part of the house hear:

'In the graveyard!'

'A little bit louder, please. Don't be afraid. You were——'

'In the graveyard.'

A contemptuous smile flitted across Injun Joe's face.

'Were you anywhere near Horse Williams's grave?'

'Yes, sir.'

'Speak up—just a trifle louder. How near were you?'

'Near as I am to you.'

'Were you hidden or not?'

'I was hid.'

'Where?'

'Behind the elms that's on the edge of the grave.'

Injun Joe gave a barely perceptible start.

'Anyone with you?'

'Yes, sir. I was there with——'

'Wait—wait a moment. Never mind mentioning your companion's name. We will produce him at the proper time. Did you carry anything there with you?'

Tom hesitated and looked confused.

'Speak out, my boy—don't be diffident. The truth is always respectable. What did you take there?'

'Only a—a—dead cat.'

There was a ripple of mirth, which the court checked.

'We will produce the skeleton of that cat. Now, my boy, tell us everything that occurred—tell it in your own way—don't skip anything, and don't be afraid.'

Tom began—hesitatingly at first, but, as he warmed to his subject his words flowed more and more easily; in a little while every sound ceased but his own voice; every eye fixed itself upon him; with parted lips and bated breath the audience hung upon his words, taking no note of time, rapt in the ghastly fascination of the tale. The strain upon pent emotion reached its climax when the boy said, 'And as the doctor fetched the board around and Muff Potter fell, Injun Joe jumped with the knife and——'

Crash! Quick as lightning the half-breed sprang for a window, tore his way through all opposers, and was gone!

CHAPTER XXIV

*Tom as the Village Hero—Days of Splendour and
Nights of Horror—Pursuit of Injun Joe*

Tom was a glittering hero once more—the pet of the old,
the envy of the young. His name even went into immor-
tal print, for the village paper magnified him. There
were some that believed he would be President yet, if he escaped
hanging.

As usual, the fickle, unreasoning world took Muff Potter to
its bosom, and fondled him as lavishly as it had abused him before.
But that sort of conduct is to the world's credit; therefore it is not
well to find fault with it.

Tom's days were days of splendour and exultation to him, but
his nights were seasons of horror. Injun Joe infested all his
dreams, and always with doom in his eye. Hardly any temptation
could persuade the boy to stir abroad after nightfall. Poor Huck
was in the same state of wretchedness and terror, for Tom had
told the whole story to the lawyer the night before the great
day of the trial, and Huck was sore afraid that his share in the
business might leak out yet, notwithstanding Injun Joe's flight
had saved him the suffering of testifying in court. The poor fellow
had got the attorney to promise secrecy, but what of that? Since
Tom's harassed conscience had managed to drive him to the
lawyer's house by night and wring a dread tale from lips that had
been sealed with the dismallest and most formidable of oaths,
Huck's confidence in the human race was well-nigh obliterated.
Daily Muff Potter's gratitude made Tom glad he had spoken:
but nightly he wished he had sealed up his tongue. Half the
time Tom was afraid Injun Joe would never be captured; the

other half he was afraid he would be. He felt sure he never could draw a safe breath again until that man was dead and he had seen the corpse.

Rewards had been offered, the country had been scoured, but no Injun Joe was found. One of those omniscient and awe-inspiring marvels, a detective, came up from St. Louis, moused around, shook his head, looked wise, and made that sort of astounding success which members of that craft usually achieve. That is to say, he 'found a clue'. But you can't hang a 'clue' for murder, and so after that detective had got through and gone home, Tom felt just as insecure as he was before.

The slow days drifted on, and each left behind it a slightly lightened weight of apprehension.

CHAPTER XXV

About Kings and Diamonds—Search for the Treasure—Dead People and Ghosts

THERE comes a time in every rightly constructed boy's life when he has a raging desire to go somewhere and dig for hidden treasure. This desire suddenly came upon Tom one day. He sallied out to find Joe Harper, but failed of success. Next he sought Ben Rogers; he had gone fishing. Presently he stumbled upon Huck Finn the Red-Handed. Huck would answer. Tom took him to a private place, and opened the matter to him confidentially. Huck was willing. Huck was always willing to take a hand in any enterprise that offered entertainment and required no capital, for he had a troublesome superabundance of that sort of time which is *not* money.

'Where'll we dig?' said Huck.

'Oh, 'most anywhere.'

'Why, is it hid all around?'

'No, indeed it ain't. It's hid in mighty particular places, Huck—sometimes on islands, sometimes in rotten chests under the end of a limb of an old dead tree, just where the shadow falls at midnight; but mostly under the floor in ha'nted houses.'

'Who hides it?'

'Why, robbers, of course—who'd you reckon? Sunday-school sup'rintendents?'

'I don't know. If 'twas mine I wouldn't hide it; I'd spend it and have a good time.'

'So would I; but robbers don't do that way, they always hide it and leave it there.'

'Don't they come after it any more?'

'No, they think they will, but they generally forget the marks, or else they die. Anyway, it lays there a long time and gets rusty; and by and by somebody finds an old yellow paper that tells how to find the marks—a paper that's got to be ciphered over about a week because it's mostly signs and hy'roglyphics.'

'Hyro—which?'

'Hy'roglyphics—pictures and things, you know, that don't seem to mean anything.'

'Have you got one of them papers, Tom?'

'No.'

'Well, then, how you going to find the marks?'

'I don't want any marks. They always bury it under a ha'nted house, or on an island, or under a dead tree that's got one limb sticking out. Well, we've tried Jackson's Island a little, and we can try it again some time; and there's the old ha'nted house up the Still House branch, and there's lots of dead-limb trees—dead loads of 'em.'

'Is it under all of them?'

'How you talk! No!'

'Then how you going to know which one to go for?'

'Go for all of 'em.'

'Why, Tom, it'll take all summer.'

'Well, what of that? Suppose you find a brass pot with a hundred dollars in it, all rusty and gay, or a rotten chest full of di'monds. How's that?'

Huck's eyes glowed.

'That's bully, plenty bully enough for me. Just you gimme the hundred dollars, and I don't want no di'monds.'

'All right. But I bet you *I* ain't going to throw off on di'monds. Some of 'em's worth twenty dollars apiece. There ain't any, hardly, but's worth six bits or a dollar.'

'No! Is that so?'

'Cert'nly—anybody'll tell you so! Hain't you ever seen one, Huck?'

'Not as I remember.'

'Oh, kings have slathers of them.'

'Well, I don't know no kings, Tom.'

'I reckon you don't. But if you was to go to Europe you'd see a raft of 'em hopping around.'

'Do they hop?'

'Hop?—your granny! No!'

'Well, what did you say they did for?'

'Shucks! I only meant you'd *see* 'em—not hopping, of course —what they want to hop for? But I mean you'd just see 'em— scattered around, you know, in a kind of a general way. Like that old hump-backed Richard.'

'Richard! What's his other name?'

'He didn't have any other name. Kings don't have any but a given name.'

'No?'

'But they don't.'

'Well, if they like it, Tom, all right; but I don't want to be a king and have only just a given name, like a nigger. But say— where you going to dig first?'

'Well, I don't know. S'pose we tackle that old dead-limb tree on the hill t'other side of Still House branch?'

'I'm agreed.'

So they got a crippled pick and a shovel, and set out in their three-mile tramp. They arrived hot and panting, and threw themselves down in the shade of a neighbouring elm to rest and have a smoke.

'I like this,' said Tom.

'So do I.'

'Say, Huck, if we find a treasure here, what you going to do with your share?'

'Well, I'll have pie and a glass of soda every day, and I'll go to every circus that comes along. I bet I'll have a gay time.'

'Well, ain't you going to save any of it?'

'Save it? What for?'

'Why, so as to have something to live on by and by.'

'Oh, that ain't any use. Pap would come back to thish-yer town some day and get his claws on it if I didn't hurry up, and I tell you he'd clean it out pretty quick. What you going to do with yourn, Tom?'

'I'm going to buy a new drum, and sure-'nough sword, and a red necktie, and a bull pup, and get married.'

'Married!'

'That's it.'

'Tom, you—why you ain't in your right mind.'

'Wait—you'll see.'

'Well, that's the foolishest thing you could do. Look at pap and my mother. Fight! why they used to fight all the time. I remember, mighty well.'

'That ain't anything. The girl I'm going to marry won't fight.'

'Tom, I reckon they're all alike. They'll all comb a body. Now you better think 'bout this a while. I tell you you better. What's the name of the gal?'

'It ain't a gal at all—it's a girl.'

'It's all the same, I reckon; some says gal, some says girl—both's right, like enough. Anyway, what's her name, Tom?'

'I'll tell you some time—not now.'

'All right—that'll do. Only if you get married I'll be more lonesomer than ever.'

'No, you won't, you'll come and live with me. Now stir out of this, and we'll go to digging.'

They worked and sweated for half an hour. No result. They toiled another half hour. Still no result. Huck said:

'Do they always bury it as deep as this?'

'Sometimes—not always. Not generally. I reckon we haven't got the right place.'

So they chose a new spot and began again. The labour

dragged a little, but still they made progress. They pegged away in silence for some time. Finally Huck leaned on his shovel, swabbed the beaded drops from his brow with his sleeve, and said:

'Where you going to dig next, after we get this one?'

'I reckon maybe we'll tackle the old tree that's over yonder on Cardiff Hill, back of the widow's.'

'I reckon that'll be a good one. But won't the widow take it away from us, Tom? It's on her land.'

'*She* take it away! Maybe she'd like to try it once. Whoever finds one of these hid treasures, it belongs to him. It don't make any difference whose land it's on.'

That was satisfactory. The work went on. By and by Huck said:

'Blame it! we must be in the wrong place again. What do you think?'

'It *is* mighty curious, Huck. I don't understand it. Sometimes witches interfere. I reckon maybe that's what's the trouble now.'

'Shucks! witches ain't got no power in the daytime.'

'Well, that's so. I didn't think of that. Oh, *I* know what the matter is! What a blamed lot of fools we are! You got to find out where the shadow of the limb falls at midnight, and that's where you dig!'

'Then, confound it, we've fooled away all this work for nothing. Now, hang it all, we got to come back in the night. It's an awful long way. Can you get out?'

'I bet I will. We've got to do it to-night, too, because if somebody sees these holes they'll know in a minute what's here and they'll go for it.'

'Well, I'll come around and meow to-night.'

'All right. Let's hide the tools in the bushes.'

The boys were there that night about the appointed time. They sat in the shadow waiting. It was a lonely place, and an hour made solemn by old traditions. Spirits whispered in the rustling leaves, ghosts lurked in the murky nooks, the deep baying of a hound floated up out of the distance, an owl answered with his sepulchral note. The boys were subdued by these solemnities, and talked little. By and by they judged that twelve had come; they marked where the shadow fell and began to dig. Their hopes commenced to rise. Their interest grew stronger, and their industry kept pace with it. The hole deepened and still deepened, but every time their hearts jumped to hear the pick strike upon something, they only suffered a new disappointment. It was only a stone or a chunk. At last Tom said:

'It ain't any use, Huck, we're wrong again.'

'Well, but we *can't* be wrong. We spotted the shadder to a dot.'

'I know it, but then there's another thing.'

'What's that?'

'Why we only guessed at the time. Like enough it was too late or too early.'

Huck dropped his shovel.

'That's it,' said he. 'That's the very trouble. We got to give this one up. We can't ever tell the right time, and besides, this kind of thing's too awful, here this time of night with witches and ghosts a fluttering around so. I feel as if something's behind me all the time; and I'm afeard to turn around, becuz maybe there's others in front a waiting for a chance. I been creeping all over ever since I got here.'

'Well, I've been pretty much so too, Huck. They 'most always put in a dead man when they bury a treasure under a tree, to look out for it.'

'Lordy!'

'Yes, they do. I've always heard that.'

'Tom, I don't like to fool around much where there's dead people. A body's bound to get into trouble with 'em, sure.'

'I don't like to stir 'em up, either. S'pose this one here was to stick his skull out and say something!'

'Don't, Tom! It's awful!'

'Well it just is. Huck, I don't feel comfortable a bit.'

'Say, Tom, let's give this place up, and try somewhere else.'

'All right, I reckon we better.'

'What'll it be?'

Tom considered a while, and then said:

'The ha'nted house. That's it.'

'Blame it, I don't like ha'nted houses, Tom. Why, they're a dern sight worse'n dead people. Dead people might talk, maybe, but they don't come sliding around in a shroud when you ain't noticing, and peep over your shoulder all of a sudden and grit their teeth the way a ghost does. I couldn't stand such a thing as that, Tom—nobody could.'

'Yes; but Huck, ghosts don't travel around only at night—they won't hender us from digging there in the daytime.'

'Well, that's so. But you know mighty well people don't go about that ha'nted house in the day nor the night.'

'Well, that's mostly because they don't like to go where a man's been murdered, anyway. But nothing's ever been seen around that house except in the night—just some blue light slipping by the windows—no regular ghosts.'

'Well, where you see one of them blue lights flickering around, Tom, you can bet there's a ghost mighty close behind it. It stands to reason. Becuz *you* know that they don't anybody but ghosts use 'em.'

'Yes, that's so. But anyway they don't come around in the daytime, so what's the use of our being afeard?'

'Well, all right. We'll tackle the ha'nted house if you say so; but I reckon it's taking chances.'

They had started down the hill by this time. There in the middle of the moonlit valley below them stood the 'ha'nted, house, utterly isolated, its fences gone long ago, rank weeds smothering the very door-steps, the chimney crumbled to ruin' the window-sashes vacant, a corner of the roof caved in. The boys gazed a while, half expecting to see a blue light flit past a window; then talking in a low tone, as befitted the time and the circumstances, they struck far off to the right, to give the haunted house a wide berth, and took their way homeward through the woods that adorned the rearward side of Cardiff Hill.

CHAPTER XXVI

The Haunted House—Sleepy Ghosts—A Box of Gold—Bitter Luck

ABOUT noon the next day the boys arrived at the dead tree; they had come for their tools. Tom was impatient to go to the haunted house; Huck was measurably so, also, but suddenly said:

'Looky here, Tom, do you know what day it is?'

Tom mentally ran over the days of the week, and then quickly lifted his eyes with a startled look in them:

'My! I never once thought of it, Huck!'

'Well, I didn't, neither, but all at once it popped on to me that it was Friday.'

'Blame it; a body can't be too careful, Huck. We might a got into an awful scrape, tackling such a thing on a Friday.'

'*Might!* Better say we *would*! There's some lucky days, maybe, but Friday ain't.'

'Any fool knows that. I don't reckon *you* was the first that found it out, Huck.'

'Well, I never said I was, did I? And Friday ain't all, neither. I had a rotten bad dream last night—dreamt about rats.'

'No! Sure sign of trouble. Did they fight?'

'No.'

'Well, that's good, Huck. When they don't fight it's only a sign that there's trouble around, you know. All we got to do is to look mighty sharp and keep out of it. We'll drop this thing for to-day, and play. Do you know Robin Hood, Huck?'

'No. Who's Robin Hood?'

'Why, he was one of the greatest men that was ever in England—and the best. He was a robber.'

'Cracky, I wisht I was. Who did he rob?'

'Only sheriffs and bishops and rich people and kings, and such like. But he never bothered the poor. He loved 'em. He always divided up with 'em perfectly square.'

'Well, he must 'a' been a brick.'

'I bet you he was, Huck. Oh, he was the noblest man that ever was. They ain't any such men now, I can tell you. He could lick any man in England with one hand tied behind him; and he could take his yew bow and plug a ten cent piece every time, a mile and a half.'

'What's a *yew* bow?'

'*I* don't know. It's some kind of a bow, of course. And if he hit that dime only on the edge he would set down and cry—and curse. But we'll play Robin Hood —it's noble fun. I'll learn you.'

'I'm agreed.'

So they played Robin Hood all the afternoon, now and then casting a yearning eye down upon the haunted house and passing a remark about the morrow's prospects and possibilities there. As the sun began to sink into the west they took their way homeward athwart the long shadows of the trees, and soon were buried from sight in the forests of Cardiff Hill.

On Saturday, shortly after noon, the boys were at the dead tree again. They had a smoke and a chat in the shade, and then dug a little in their last hole, not with great hope, but merely because Tom said there were so many cases where people had given up a treasure after getting down within six inches of it, and then somebody else had come along and turned it up with a single thrust of a shovel. The thing failed this time, however, so the boys shouldered their tools and went away feeling that they had not trifled with fortune, but had fulfilled all the requirements that belong to the business of treasure-hunting.

When they reached the haunted house, there was something

so weird and grisly about the dead silence that reigned there under the baking sun, and something so depressing about the loneliness and desolation of the place, that they were afraid, for a moment, to venture in. Then they crept to the door and took a trembling peep. They saw a weed-grown, floorless room, unplastered, an ancient fire-place, vacant windows, a ruinous staircase; and here, there, and everywhere, hung ragged and abandoned cobwebs. They presently entered softly, with quickened pulses, talking in whispers, ears alert to catch the slightest sound and muscles tense and ready for instant retreat.

In a little while familiarity modified their fears, and they gave the place a critical and interested examination, rather admiring their own boldness, and wondering at it, too. Next they wanted to look upstairs. This was something like cutting off retreat, but they got to daring each other, and of course there could be but one result—they threw their tools into a corner and made the ascent. Up there were the same signs of decay. In one corner they found a closet that promised mystery, but the promise was a fraud—there was nothing in it. Their courage was up now, and well in hand. They were about to go down and begin work when—

'*Sh!*' said Tom.

'What is it?' whispered Huck, blanching with fright.

'*Sh!* There! Hear it?'

'Yes! Oh, my! Let's run!'

'Keep still! Don't you budge! They're coming right towards the door.'

The boys stretched themselves upon the floor with their eyes to knot-holes in the planking, and lay waiting in a misery of fear.

'They've stopped—— No—coming—— Here they are. Don't whisper another word, Huck. My goodness, I wish I was out of this!'

Two men entered. Each boy said to himself:

'There's the old deaf and dumb Spaniard that's been about town once or twice lately—never saw t'other man before.'

'T'other' was a ragged, unkempt creature, with nothing very pleasant in his face. The Spaniard was wrapped in a *serapé*; he had bushy white whiskers, long white hair flowed from under his sombrero, and he wore green goggles. When they came in, 't'other' was talking in a low voice; they sat down on the ground, facing the door, with their backs to the wall, and the speaker continued his remarks. His manner became less guarded, and his words more distinct as he proceeded.

'No,' said he, 'I've thought it all over, and I don't like it. It's dangerous.'

'Dangerous!' grunted the 'deaf and dumb' Spaniard, to the vast surprise of the boys. 'Milksop!'

This voice made the boys gasp and quake. It was Injun Joe's! There was silence for some time. Then Joe said:

'What's any more dangerous than that job up yonder?—but nothing's come of it.'

'That's different. Away up the river so, and not another house about. 'Twon't ever be known that we tried, anyway, long as we didn't succeed.'

'Well, what's more dangerous than coming here in the day-time?—anybody would suspicion us that saw us.'

'*I* know that. But there warn't any other place as handy after that fool of a job. I want to quit this shanty. I wanted to yester-day, only it warn't any use trying to stir out of here with those infernal boys playing over there on the hill right in full view.'

'Those infernal boys,' quaked again under the inspiration of this remark, and thought how lucky it was that they had remem-bered it was Friday and concluded to wait a day. They wished in their hearts they had waited a year. The two men got out some food and made a luncheon. After a long and thoughtful silence, Injun Joe said:

'Look here, lad, you go back up the river where you belong. Wait there till you hear from me. I'll take the chances on drop-ping into this town just once more, for a look. We'll do that "dangerous" job after I've spied around a little and think things look well for it. Then for Texas! We'll leg it together!'

This was satisfactory. Both men presently fell to yawning, and Injun Joe said:

'I'm dead for sleep! It's your turn to watch.'

He curled down in the weeds and soon began to snore. His comrade stirred him once or twice, and he became quiet. Presently the watcher began to nod; his head drooped lower and lower; both men began to snore now.

The boys drew a long grateful breath. Tom whispered:

'Now's our chance—come!'

Huck said: 'I can't—I'd die if they was to wake.'

Tom urged—Huck held back. At last Tom rose slowly and softly, and started alone. But the first step he made wrung such a hideous creak from the crazy floor that he sank down almost dead with fright. He never made a second attempt. The boys lay there counting the dragging moments till it seemed to them that time must be done and eternity growing grey; and then they were grateful to note that at last the sun was setting.

Now one snore ceased. Injun Joe sat up, stared around— smiled grimly upon his comrade, whose head was drooping upon his knees—stirred him up with his foot, and said:

'Here! *You're* a watchman, ain't you! All right, though— nothing's happened.'

'My! Have I been asleep?'

'Oh, partly, partly. Nearly time for us to be moving, pard. What'll we do with what little swag we've got left?'

'I don't know—leave it here as we've always done, I reckon. No use to take it away till we start south. Six hundred and fifty in silver's something to carry.'

'Well—all right—it won't matter to come here once more.'

'No—but I'd say come in the night as we used to do—it's better.'

'Yes, but look here; it may be a good while before I get the

183

right chance at the job; accidents might happen, 'tain't in such a very good place; we'll just regularly bury it—and bury it deep.'

'Good idea,' said the comrade, who walked across the room, knelt down, raised one of the rearward hearthstones, and took out a bag that jingled pleasantly. He subtracted from it twenty or thirty dollars for himself and as much for Injun Joe, and passed the bag to the latter, who was on his knees in the corner, now, digging with his bowie-knife.

The boys forgot all their fears, all their miseries in an instant. With gloating eyes they watched every movement. Luck!— the splendour of it was beyond all imagination! Six hundred dollars was money enough to make half a dozen boys rich! Here was treasure-hunting under the happiest auspices—there would not be any bothersome uncertainty as to where to dig. They nudged each other every moment—eloquent nudges and easily understood, for they simply meant, 'Oh, but ain't you glad *now* we're here!'

Joe's knife struck upon something.

'Hello!' said he.

'What is it?' said his comrade.

'Half-rotten plank—no, it's a box, I believe. Here, bear a hand, and we'll see what it's here for. Never mind, I've broke a hole.'

He reached his hand in and drew it out.

'Man, it's money!'

The two men examined the handful of coins. They were gold. The boys above were as excited as themselves, and as delighted.

Joe's comrade said:

'We'll make quick work of this. There's an old rusty pick over amongst the weeds in the corner, the other side of the fire-place —I saw it a minute ago.'

He ran and brought the boys' pick and shovel. Injun Joe took the pick, looked it over critically, shook his head, muttered something to himself, and then began to use it.

The box was soon unearthed. It was not very large; it was iron-bound and had been very strong before the slow years had injured it. The men contemplated the treasure a while in blissful silence.

'Pard, there's thousands of dollars here,' said Injun Joe.

"'Twas always said that Murrel's gang* used around here one summer,' the stranger observed.

'I know it,' said Injun Joe; 'and this looks like it, I should say.'

'*Now* you won't need to do that job.'

The half-breed frowned. Said he:

'You don't know me. Least you don't know all about that thing. 'Tain't robbery altogether—it's *revenge*!' and a wicked light flamed in his eyes. 'I'll need your help in it. When it's finished—then Texas. Go home to your Nance and your kids, and stand by till you hear from me.'

'Well, if you say so. What'll we do with this—bury it again?'

'Yes' [ravishing delight overhead]. '*No*! by the great Sachem, no!' [profound distress overhead.] 'I'd nearly forgot. That pick had fresh earth on it!' [The boys were sick with terror in a moment.] 'What business has a pick and a shovel here? What business with fresh earth on them? Who brought them here—and where are they gone? Have you heard anybody?—seen anybody? What! bury it again and leave them to come and see the ground disturbed? Not exactly—not exactly. We'll take it to my den.'

'Why, of course! Might have thought of that before. You mean Number One?'

'No—Number Two—under the cross. The other place is bad —too common.'

'All right. It's nearly dark enough to start.'

185

Injun Joe got up and went about from window to window, cautiously peeping out. Presently he said:

'Who could have brought those tools here? Do you reckon they can be upstairs?'

The boys' breath forsook them. Injun Joe put his hand on his knife, halted a moment, undecided, and then turned towards the stairway. The boys thought of the closet, but their strength was gone. The steps came creaking up the stairs—the intolerable distress of the situation woke the stricken resolution of the lads —they were about to spring for the closet, when there was a crash of rotten timbers, and Injun Joe landed on the ground amid the débris of the ruined stairway. He gathered himself up cursing, and his comrade said:

'Now what's the use of all that? If it's anybody, and they're up there, let them *stay* there—who cares? If they want to jump down, now, and get into trouble, who objects? It will be dark in fifteen minutes—and then let them follow us if they want to; I'm willing. In my opinion, whoever hove those things in here caught a sight of us, and took us for ghosts or devils or something. I'll bet they're running yet.'

Joe grumbled a while; then he agreed with his friend that what daylight was left ought to be economized in getting things ready for leaving. Shortly afterwards they slipped out of the house in the deepening twilight, and moved towards the river with their precious box.

Tom and Huck rose up, weak but vastly relieved, and stared after them through the chinks between the logs of the house. Follow? Not they—they were content to reach ground again without broken necks, and take the townward track over the hill. They did not talk much, they were too much absorbed in hating themselves—hating the ill-luck that made them take the spade and the pick there. But for that Injun Joe never would have suspected. He would have hidden the silver with the gold to wait there till his 'revenge' was satisfied, and then he would have had the misfortune to find that money turn up missing. Bitter, bitter luck that the tools were ever brought there! They resolved to keep a lookout for that Spaniard when he should come to town spying out for chances to do his revengeful job, and follow him to 'Number Two', wherever that might be. Then a ghastly thought occurred to Tom:

'Revenge? What if he means *us*, Huck!'

'Oh, don't!' said Huck, nearly fainting.

They talked it all over, and as they entered town they agreed to believe that he might possibly mean somebody else—at least that he might at least mean nobody but Tom, since only Tom had testified.

Very, very small comfort it was to Tom to be alone in danger! Company would be a palpable improvement, he thought.

CHAPTER XXVII

Doubts to be Settled—The Young Detectives

THE adventure of the day mightily tormented Tom's dreams that night. Four times he had his hands on that rich treasure, and four times it wasted to nothingness in his fingers as sleep forsook him, and wakefulness brought back the hard reality of his misfortune. As he lay in the early morning recalling the incidents of his great adventure, he noticed that they seemed curiously subdued and far away, somewhat as if they had happened in another world, or in a time long gone by. Then it occurred to him that the great adventure itself must be a dream! There was one very strong argument in favour of this idea——namely, that the quantity of coin he had seen was too vast to be real. He had never seen as much as fifty dollars in one mass before, and he was like all boys of his age and station in life, in that he imagined that all references to 'hundreds' and 'thousands' were mere fanciful forms of speech, and that no such sums really existed in the world. He never had supposed for a moment that so large a sum as a hundred dollars was to be found in actual money in anyone's possession. If his notions of hidden treasure had been analysed they would have been found to consist of a handful of real dimes, and a bushel of vague, splendid, ungraspable dollars.

But the incidents of his adventure grew sensibly sharper and clearer under the attrition of thinking them over, and so he presently found himself leaning to the impression that the thing might not have been a dream after all. This uncertainty must be swept away. He would snatch a hurried breakfast, and go and find Huck.

Huck was sitting on the gunwale of a flat boat, listlessly dangling his feet in the water, and looking very melancholy. Tom concluded to let Huck lead up to the subject. If he did not do it, then the adventure would be proved to have been only a dream.

'Hello, Huck!'

'Hello, yourself.'

Silence for a minute.

'Tom, if we'd a left the blame tools at the dead tree we'd 'a' got the money. Oh, ain't it awful?'

''Tain't a dream, then, 'tain't a dream! Somehow I 'most wish it was. Dog'd if I don't, Huck.'

'What ain't a dream?'

'Oh, that thing yesterday. I been half thinking it was.'

'Dream! If them stairs hadn't broke down you'd 'a' seen how much dream it was! I've had dreams enough all night, with that patch-eyed Spanish devil going for me all through 'em—rot him!'

'No, not rot him. *Find* him! Track the money!'

'Tom, we'll never find him. A feller don't have only one chance for such a pile, and that one's lost. I'd feel mighty shakey if I was to see him, anyway.'

'Well, so'd I; but I'd like to see him, anyway, and track him out—to his Number Two.'

'Number Two; yes, that's it. I ben thinking 'bout that. But I can't make nothing out of it. What do you reckon it is?'

'I dono. It's too deep. Say, Huck—maybe it's the number of a house!'

'Goody!—No, Tom, that ain't it. If it is, it ain't in this one-horse town. They ain't no numbers here.'

'Well, that's so. Lemme think a minute. Here—it's the number of a room—in a tavern, you know!'

'Oh, that's the trick! They ain't only two taverns. We can find out quick.'

'You stay here, Huck, till I come.'

Tom was off at once. He did not care to have Huck's company in public places. He was gone half an hour. He found that in the best tavern, Number Two had long been occupied by a young lawyer, and was still so occupied. In the less ostentatious house Number Two was a mystery. The tavern-keeper's young son said it was kept locked all the time, and he never saw anybody go into it or come out of it except at night; he did not know any particular reason for this state of things; had had some little curiosity, but it was rather feeble; had made the most of the mystery by entertaining himself with the idea that that room was 'ha'nted'; had noticed that there was a light in there the night before.

'That's what I've found out, Huck. I reckon that's the very Number Two we're after.'

'I reckon it is, Tom. Now what you going to do?'

'Lemme think.'

Tom thought a long time. Then he said:

'I'll tell you. The back door of that Number Two is the door that comes out into that little close alley between the tavern and the old rattle-trap of a brick store. Now you get hold of all the door keys you can find, and I'll nip all of auntie's, and the first dark night we'll go there and try 'em. And mind you keep a lookout for Injun Joe, because he said he was going to drop into town and spy around once more for a chance to get his revenge. If you see him, you just follow him; and if he don't go to that Number Two, that ain't the place.'

'Lordy, I don't want to foller him by myself!'

'Why, it'll be night, sure. He mightn't ever see you—and if he did, maybe he'd never think anything.'

'Well, if it's pretty dark I reckon I'll track him. I dono—I dono. I'll try.'

'You bet I'll follow him, if it's dark, Huck! Why, he might

'a' found out he couldn't get his revenge, and be going right after that money.'

'It's so, Tom, it's so. I'll foller him; I will, by jingoes!'

'Now, you're *talking*! Don't you ever weaken, Huck, and I won't.'

CHAPTER XXVIII

An Attempt at Number Two—Huck mounts Guard

THAT night Tom and Huck were ready for their adventure. They hung about the neighbourhood of the tavern until after nine, one watching the alley at a distance and the other the tavern door. Nobody entered the alley or left it, nobody resembling the Spaniard entered or left the tavern door. The night promised to be a fair one; so Tom went home, with the understanding that if a considerable degree of darkness came on, Huck was to come and 'meow', whereupon he would slip out and try the keys. But the night remained clear, and Huck closed his watch and retired to bed in an empty sugar hogshead about twelve.

Tuesday the boys had the same ill-luck. Also Wednesday. But Thursday night promised better. Tom slipped out in good season with his aunt's old tin lantern, and a large towel to blindfold it with. He hid the lantern in Huck's sugar hogshead, and the watch began. An hour before midnight the tavern closed up, and its lights (the only ones thereabouts) were put out. No Spaniard had been seen. Nobody had entered or left the alley. Everything was auspicious. The blackness of darkness reigned; the perfect stillness was interrupted only by occasional mutterings of distant thunder.

Tom got his lantern, lit it in the hogshead, wrapped it closely in the towel, and the two adventurers crept in the gloom towards the tavern. Huck stood sentry and Tom felt his way into the alley. Then there was a season of waiting anxiety that weighed upon Huck's spirits like a mountain. He began to wish he could see a flash from the lantern—it would frighten him, but it would at least tell him that Tom was alive yet.

It seemed hours since Tom had disappeared. Surely he must have fainted; maybe he was dead; maybe his heart had burst under terror and excitement. In his uneasiness Huck found himself drawing closer and closer to the alley, fearing all sorts of dreadful things, and momentarily expecting some catastrophe to happen that would take away his breath. There was not much to take away, for he seemed only able to inhale it by thimblefuls, and his heart would soon wear itself out, the way it was beating. Suddenly there was a flash of light, and Tom came tearing by him:

'Run!' said he; 'run, for your life!'

He needn't have repeated it; once was enough; Huck was making thirty or forty miles an hour before the repetition was uttered. The boys never stopped till they reached the shed of a deserted slaughter-house at the lower end of the village. Just as they got within its shelter the storm burst and the rain poured down. As soon as Tom got his breath he said:

'Huck, it was awful! I tried two of the keys just as soft as I could; but they seemed to make such a power of racket that I couldn't hardly get my breath, I was so scared. They wouldn't turn in the lock, either. Well, without noticing what I was doing, I took hold of the knob, and open comes the door! It warn't locked! I hopped in, and shook off the towel, and, *great Cæsar's ghost!*'

'What!—what'd you see, Tom?'

'Huck, I most stepped on to Injun Joe's hand!'

'No!'

'Yes. He was laying there, sound asleep on the floor, with his old patch on his eye and his arms spread out.'

'Lordy, what did you do? Did he wake up?'

'No, never budged. Drunk, I reckon. I just grabbed that towel and started!'

'I'd never 'a' thought of the towel, I bet!'

'Well, I would. My aunt would make me mighty sick if I lost it.'

'Say, Tom, did you see that box?'

'Huck, I didn't wait to look around. I didn't see the box, I didn't see the cross. I didn't see anything but a bottle and a tin cup on the floor by Injun Joe! Yes, and I saw two barrels and lots more bottles in the room. Don't you see, now, what's the matter with that ha'nted room?'

'How?'

'Why, it's ha'nted with whisky! Maybe *all* the Temperance Taverns have got a ha'nted room, hey, Huck?'

'Well, I reckon maybe that's so. Who'd 'a' thought such a thing? But say, Tom, now's a mighty good time to get that box, if Injun Joe's drunk.'

'It is that! You try it!'

Huck shuddered.

'Well, no—I reckon not.'

'And *I* reckon not, Huck. Only one bottle alongside of Injun Joe ain't enough. If there'd been three he'd be drunk enough, and I'd do it.'

There was a long pause for reflection, and then Tom said:

'Looky here, Huck, let's not try that thing any more till we know Injun Joe's not in there. It's too scary. Now if we watch every night, we'll be dead sure to see him go out some time or other, then we'll snatch that box quickern' lightning.'

'Well, I'm agreed. I'll watch the whole night long, and I'll do it every night, too, if you'll do the other part of the job.'

'All right, I will. All you got to do is to trot up Hooper Street a block and meow—and if I'm asleep you throw some gravel at the window, and that'll fetch me.'

'Agreed, and good as wheat!'

'Now, Huck, the storm's over, and I'll go home. It'll begin

to be daylight in a couple of hours. You go back and watch that long, will you?'

'I said I would, Tom, and I will. I'll ha'nt that tavern every night for a year. I'll sleep all day and I'll stand watch all night.'

'That's all right. Now where are you going to sleep?'

'In Ben Roger's hay-loft. He lets me, and so does his pap's nigger man, Uncle Jake. I tote water for Uncle Jake whenever he wants me to, and any time I ask him he gives me a little something to eat if he can spare it. That's a mighty good nigger. Tom. He likes me, becuz I don't ever act as if I was above him, Sometimes I've set right down and eat *with* him. But you needn't tell that. A body's got to do things when he's awful hungry he wouldn't want to do as a steady thing.'

'Well, if I don't want you in the daytime I'll let you sleep. I won't come bothering around. Any time you see something's up in the night, just skip right around and meow.'

CHAPTER XXIX

The Picnic—Huck on Injun Joe's Track—The 'Revenge' Job—Aid for the Widow

THE first thing Tom heard on Friday morning was a glad piece of news—Judge Thatcher's family had come back to town the night before. Both Injun Joe and the treasure sunk into secondary importance for a moment, and Becky took the chief place in the boy's interest. He saw her, and they had an exhausting good time playing 'hi-spy' and 'gully-keeper' with a crowd of their schoolmates. The day was completed and crowned in a peculiarly satisfactory way: Becky teased her mother to appoint the next day for the long-promised and long-delayed picnic, and she consented. The child's delight was boundless, and Tom's not more moderate. The invitations were sent out before sunset, and straightway the young folks of the village were thrown into a fever of preparation and pleasurable anticipation. Tom's excitement enabled him to keep awake until a pretty late hour, and he had good hopes of hearing Huck's 'meow' and of having his treasure to astonish Becky and the picnickers with, the next day; but he was disappointed. No signal came that night.

Morning came eventually, and by ten or eleven o'clock a giddy and rollicking company were gathered at Judge Thatcher's and everything was ready for a start. It was not the custom for elderly people to mar picnics with their presence. The children were considered safe enough under the wings of a few young ladies of eighteen and a few young gentlemen of twenty-three or thereabouts. The old steam ferry-boat was chartered for the occasion: presently the gay throng filed up the main street laden with provision baskets. Sid was sick and had to miss the fun; Mary remained at home to entertain him. The last thing Mrs. Thatcher said to Becky was:

'You'll not get back till late. Perhaps you'd better stay all night with some of the girls that live near the ferry landing, child!'

'Then I'll stay with Susy Harper, mamma.'

'Very well. And mind and behave yourself, and don't be any trouble.'

Presently, as they tripped along, Tom said to Becky:

'Say—I'll tell you what we'll do. 'Stead of going to Joe Harper's, we'll climb right up the hill and stop at the Widow Douglas's. She'll have ice-cream! She has it 'most every day— dead loads of it. And she'll be awful glad to have us.'

'Oh, that will be fun!'

Then Becky reflected a moment, and said:

'But what will mamma say?'

'How'll she ever know?'

The girl turned the idea over in her mind, and said reluctantly:

'I reckon it's wrong—but——'

'But; shucks! Your mother won't know, and so what's the harm? All she wants is that you'll be safe; and I bet you she'd 'a' said go there if she'd 'a' thought of it. I know she would!'

The Widow Douglas's splendid hospitality was a tempting bait. It and Tom's persuasions presently carried the day. So it was decided to say nothing to anybody about the night's programme.

Presently it occurred to Tom that maybe Huck might come this very night and give the signal. The thought took a deal of the spirit out of his anticipations. Still he could not bear to give up the fun at Widow Douglas's. And why should he give it up, he reasoned—the signal did not come the night before, so why should it be any more likely to come to-night? The sure fun of the evening outweighed the uncertain treasure; and, boy like, he determined to yield to the stronger inclination and not allow himself to think of the box of money another time that day.

Three miles below town the ferry-boat stopped at the mouth of a woody hollow and tied up. The crowd swarmed ashore, and soon the forest distances and craggy heights echoed far and near with shoutings and laughter. All the different ways of getting hot and tired were gone through with, and by and by the rovers straggled back to camp fortified with responsible appetites, and the destruction of the good things began. After the feast there was a refreshing season of rest and chat in the shade of spreading oaks. By and by somebody shouted:

'Who's ready for the cave?'

Everybody was. Bundles of candles were procured, and straightway there was a general scamper up the hill. The mouth of the cave was up the hillside—an opening shaped like a letter A. Its massive oaken door stood unbarred. Within was a small chamber, chilly as an ice-house, and walled by Nature with solid limestone that was dewy with a cold sweat. It was romantic and mysterious to stand here in the deep gloom and look out upon the green valley shining in the sun. But the impressiveness of the situation quickly wore off, and the romping began again. The moment a candle was lighted there was a general rush upon the owner of it; a struggle and a gallant defence followed, but the candle was soon knocked down or blown out, and then there was a glad clamour of laughter and a new chase. But all things have an end. By and by the procession went filing down the steep descent of the main avenue, the flickering rank of lights dimly revealing the lofty walls of rock almost to their point of junction sixty feet overhead. This main avenue was not more than eight or ten feet wide. Every few steps other lofty and still narrower crevices branched from it on either hand, for McDougal's cave was but a vast labyrinth of crooked aisles that ran into each other and out again and led nowhere. It was said that one might wander days and nights together through its intricate tangle of rifts and chasms, and never find the end of the cave; and that he might go down and down, and still down into the earth, and it was just the same—labyrinth underneath labyrinth, and no end to any of them. No man 'knew' the cave. That was an impossible thing. Most of the young men knew a portion of it, and it was not customary to venture much beyond this known portion. Tom Sawyer knew as much of the cave as anyone.

The procession moved along the main avenue some three-quarters of a mile, and then groups and couples began to slip aside into branch avenues, fly along the dismal corridors, and take each other by surprise at points where the corridors joined again. Parties were able to elude each other for the space of half an hour without going beyond the 'known' ground.

By and by, one group after another came straggling back to the mouth of the cave, panting, hilarious, smeared from head to foot with tallow drippings, daubed with clay, and entirely delighted with the success of the day. Then they were astonished to find that they had been taking no note of time, and that night was about at hand. The clanging bell had been calling for half an hour. However, this sort of close to the day's adventures was romantic and therefore satisfactory. When the ferry-boat with her wild freight pushed into the stream, nobody cared sixpence for the wasted time but the captain of the craft.

Huck was already upon his watch when the ferry-boat's light went glinting past the wharf. He heard no noise on board, for the young people were as subdued and still as people usually are who are nearly tired to death. He wondered what boat it was, and why she did not stop at the wharf—and then he dropped her out of his mind and put his attention upon his business. The night was growing cloudy and dark. Ten o'clock came, and the noise of vehicles ceased, scattered lights began to wink out, all straggling foot-passengers disappeared, the village betook itself to its slumbers and left the small watcher alone with the silence and the ghosts. Eleven o'clock came, and the tavern lights were put out; darkness everywhere, now. Huck waited what seemed a weary long time, but nothing happened. His faith was weakening. Was there any use? Was there really any use? Why not give it up and turn in?

A noise fell upon his ear. He was all attention in an instant. The alley door closed softly. He sprang to the corner of the brick store. The next moment two men brushed by him, and one seemed to have something under his arm. It must be that box! So they were going to remove the treasure. Why call Tom now? It would be absurd—the men would get away with the box and never be found again. No, he would stick to their wake and follow them; he would trust to the darkness for security from discovery. So communing with himself, Huck stepped out and glided along behind the men, cat-like, with bare feet, allowing them to keep just far enough ahead not to be invisible.

They moved up the river street three blocks, then turned to the left up a cross street. They went straight ahead, then, until they came to the path that led up Cardiff Hill; this they took. They passed by the old Welshman's house, half-way up the hill, without hesitating, and still climbed upward. Good, thought Huck, they will bury it in the old quarry. But they never stopped at the quarry. They passed on, up the summit. They plunged into the narrow path between the tall sumach bushes, and were at once hidden in the gloom. Huck closed up and shortened his distance, now, for they would never be able to see him. He trotted along a while; then slackened his pace, fearing he was gaining too fast; moved on a piece, then stopped altogether; listened; no sound; none, save that he seemed to hear the beating of his own heart. The hooting of an owl came from over the hill—ominous sound! But no footsteps. Heavens, was everything lost? He was about to spring with winged feet, when a man cleared his throat not four feet from him! Huck's heart shot into his throat, but he swallowed it again; and then he stood there shaking as if a dozen agues had taken charge of him at once, and so weak that he thought he must surely fall to the ground. He knew where he was. He knew he was within five steps of the stile leading into Widow Douglas's grounds. 'Very well,' he thought, 'let them bury it there; it won't be hard to find.'

Now there was a voice—a very low voice—Injun Joe's:

'Damn her! maybe she's got company—there's lights, late as it is.'

'I can't see any.'

This was that stranger's voice—the stranger of the haunted house. A deadly chill went to Huck's heart—this, then, was the revenge' job! His thought was to fly. Then he remembered that the Widow Douglas had been kind to him more than once, and maybe these men were going to murder her. He wished he dared venture to warn her; but he knew he didn't dare—they might come and catch him. He thought all this and more in the moment that elapsed between the stranger's remark and Injun Joe's next—which was:

'Because the bush is in your way. Now—this way—now you see, don't you?'

'Yes. Well, there *is* company there, I reckon. Better give it up.'

'Give it up, and I just leaving this country for ever! Give it up, and maybe never have another chance. I tell you again, as I've told you before, I don't care for her swag—you may have it. But her husband was rough on me—many times he was rough on me—and mainly he was the justice of the peace that jugged me for a vagrant. And that ain't all! It ain't all! It ain't a millionth part of it! He had me *horsewhipped*!—horsewhipped in front of the jail, like a nigger!—with all the town looking on! HORSEWHIPPED!—do you understand? He took advantage of me and died. But I'll take it out of *her*!'

'Oh, don't kill her! Don't do that!'

'Kill! Who said anything about killing? I would kill *him* if he was here; but not her. When you want to get revenge on a woman you don't kill her—bosh! you go for her looks. You slit her nostrils—you notch her ears like a sow!'

'By God, that's——'

'Keep your opinion to yourself! It will be safest for you. I'll tie her to the bed. If she bleeds to death, is that my fault? I'll not cry if she does. My friend, you'll help in this thing—for *my* sake—that's why you're here—I mightn't be able alone. If you flinch, I'll kill you! Do you understand that? And if I have to kill you, I'll kill her—and then I reckon nobody'll ever know much about who done this business.'

'Well, if it's got to be done, let's get at it. The quicker the better—I'm all in a shiver.'

'Do it *now*!—and company there! Look here—I'll get suspicious of you, first thing you know. No—we'll wait till the lights are out—there's no hurry.'

Huck felt that a silence was going to ensue—a thing still more awful than any amount of murderous talk; so he held his breath and stepped gingerly back: planted his foot carefully and firmly, after balancing, one-legged, in a precarious way and almost toppling over, first on one side and then on the other. He took another step back with the same elaboration and the same risks; then another and another, and—a twig snapped under his foot! His breath stopped and he listened. There was no sound —the stillness was perfect. His gratitude was measureless. Now he turned in his tracks between the walls of sumach bushes— turned himself as carefully as if he were a ship—and then stepped quickly but cautiously along. When he emerged at the quarry he felt secure, so he picked up his nimble heels and flew. Down, down he sped till he reached the Welshman's. He banged at the door, and presently the heads of the old man and his two stalwart sons were thrust from windows.

'What's the row there? Who's banging? What do you want?'

'Let me in—quick! I'll tell everything.'

'Why, who are you?'

'Huckleberry Finn—quick, let me in!'

'Huckleberry Finn, indeed! It ain't a name to open many doors, I judge! But let him in, lads, and let's see what's the trouble.'

'Please don't ever tell *I* told you,' were Huck's first words when he got in. 'Please don't—I'd be killed sure—but the Widow's been good friends to me sometimes, and I want to tell —I *will* tell if you'll promise you won't ever say it was me.'

'By George, he *has* got something to tell, or he wouldn't act so!' exclaimed the old man. 'Out with it, and nobody here'll ever tell, lad.'

Three minutes later the old man and his sons, well armed, were up the hill, and just entering the sumach path on tip-toe, their weapons in their hands. Huck accompanied them no further. He hid behind a great boulder and fell to listening. There was a lagging, anxious silence, and then all of a sudden there was an explosion of firearms and a cry. Huck waited for no particulars. He sprang away and sped down the hill as fast as his legs could carry him.

CHAPTER XXX

*The Welshman's Reports—Huck under Fire—
The Story circulated—A New Sensation—Hope
giving way to Despair*

As the earliest suspicion of dawn appeared on Sunday morning, Huck came groping up the hill and rapped gently at the old Welshman's door. The inmates were asleep, but it was a sleep that was set on a hair-trigger, on account of the exciting episode of the night. A call came from a window:

'Who's there?'

Huck's scared voice answered in a low tone:

'Please let me in! It's only Huck Finn!'

'It's a name that can open this door night or day, lad!—and welcome!'

These were strange words to the vagabond boy's ears, and the pleasantest he had ever heard. He could not recollect that the closing word had ever been applied in his case before.

The door was quickly unlocked, and he entered. Huck was given a seat, and the old man and his brace of tall sons speedily dressed themselves.

'Now, my boy, I hope you're good and hungry, because breakfast will be ready as soon as the sun's up, and we'll have a piping hot one, too—make yourself easy about that. I and the boys hoped you'd turn up and stop here last night.'

'I was awful scared,' said Huck, 'and I run. I took out when the pistols went off, and I didn't stop for three mile. I've come now becuz I wanted to know about it, you know; and I come before daylight becuz I didn't want to run acrost them devils, even if they was dead.'

'Well, poor chap, you do look as if you'd had a hard night of it
—but there's a bed here for you when you've had your breakfast.
No, they ain't dead, lad—we are sorry enough for that. You see,
we knew right where to put our hands on them, by your description; so we crept along on tip-toe till we got within fifteen feet of
them—dark as a cellar that sumach path was—and just then I
found I was going to sneeze. It was the meanest kind of luck! I
tried to keep it back, but no use—'twas bound to come, and it
did come! I was in the lead, with my pistol raised, and when the
sneeze started those scoundrels a-rustling to get out of the path,
I sang out "Fire, boys!" and blazed away at the place where the
rustling was. So did the boys. But they were off in a jiffy, those
villains, and we after them, down through the woods. I judge we
never touched them. They fired a shot apiece as they started, but
their bullets whizzed by and didn't do us any harm. As soon as
we lost the sound of their feet we quit chasing, and went down and
stirred up the constables. They got a posse together, and went
off to guard the river bank, and as soon as it is light the sheriff
and a gang are going to beat up the woods. My boys will be
with them presently. I wish we had some sort of a description
of those rascals—'twould help a good deal. But you couldn't see
what they were like in the dark, lad, I suppose?'

'Oh, yes, I saw them down town, and follered them.'

'Splendid! Describe them—describe them, my boy!'

'One's the old deaf and dumb Spaniard that's ben around here
once or twice, and t'other's a mean-looking, ragged——'

'That's enough, lad, we know the men! Happened on them in
the woods back of the widow's one day, and they slunk away.
Off with you, boys, and tell the sheriff—get your breakfast
to-morrow morning!'

The Welshman's sons departed at once. As they were leaving
the room Huck sprang up and exclaimed:

'Oh, please don't tell *any*body it was me that blowed on them!
Oh, please!'

'All right if you say it, Huck, but you ought to have the credit of what you did.'

'Oh, no, no! Please don't tell!'

When the young men were gone, the old Welshman said:

'They won't tell—and I won't. But why don't you want it known?'

Huck would not explain further than to say that he already knew too much about one of those men, and would not have the man know that he knew anything against him for the whole world—he would be killed for knowing it, sure.

The old man promised secrecy once more, and said:

'How did you come to follow these fellows, lad? Were they looking suspicious?'

Huck was silent, while he framed a duly cautious reply. Then he said:

'Well, you see, I'm a kind of a hard lot—least everybody says so, and I don't see nothing agin it—and sometimes I can't sleep much, on account of thinking about it, and sort of trying to strike out a new way of doing. That was the way of it last night. I couldn't sleep, and so I come along up street 'bout midnight a turning it all over, and when I got to that old shackly brick-store by the Temperance Tavern, I backed up agin the wall to have another think. Well, just then along comes these two chaps slipping along close by me, with something under their arm, and I reckoned they'd stole it. One was a smoking, and t'other wanted a light; so they stopped right before me, and the cigars lit up their faces, and I see that the big one was the deaf and dumb Spaniard, by his white whiskers and the patch on his eye, and t'other one was a rusty, ragged-looking devil.'

'Could you see the rags by the light of the cigars?'

This staggered Huck for a moment. Then he said:

'Well, I don't know—but somehow it seems as if I did.'

'Then they went on, and you——'

'Followed 'em—yes. That was it. I wanted to see what was

up—they sneaked along so. I dogged 'em to the widder's stile, and stood in the dark, and heard the ragged one beg for the widder, and the Spaniard swear he'd spile her looks, just as I told you and your two——'

'What! The *deaf and dumb* man said all that!'

Huck had made another terrible mistake! He was trying his best to keep the old man from getting the faintest hint of who the Spaniard might be, and yet his tongue seemed determined to get him into trouble in spite of all he could do. He made several efforts to creep out of his scrape, but the old man's eye was upon him, and he made blunder after blunder. Presently the Welshman said:

'My boy, don't be afraid of me, I wouldn't hurt a hair of your head for all the world—No—I'd protect you—I'd protect you. This Spaniard is not deaf and dumb; you've let that slip without intending it; you can't cover that up now. You know something about that Spaniard that you want to keep dark. Now trust me —tell me what it is, and trust me—I won't betray you.'

Huck looked into the old man's honest eyes a moment, then bent over and whispered in his ear·

''Tain't a Spaniard—it's Injun Joe!'

The Welshman almost jumped out of his chair. In a moment he said:

'It's all plain enough now. When you talked about notching ears and slitting noses, I judged that that was your own embellishment, because white men don't take that sort of revenge. But an Injun! That's a different matter altogether.'

During breakfast the talk went on, and in the course of it the old man said that the last thing which he and his sons had done before going to bed was to get a lantern and examine the stile and its vicinity for marks of blood. They found none, but captured a bulky bundle of——

'Of *w h a t?*'

If the words had been lightning, they could not have leaped

with a more stunning suddenness from Huck's blanched lips. His eyes were staring wide, now, and his breath suspended— waiting for the answer. The Welshman started—stared in return —three seconds—five seconds—ten—then replied:

'Of burglars' tools. Why, what's the *matter* with you!'

Huck sank back, panting gently, but deeply, unutterably grateful. The Welshman eyed him gravely, curiously—and presently said:

'Yes, burglars' tools. That appears to relieve you a good deal. But what did give you that turn? What were *you* expecting we'd found?'

Huck was in a close place; the inquiring eye was upon him— he would have given anything for material for a plausible answer. Nothing suggested itself; the inquiring eye was boring deeper and deeper—a senseless reply offered—there was no time to weigh it, so at a venture he uttered it, feebly:

'Sunday-school books, maybe.'

Poor Huck was too distressed to smile, but the old man laughed loud and joyously, shook up the details of his anatomy from head to foot, and ended by saying that such a laugh was money in a man's pocket, because it cut down the doctor's bills like everything. Then he added:

'Poor old chap, you're white and jaded; you ain't well a bit. No wonder you're a little flighty and off your balance. But you'll come out of it. Rest and sleep will fetch you all right, I hope.'

Huck was irritated to think he had been such a goose and betrayed such a suspicious excitement, for he had dropped the idea that the parcel brought from the tavern was the treasure, as soon as he had heard the talk at the widow's stile. He had only *thought* it was not the treasure, however; he had not known that it wasn't; and so the suggestion of a captured bundle was too much for his self-possession. But on the whole he felt glad the little episode had happened, for now he knew beyond all question that that bundle was not *the* bundle, and so his mind was at rest and exceedingly comfortable. In fact, everything seemed to be drifting just in the right direction now; the treasure must be still in Number Two, the men would be captured and jailed that day, and he and Tom could seize the gold that night without any trouble or any fear of interruption.

Just as breakfast was completed there was a knock at the door. Huck jumped for a hiding-place, for he had no mind to be connected even remotely with the late event. The Welshman admitted several ladies and gentlemen, among them the Widow Douglas, and noticed that groups of citizens were climbing up the hill to stare at the stile. So the news had spread.

The Welshman had to tell the story of the night to the visitors. The widow's gratitude for her preservation was out-spoken.

'Don't say a word about it, madam. There's another that you're more beholden to than you are to me and my boys maybe, but he don't allow me to tell his name. We wouldn't have been there but for him.'

Of course this excited a curiosity so vast that it almost belittled the main matter; but the Welshman allowed it to eat into the vitals of his visitors, and through them be transmitted to the whole town, for he refused to part with his secret. When all else had been learned the widow said:

'I went to sleep reading in bed, and slept straight through all that noise. Why didn't you come and wake me?'

'We judged it warn't worth while. Those fellows waren't likely to come again; they hadn't any tools left to work with, and what was the use of waking you up and scaring you to death? My three negro men stood guard at your house all the rest of the night. They've just come back.'

More visitors came, and the story had to be told and retold for a couple of hours more.

There was no Sabbath-school during day-school vacation, but everybody was early at church. The stirring event was well canvassed. News came that not a sign of the two villains had been yet discovered. When the sermon was finished Judge Thatcher's wife dropped alongside of Mrs. Harper as she moved down the aisle with the crowd, and said:

'Is my Becky going to sleep all day? I just expected she would be tired to death.'

'Your Becky?'

'Yes,' with a startled look. 'Didn't she stay with you last night?'

'Why, no.'

Mrs. Thatcher turned pale, and sank into a pew just as Aunt Polly, talking briskly with a friend, passed by. Aunt Polly said:

'Good morning, Mrs. Thatcher. Good morning, Mrs. Harper. I've got a boy that's turned up missing. I reckon my Tom stayed at your house last night—one of you. And now he's afraid to come to church. I've got to settle with him.'

Mrs. Thatcher shook her head feebly and turned paler than ever.

'He didn't stay with us,' said Mrs. Harper, beginning to look uneasy. A marked anxiety came into Aunt Polly's face.

'Joe Harper, have you seen my Tom this morning?'

'No'm.'

'When did you see him last?'

Joe tried to remember, but was not sure he could say. The people had stopped moving out of church. Whispers passed along, and a boding uneasiness took possession of every countenance. Children were anxiously questioned, and young teachers. They all said they had not noticed whether Tom and Becky were on board the ferry-boat on the homeward trip; it was dark; no one thought of inquiring if anyone was missing. One young man finally blurted out his fear that they were still in the cave! Mrs. Thatcher swooned away; Aunt Polly fell to crying and wringing her hands.

The alarm swept from lip to lip, from group to group, from

street to street; and within five minutes the bells were wildly clanging, and the whole town was up! The Cardiff Hill episode sank into instant insignificance, the burglars were forgotten, horses were saddled, skiffs were manned, the ferry-boat ordered out, and before the horror was half an hour old two hundred men were pouring down high-road and river towards the cave.

All the long afternoon the village seemed empty and dead. Many women visited Aunt Polly and Mrs. Thatcher, and tried to comfort them. They cried with them, too, and that was still better than words.

All the tedious night the town waited for news; but when the morning dawned at last, all the word that came was 'Send more candles, and send food'. Mrs. Thatcher was almost crazed, and Aunt Polly also. Judge Thatcher sent messages of hope and encouragement from the cave, but they conveyed no real cheer.

The old Welshman came home towards daylight, spattered with candle-grease, smeared with clay, and almost worn out. He found Huck still in the bed that had been provided for him, and delirious with fever. The physicians were all at the cave, so the Widow Douglas came and took charge of the patient. She said she would do her best by him, because, whether he was good, bad, or indifferent, he was the Lord's, and nothing that was the Lord's was a thing to be neglected. The Welshman said Huck had good spots in him, and the widow said:

'You can depend on it. That's the Lord's mark. He don't leave it off. He never does. Puts it somewhere on every creature that comes from His hands.'

Early in the forenoon parties of jaded men began to straggle into the village, but the strongest of the citizens continued searching. All the news that could be gained was that remotenesses of the cavern were being ransacked that had never been visited before; that every corner and crevice was going to be thoroughly searched; that wherever one wandered through the maze of passages, lights were to be seen flitting hither and thither in the distance, and shoutings and pistol-shots sent their hollow reverberations to the ear down the sombre aisles. In one place, far from the section usually traversed by tourists, the names 'BECKY & TOM' had been found traced upon the rocky wall with candle smoke, and near at hand a grease-soiled bit of ribbon. Mrs. Thatcher recognized the ribbon and cried over it. She said it was the last relic she should ever have of her child; and that no other memorial of her could ever be so precious, because this one parted latest from the living body before the awful death came. Some said that now and then in the cave a far-away speck of light would glimmer, and then a glorious shout would burst forth and a score of men go trooping down the echoing aisle— and then a sickening disappointment always followed; the children were not there; it was only a searcher's light.

Three dreadful days and nights dragged their tedious hours along, and the village sank into a hopeless stupor. No one had heart for anything. The accidental discovery, just made, that the proprietor of the Temperance Tavern kept liquor on his premises scarcely fluttered the public pulse, tremendous as the fact was. In a lucid interval Huck feebly led up to the subject of taverns, and finally asked, dimly dreading the worst, if anything had been discovered at the Temperance Tavern since he had been ill?

'Yes,' said the widow.

Huck started up in bed, wild-eyed:

'What! What was it?'

'Liquor!—and the place has been shut up. Lie down, child —what a turn you did give me!'

'Only tell me just one thing—only just one—please! Was it Tom Sawyer that found it?'

The widow burst into tears.

'Hush, hush, child, hush! I've told you before, you must *not* talk. You are very, very sick!'

Then nothing but liquor had been found; there would have

been a great pow-wow if it had been the gold. So the treasure was gone for ever—gone for ever! But what could she be crying about? Curious that she should cry.

These thoughts worked their dim way through Huck's mind, and under the weariness they gave him he fell asleep. The widow said to herself:

'There—he's asleep, poor wreck. Tom Sawyer find it! Pity but somebody could find Tom Sawyer! Ah, there ain't many left now that's got hope enough, or strength enough either, to go on searching.'

CHAPTER XXXI

An Exploring Expedition—Trouble commences—
Lost in the Cave—Total Darkness—Found but
not Saved

Now to return to Tom and Becky's share in the picnic. They tripped along the murky aisles with the rest of the company, visiting the familiar wonders of the cave—wonders dubbed with rather over-descriptive names, such as 'The Drawing Room', 'The Cathedral', 'Aladdin's Palace', and so on. Presently the hide-and-seek frolicking began, and Tom and Becky engaged in it with zeal until the exertion began to grow a trifle wearisome; then they wandered down a sinuous avenue, holding their candles aloft and reading the tangled web-work of names, dates, post-office addresses, and mottoes with which the rocky walls had been frescoed (in candle smoke). Still drifting along and talking, they scarcely noticed that they were now in a part of the cave whose walls were not frescoed. They smoked their own names under an overhanging shelf and moved on. Presently they came to a place where a little stream of water, trickling over a ledge and carrying a limestone sediment with it, had, in the slow dragging ages, formed a laced and ruffled Niagara in gleaming and imperishable stone. Tom squeezed his small body behind it in order to illuminate it for Becky's gratification. He found that it curtained a sort of steep natural stairway which was enclosed between narrow walls, and at once the ambition to be a discoverer seized him. Becky responded to his call, and they made a smoke mark for future guidance, and started upon their quest. They wound this way and that, far down into the secret depths of the cave, made another mark, and branched off in search of novelties to tell the upper world about. In one place they found a spacious cavern, from whose ceiling depended a multitude of shining stalactites of the length and circumference of a man's leg; they walked all about it, wondering and admiring, and presently left it by one of the numerous passages that opened into it. This shortly brought them to a bewitching spring, whose basin was encrusted with a frostwork of glittering crystals; it was in the midst of a cavern whose walls were supported by many fantastic pillars which had been formed by the joining of great stalactites and stalagmites together, the result of the ceaseless water-drip of centuries. Under the roof vast knots of bats had packed themselves together, thousands in a bunch; the lights disturbed the creatures, and they came flocking down by hundreds, squeaking and darting furiously at the candles. Tom knew their ways, and the danger of this sort of conduct. He seized Becky's hand, and hurried her into the first corridor that offered; and none too soon, for a bat struck Becky's light out with its wing while she was passing out of the cavern. The bats chased the children a good distance; but the fugitives plunged into every new passage that offered, and at last got rid of the perilous things. Tom found a subterranean lake, shortly, which stretched its dim length away until its shape was lost in the shadows. He wanted to explore its borders, but concluded that it would be best to sit down and rest a while first. Now for the first time the deep stillness of the place laid a clammy hand upon the spirits of the children. Becky said:

'Why, I didn't notice, but it seems ever so long since I heard any of the others.'

'Come to think, Becky, we are away down below them, and I don't know how far away north, or south, or east, or whichever it is. We couldn't hear them here.'

Becky grew apprehensive.

'I wonder how long we've been down here, Tom. We better start back.'

'Yes, I reckon we better. P'haps we better.'

'Can you find the way, Tom? Its all a mixed-up crookedness to me.'

'I reckon I could find it, but then the bats. If they put both our candles out it will be an awful fix. Let's try some other way, so as not to go through there.'

'Well, but I hope we won't get lost. It would be so awful!' and the girl shuddered at the thought of the dreadful possibilities.

They started through a corridor, and traversed it in silence a long way, glancing at each new opening, to see if there was anything familiar about the look of it; but they were all strange. Every time Tom made an examination, Becky would watch his face for an encouraging sign, and he would say cheerily:

'Oh, it's all right. This ain't the one, but we'll come to it right away!'

But he felt less and less hopeful with each failure and presently began to turn off into diverging avenues at sheer random, in desperate hope of finding the one that was wanted. He still said it was 'All right,' but there was such a leaden dread at his heart, that the words had lost their ring, and sounded just as if he had said, 'All is lost!' Becky clung to his side in an anguish of fear, and tried hard to keep back the tears, but they would come. At last she said:

'Oh, Tom, never mind the bats; let's go back that way! We seem to get worse and worse off all the time.'

Tom stopped.

'Listen!' said he.

Profound silence; silence so deep that even their breathings were conspicuous in the hush. Tom shouted. The call went echoing down the empty aisles, and died out in the distance in a faint sound that resembled a ripple of mocking laughter.

'Oh, don't do it again, Tom, it is too horrid,' said Becky.

'It is horrid, but I better, Becky; they *might* hear us, you know,' and he shouted again.

The 'might' was even a chillier horror than the ghostly laughter, it so confessed a perishing hope. The children stood still and listened; but there was no result. Tom turned upon the back track at once, and hurried his steps. It was but a little while before a certain indecision in his manner revealed another fearful fact to Becky; he could not find his way back!

'Oh, Tom, you didn't make any marks!'

'Becky, I was such a fool! such a fool! I never thought we might want to come back! No, I can't find the way. It's all mixed up.'

'Tom, Tom, we're lost! we're lost! We never can get out of this awful place! Oh, why *did* we ever leave the others?'

She sank to the ground, and burst into such a frenzy of crying that Tom was appalled with the idea that she might die, or lose her reason. He sat down by her and put his arms around her; she buried her face in his bosom, she clung to him, she poured out her terrors, her unavailing regrets, and the far echoes turned them all to jeering laughter. Tom begged her to pluck up hope again, and she said she could not. He fell to blaming and abusing himself for getting her into this miserable situation; this had a better effect. She said she would try to hope again, she would get up and follow wherever he might lead, if only he would not talk like that any more. For he was no more to blame than she, she said.

So they moved on again—aimlessly—simply at random—all they could do was to move, keep moving. For a little while hope made a show of reviving—not with any reason to back it, but only because it is its nature to revive when the spring has not been taken out of it by age and familiarity with failure.

By and by Tom took Becky's candle, and blew it out. This economy meant so much. Words were not needed. Becky understood, and her hope died again. She knew that Tom had a whole candle and three or four pieces in his pocket—yet he must economize.

By and by fatigue began to assert its claims; the children tried to pay no attention, for it was dreadful to think of sitting down when time was grown to be so precious; moving, in some direction, in any direction, was at least progress and might bear fruit; but to sit down was to invite death and shorten its pursuit.

At last Becky's frail limbs refused to carry her farther. She sat down. Tom rested with her, and they talked of home, and friends there, and the comfortable beds, and above all, the light! Becky cried, and Tom tried to think of some way of comforting her, but all his encouragements were grown threadbare with use, and sounded like sarcasms. Fatigue bore so heavily upon Becky that she drowsed off to sleep. Tom was grateful. He sat looking into her drawn face and saw it grow smooth and natural under the influence of pleasant dreams; and by and by a smile dawned and rested there. The peaceful face reflected somewhat of peace and healing into his own spirit, and his thoughts wandered away to bygone times and dreamy memories. While he was deep in his musings Becky woke up with a breezy little laugh; but it was stricken dead upon her lips, and a groan followed it.

'Oh, how *could* I sleep! I wish I never, never had waked! No, no, I don't, Tom! Don't look so! I won't say it again.'

'I'm glad you've slept, Becky; you'll feel rested, now, and we'll find the way out.'

'We can try, Tom; but I've seen such a beautiful country in my dream. I reckon we are going there.'

'Maybe not, maybe not. Cheer up, Becky, and let's go on trying.'

They rose up and wandered along, hand in hand and hopeless. They tried to estimate how long they had been in the cave, but all they knew was that it seemed days and weeks, and yet it was plain that this could not be, for their candles were not gone yet.

A long time after this—they could not tell how long—Tom said they must go softly and listen for dripping water—they must find a spring. They found one presently, and Tom said it was time to rest again. Both were cruelly tired, yet Becky said she thought she could go on a little farther. She was surprised to hear Tom dissent. She could not understand it. They sat down, and Tom fastened his candle to the wall in front of them with some clay. Thought was soon busy; nothing was said for some time. Then Becky broke the silence:

'Tom, I am so hungry!'

Tom took something out of his pocket.

'Do you remember this?' said he.

Becky almost smiled.

'It's our wedding cake, Tom.'

'Yes—I wish it was as big as a barrel, for it's all we've got.'

'I saved it from the picnic for us to dream on, Tom, the way grown-up people do with wedding cake—but it'll be our——'

She dropped the sentence where it was. Tom divided the cake, and Becky ate with good appetite, while Tom nibbled at his moiety. There was abundance of cold water to finish the feast with. By and by Becky suggested that they should move on again. Tom was silent a moment. Then he said:

'Becky, can you bear it if I tell you something?'

Becky's face paled, but she said she thought she could.

'Well, then, Becky, we must stay here, where there's water to drink. That little piece is our last candle!'

Becky gave loose to tears and wailings. Tom did what he could to comfort her, but with little effect. At length Becky said:

'Tom.'

'Well, Becky?'

'They'll miss us and hunt for us!'

'Yes, they will! Certainly they will!'

'Maybe they're hunting for us now, Tom.'

'Why, I reckon maybe they are! I hope they are.'

'When would they miss us, Tom?'

'When they get back to the boat, I reckon.'

'Tom, it might be dark, then—would they notice we hadn't come?'

'I don't know. But anyway, your mother would miss you as soon as they got home.'

A frightened look in Becky's face brought Tom to his senses, and he saw that he had made a blunder. Becky was not to have gone home that night! The children became silent and thoughtful. In a moment a new burst of grief from Becky showed Tom that the thing in his mind had struck hers also—that the Sabbath morning might be half spent before Mrs. Thatcher discovered that Becky was not at Mrs. Harper's.

The children fastened their eyes upon their bit of candle and watched it melt slowly and pitilessly away; saw the half inch or wick standing alone at last: saw the feeble flame rise and fall, climb the thin column of smoke, linger at its top a moment, and then—the horror of utter darkness reigned!

How long afterwards it was that Becky came to a slow consciousness that she was crying in Tom's arms, neither could tell. All that they knew was, that after what seemed a mighty stretch of time, both awoke out of a dead stupor of sleep, and resumed their miseries once more. Tom said it might be Sunday now—maybe Monday. He tried to get Becky to talk, but her sorrows were too oppressive, all her hopes were gone. Tom said that they must have been missed long ago, and no doubt the search was going on. He would shout, and maybe some one would come. He tried it; but in the darkness the distant echoes sounded so hideously that he tried it no more.

The hours wasted away, and hunger came to torment the captives again. A portion of Tom's half of the cake was left, they divided and ate it. But they seemed hungrier than before. The poor morsel of food only whetted desire.

By and by Tom said:

'*Sh!* Did you hear that?'

Both held their breath and listened. There was a sound like

the faintest, far-off shout. Instantly Tom answered it, and leading Becky by the hand, started groping down the corridor in its
direction. Presently he listened again; again the sound was heard,
and apparently a little nearer.

'It's them!' said Tom; 'they're coming! Come along, Becky
—we're all right now!'

The joy of the prisoners was almost overwhelming. Their
speed was slow, however, because pitfalls were somewhat common, and had to be guarded against. They shortly came to one,
and had to stop. It might be three feet deep, it might be a hundred—there was no passing it, at any rate. Tom got down on his
breast, and reached as far down as he could. No bottom. They
must stay there and wait until the searchers came. They listened;
evidently the distant shoutings were growing more distant! A
moment or two more, and they had gone altogether. The heart-
sinking misery of it! Tom whooped until he was hoarse, but it
was of no use. He talked hopefully to Becky; but an age of anxious
waiting passed and no sounds came again.

The children groped their way back to the spring. The weary
time dragged on; they slept again, and awoke famished and woe-
stricken. Tom believed it must be Tuesday by this time.

Now an idea struck him. There were some side-passages near
at hand. It would be better to explore some of these than bear
the weight of the heavy time in idleness. He took a kite-line
from his pocket, tied it to a projection, and he and Becky started,
Tom in the lead, unwinding the line as he groped along. At
the end of twenty steps the corridor ended in a 'jumping-off
place'. Tom got down on his knees and felt below, and then
as far around the corner as he could reach with his hands conveniently; he made an effort to stretch yet a little further to the
right, and at that moment, not twenty yards away, a human
hand, holding a candle, appeared from behind a rock! Tom lifted
up a glorious shout, and instantly that hand was followed by the
body it belonged to—Injun Joe's! Tom was paralysed; he could

not move. He was vastly gratified the next moment to see the 'Spaniard' take to his heels and get himself out of sight. Tom wondered that Joe had not recognized his voice and come over and killed him for testifying in court. But the echoes must have disguised the voice. Without doubt that was it, he reasoned. Tom's fright weakened every muscle in his body. He said to himself that if he had strength enough to get back to the spring he would stay there, and nothing should tempt him to run the risk of meeting Injun Joe again. He was careful to keep from Becky what it was he had seen. He told her he had only shouted 'for luck'.

But hunger and wretchedness rise superior to fears in the long run. Another tedious wait at the spring, and another long sleep brought changes. The children awoke, tortured with a raging hunger. Tom believed that it must be Wednesday or Thursday, or even Friday or Saturday, now, and that the search had been given over. He proposed to explore another passage. He felt willing to risk Injun Joe and all other terrors. But Becky was very weak. She had sunk into a dreary apathy, and would not be roused. She said she would wait, now, where she was, and die—it would not be long. She told Tom to go with the kite-line and explore if he chose; but she implored him to come back every little while and speak to her; and she made him promise that when the awful time came, he would stay by her and hold her hand until all was over.

Tom kissed her, with a choking sensation in his throat, and made a show of being confident of finding the searchers or an escape from the cave; then he took the kite-line in his hand and went groping down one of the passages on his hands and knees, distressed with hunger and sick with bodings of coming doom.

CHAPTER XXXII

Tom tells the Story of Their Escape—Tom's Enemy in Safe Quarters

TUESDAY afternoon came, and waned to the twilight. The village of St. Petersburg still mourned. The lost children had not been found. Public prayers had been offered up for them, and many and many a private prayer that had the petitioner's whole heart in it; but still no good news came from the cave. The majority of the searchers had given up the quest and gone back to their daily avocations, saying that it was plain the children could never be found. Mrs. Thatcher was very ill, and a great part of the time delirious. People said it was heart-breaking to hear her call her child, and raise her head and listen a whole minute at a time, then lay it wearily down again with a moan. Aunt Polly had dropped into a settled melancholy, and her grey hair had grown almost white. The village went to its rest on Tuesday night, sad and forlorn.

Away in the middle of the night a wild peal burst from the village bells, and in a moment the streets were swarming with frantic half-clad people, who shouted, 'Turn out! turn out! they're found! they're found!' Tin pans and horns were added to the din, the population massed itself and moved toward the river, met the children coming in an open carriage drawn by shouting citizens, thronged around it, joined its homeward march, and swept magnificently up the main street roaring huzzah after huzzah!

The village was illuminated; nobody went to bed again; it was the greatest night the little town had ever seen. During the first half-hour a procession of villagers filed through Judge

Thatcher's house, seized the saved ones and kissed them, squeezed Mrs. Thatcher's hand, tried to speak but couldn't, and drifted out raining tears all over the place.

Aunt Polly's happiness was complete, and Mrs. Thatcher's nearly so. It would be complete, however, as soon as the messenger despatched with the great news to the cave should get the word to her husband.

Tom lay upon a sofa with an eager auditory about him, and told the history of the wonderful adventure, putting in many striking additions to adorn it withal; and closed with a description of how he left Becky and went on an exploring expedition; how he followed two avenues as far as his kiteline would reach; how he followed a third to the fullest stretch of the kite-lines and was about to turn back when he glimpsed a far-off speck that looked like daylight; dropped the line and groped toward it, pushed his head and shoulders through a small hole, and saw the broad Mississippi rolling by! And if it had only happened to be night he would not have seen that speck of daylight, and would not have explored that passage any more! He told how he went back for Becky and broke the good news, and she told him not to fret her with such stuff, for she was tired, and knew she was going to die, and wanted to. He described how he laboured with her and convinced her, and how she almost died for joy when she had groped to where she actually saw the blue speck of daylight; how he pushed his way out at the hole and then helped her out; how they sat there and cried for gladness; how some men came along in a skiff, and Tom hailed them and told them their situation and their famished condition; how the men didn't believe the wild tale at first, 'because', said they, 'you are five miles down the river below the valley the cave is in'; then took them aboard, rowed to a house, gave them supper, made them rest till two or three hours after dark, and then brought them home.

Before day-dawn Judge Thatcher and the handful of searchers

with him were tracked out in the cave by the twine clues they had strung behind them, and informed of the great news.

Three days and nights of toil and hunger in the cave were not to be shaken off at once, as Tom and Becky soon discovered. They were bedridden all of Wednesday and Thursday, and seemed to grow more and more tired and worn all the time. Tom got about a little on Thursday, was down town Friday, and nearly as whole as ever Saturday, but Becky did not leave her room until Sunday, and then she looked as if she had passed through a wasting illness.

Tom learned of Huck's sickness, and went to see him on Friday, but could not be admitted to the bedroom; neither could he on Saturday or Sunday. He was admitted daily after that, but was warned to keep still about his adventure and introduce no exciting topic. The Widow Douglas stayed by to see that he obeyed. At home Tom learned of the Cardiff Hill event; also that the 'ragged man's' body had eventually been found in the river near the ferry landing; he had been drowned while trying to escape perhaps.

About a fortnight after Tom's rescue from the cave he started off to visit Huck, who had grown plenty strong enough, now, to hear exciting talk, and Tom had some that would interest him, he thought. Judge Thatcher's house was on Tom's way, and he stopped to see Becky. The Judge and some friends set Tom to talking, and someone asked him ironically if he wouldn't like to go to the cave again. Tom said he thought he wouldn't mind it. The Judge said:

'Well, there are others just like you, Tom, I've not the least doubt. But we have taken care of that. Nobody will get lost in that cave any more.'

'Why?'

'Because I had its big door sheathed with boiler iron two weeks ago, and triple locked; and I've got the keys.'

Tom turned as white as a sheet.

'What's the matter, boy? Here, run, somebody! Fetch a glass of water!'

The water was brought and thrown into Tom's face.

'Ah, now you're all right. What was the matter with you, Tom?'

'Oh, Judge, Injun Joe's in the cave!'

CHAPTER XXXIII

The Fate of Injun Joe—Huck and Tom compare Notes—An Expedition to the Cave—Protection against Ghosts—'An Awful Snug Place'—A Reception at the Widow Douglas's

WITHIN a few minutes the news had spread, and a dozen skiff-loads of men were on their way to McDougal's Cave, and the ferry-boat, well filled with passengers, soon followed. Tom Sawyer was in the skiff that bore Judge Thatcher. When the cave door was unlocked, a sorrowful sight presented itself in the dim twilight of the place. Injun Joe lay stretched upon the ground, dead, with his face close to the crack of the door, as if his longing eyes had been fixed to the latest moment upon the light and the cheer of the world outside. Tom was touched, for he knew by his own experience how this wretch had suffered. His pity was moved, but nevertheless he felt an abounding sense of relief and security, now, which revealed to him in a degree which he had not fully appreciated before, how vast a weight of dread had been lying upon him since the day he lifted his voice against this bloody-minded outcast.

Injun Joe's bowie-knife lay close by, its blade broken in two. The great foundation-beam of the door had been chipped and hacked through with tedious labour; useless labour, too, it was, for the native rock formed a sill outside it, and upon that stubborn material the knife had wrought no effect; the only damage done was to the knife itself. But if there had been no stony obstruction there, the labour would have been useless still, for if the beam had been wholly cut away Injun Joe could not have squeezed his body under the door, and he knew it. So he had only hacked that place in order to be doing something—in order to pass the weary time—in order to employ his tortured faculties. Ordinarily one could find half a dozen bits of candle stuck around in the crevices of this vestibule, left there by tourists; but there were none now. The prisoner had searched them out and eaten them. He had also contrived to catch a few bats, and these, also, he had eaten, leaving only their claws. The poor unfortunate had starved to death. In one place near at hand a stalagmite had been slowly growing up from the ground for ages, builded by the water-drip from a stalactite overhead. The captive had broken off the stalagmite, and upon the stump had placed a stone, wherein he had scooped a shallow hollow to catch the precious drop that fell once in every three minutes with the dreary regularity of a clock-tick—a dessert-spoonful once in four-and-twenty hours. That drop was falling when the Pyramids were new; when Troy fell, when the foundations of Rome were laid, when Christ was crucified; when the Conqueror created the British Empire; when Columbus sailed; when the massacre at Lexington was 'news.' It is falling now; it will still be falling when all these things shall have sunk down the afternoon of history and the twilight of tradition, and been swallowed up in the thick night of oblivion. Has everything a purpose and a mission? Did this drop fall patiently during five thousand years to be ready for this flitting human insect's need, and has it another important object to accomplish ten thousand years to come? No matter. It is many and many a year since the hapless half-breed scooped out the stone to catch the priceless drops, but to this day the tourist stares longest at that pathetic stone and that slow-dropping water when he comes to see the wonders of McDougal's Cave. Injun Joe's Cup stands first in the list of the cavern's marvels; even 'Aladdin's Palace' cannot rival it.

Injun Joe was buried near the mouth of the cave; and people

flocked there in boats and waggons from the towns and from all the farms and hamlets for seven miles around; they brought their children, and all sorts of provisions, and confessed that they had had almost as satisfactory a time at the funeral as they could have had at the hanging.

This funeral stopped the further growth of one thing—the petition to the Governor for Injun Joe's pardon. The petition had been largely signed; many tearful and eloquent meetings had been held, and a committee of sappy women been appointed to go in deep mourning and wail around the Governor, and implore him to be a merciful ass, and trample his duty under foot. Injun Joe was believed to have killed five citizens of the village, but what of that? If he had been Satan himself there would have been plenty of weaklings ready to scribble their names to a pardon-petition, and drip a tear on it from their permanently impaired and leaky waterworks.

The morning after the funeral Tom took Huck to a private place to have an important talk. Huck had learned all about Tom's adventure from the Welshman and the Widow Douglas by this time, but Tom said he reckoned there was one thing they had not told him; that thing was what he wanted to talk about now. Huck's face saddened. He said:

'I know what it is. You got into Number Two, and never found anything but whisky. Nobody told me it was you, but I just knowed it must 'a' ben you, soon as I heard 'bout that whisky business; and I knowed you hadn't got the money becuz you'd 'a' got at me some way or other, and told me, even if you was mum to everybody else. Tom, something's always told me we'd never get holt of that swag.'

'Why, Huck, *I* never told on that tavern-keeper. *You* know his tavern was all right the Saturday I went to the picnic. Don't you remember you was to watch there that night?'

'Oh, yes! Why, it seems 'bout a year ago. It was that very night that I follered Injun Joe to the widder's.'

'*You* followed him?'

'Yes—but you keep mum. I reckon Injun Joe's left friends behind him, and I don't want 'em souring on me, and doing me mean tricks. If it hadn't ben for me he'd be down in Texas now, all right.'

Then Huck told his entire adventure in confidence to Tom, who had only heard of the Welshman's part of it before.

'Well,' said Huck, presently, coming back to the main question, 'whoever nipped the whisky in Number Two nipped the money, too, I reckon—anyways it's a goner for us, Tom.'

'Huck, that money wasn't ever in Number Two!'

'What!' Huck searched his comrade's face keenly. 'Tom, have you got on the track of that money again?'

'Huck, it's in the cave!'

Huck's eyes blazed.

'Say it again, Tom!'

'The money's in the cave!'

'Tom—honest injun, now—is it fun or earnest?'

'Earnest, Huck—just as earnest as ever I was in my life. Will you go in there with me and help get it out?'

'I bet I will! I will if it's where we can blaze our way to it and not get lost.'

'Huck, we can do that without the least little bit of trouble in the world.'

'Good as wheat! What makes you think the money's——'

'Huck, you just wait till we get in there. If we don't find it, I'll agree to give you my drum and everything I've got in the world. I will, by jings.'

'All right—it's a whiz. When do you say?'

'Right now, if you say it. Are you strong enough?'

'Is it far in the cave? I ben on my pins a little three of four days, now, but I can't walk more'n a mile, Tom—least I don't think I could.'

'It's about five miles into there the way anybody but me would

230

go, Huck, but there's a mighty short cut that they don't anybody but me know about Huck, I'll take you right to it in a skiff. I'll float the skiff down there, and I'll pull it back again, all by myself. You needn't ever turn your hand over.'

'Less start right off, Tom.'

'All right. We want some bread and meat, and our pipes, and a little bag or two, and two or three kite-strings, and some of these new-fangled things they call lucifer-matches.* I tell you many's the time I wished I had some when I was in there before.'

A trifle after noon the boys borrowed a small skiff from a citizen who was absent, and got under way at once. When they were several miles below 'Cave Hollow,' Tom said:

'Now you see this bluff here looks all alike all the way down from the cave hollow—no houses, no woodyards, bushes all alike. But do you see that white place up yonder where there's been a land-slide? Well, that's one of my marks. We'll get ashore now.'

They landed.

'Now, Huck, where we're a standing you could touch that hole I got out of with a fishing-pole. See if you can find it.'

Huck searched all the place about, and found nothing. Tom proudly marched into a thick clump of sumach bushes and said:

'Here you are! Look at it, Huck, it's the snuggest hole in this country. You just keep mum about it. All along I've been wanting to be a robber, but I knew I'd got to have a thing like this, and where to run across it was the bother. We've got it now, and we'll keep it quiet, only we'll let Joe Harper and Ben Rogers in—because of course there's got to be a Gang, or else there wouldn't be any style about it. Tom Sawyer's Gang—it sounds splendid, don't it, Huck?'

'Well, it just does, Tom. And who'll we rob?'

'Oh, 'most anybody. Waylay people—that's mostly the way.'

'And kill them.'

'No—not always. Hide them in the cave till they raise a ransom!'

'What's a ransom?'

'Money. You make them raise all they can off'n their friends, and after you've kept them a year, if it ain't raised then you kill them. That's the general way. Only you don't kill the women. You shut up the women, but you don't kill them. They're always beautiful and rich, and awfully scared. You take their watches and things, but you always take your hat off and talk polite. They ain't anybody as polite as robbers—you'll see that in any book. Well, the women get to loving you, and after they've been in the cave a week or two weeks they stop crying, and after that you couldn't get them to leave. If you drove them out, they'd turn right around and come back. It's so in all the books.'

'Why, it's real bully, Tom. I b'lieve it's better'n to be a pirate.'

'Yes, it's better in some ways, because it's close to home, and circuses, and all that.'

By this time everything was ready and the boys entered the hole, Tom in the lead. They toiled their way to the farther end of the tunnel, then made their spliced kite-strings fast and moved on. A few steps brought them to the spring, and Tom felt a shudder quiver all through him. He showed Huck the fragment of candle-wick perched on a lump of clay against the wall, and described how he and Becky had watched the flame struggle and expire.

The boys began to quiet down to whispers, now, for the stillness and gloom of the place oppressed their spirits. They went on, and presently entered and followed Tom's other corridor until they reached the 'jumping-off place'. The candles revealed the fact that it was not really a precipice, but only a steep clay hill, twenty or thirty feet high. Tom whispered:

'Now I'll show you something, Huck.'

He held his candle aloft and said:

'Look as far around the corner as you can. Do you see that? There—on the big rock over yonder—done with candle smoke?'

'Tom, it's a *cross*!'

'*Now* where's your Number Two? "*Under the cross*", hey? Right yonder's where I saw Injun Joe poke up his candle, Huck!'

Huck stared at the mystic sign a while, and then said with a shaky voice:

'Tom, less git out of here!'

'What! and leave the treasure?'

'Yes—leave it. Injun Joe's ghost is round about there, certain.'

'No it ain't, Huck, no it ain't. It would ha'nt the place where he died—away out at the mouth of the cave—five mile from here.'

'No, Tom, it wouldn't. It would hang round the money. I know the ways of ghosts, and so do you.'

Tom began to fear that Huck was right. Misgivings gathered in his mind. But presently an idea occurred to him.

'Looky here, Huck, what fools we're making of ourselves! Injun Joe's ghost ain't a going to come around where there's a cross!'

The point was well taken. It had its effect.

'Tom, I didn't think of that. But that's so. It's luck for us, that cross is. I reckon we'll climb down there and have a hunt for that box.'

Tom went first, cutting rude steps in the clay hill as he descended. Huck followed. Four avenues opened out of the small cavern which the great rock stood in. The boys examined three of them with no result. They found a small recess in the one nearest the base of the rock, with a pallet of blankets spread down in it; also an old suspender, some bacon rind, and the well-knawed bones of two or three fowls. But there was no money-box. The lads searched and re-searched this place, but in vain. Tom said:

'He said *under* the cross. Well, this comes nearest to being under the cross. It can't be under the rock itself, because that sets solid on the ground.'

They searched everywhere once more, and then sat down discouraged. Huck could suggest nothing. By and by Tom said:

'Looky here, Huck; there's foot-prints and some candle-grease on the clay about one side of this rock, but not on the other sides. Now what's that for? I bet you the money *is* under the rock. I'm going to dig in the clay.'

'That ain't no bad notion, Tom!' said Huck, with animation. Tom's 'real Barlow' was out at once, and he had not dug four inches before he struck wood.

'Hey, Huck! you hear that?'

Huck began to dig and scratch now. Some boards were soon uncovered and removed. They had concealed a natural chasm which led under the rock. Tom got into this and held his candle as far under the rock as he could, but said he could not see to the end of the rift. He proposed to explore. He stooped and passed under; the narrow way descended gradually. He followed its winding course, first to the right, then to the left, Huck at his heels. Tom turned a short curve by and by, and exclaimed:

'My goodness, Huck, looky here!'

It was the treasure-box, sure enough, occupying a snug little cavern, along with an empty powder-keg, a couple of guns in leather cases, two or three pairs of old moccasins, a leather belt, and some other rubbish well soaked with the water drip.

'Got it at last!' said Huck, ploughing among the tarnished coins with his hand. 'My, but we're rich, Tom!'

'Huck, I always reckoned we'd get it. It's just too good to believe, but we *have* got it, sure! Say, let's not fool around here, let's snake it out. Lemme see if I can lift the box.'

It weighed about fifty pounds. Tom could lift it after an awkward fashion, but could not carry it conveniently.

'I thought so,' he said; '*they* carried it like it was heavy that day at the ha'nted house—I noticed that. I reckon I was right to think of fetching the little bags along.'

The money was soon in the bags, and the boys took it up to the cross-rock.

'Now less fetch the guns and things,' said Huck.

'No, Huck, leave them there. They're just the tricks to have when we go to robbing. We'll keep them there all the time, and we hold our orgies there, too. It's an awful snug place for orgies.'

'What's orgies?'

'*I* dono. But robbers always have orgies, and of course we've got to have them too. Come along, Huck, we've been in here a long time. It's getting late, I reckon. I'm hungry, too. We'll eat and smoke when we get to the skiff.'

They presently emerged into the clump of sumach bushes, looked warily out, found the coast clear, and were soon lunching and smoking in the skiff. As the sun dipped toward the horizon they pushed out and got under way. Tom skimmed up the shore through the long twilight, chatting cheerily with Huck, and landed shortly after dark.

'Now, Huck,' said Tom, 'we'll hide the money in the loft of the widow's wood-shed, and I'll come up in the morning and we'll count it and divide, and then we'll hunt up a place out in the woods for it where it will be safe. Just you lay quiet here and watch the stuff till I run and hook Benny Taylor's little waggon. I won't be gone a minute.'

He disappeared, and presently returned with the waggon, put the two small sacks into it, threw some old rags on top of them, and started off, dragging his cargo behind him. When the boys reached the Welshman's house they stopped to rest. Just as they were about to move on the Welshman stepped out and said:

'Hallo, who's that?'

'Huck and Tom Sawyer.'

'Good! Come along with me, boys, you are keeping everybody waiting. Here, hurry up, trot ahead; I'll haul the waggon for you. Why, it's not as light as it might be. Got bricks in it or old metal?'

'Old metal,' said Tom.

'I judged so; the boys in this town will take more trouble and fool away more time hunting up six bits' worth of old iron to sell to the foundry, than they would to make twice the money at regular work. But that's human nature. Hurry along, hurry along!'

The boys wanted to know what the hurry was about.

'Never mind; you'll see when we get to the Widow Douglas's.'

Huck said, with some apprehension, for he was long used to being falsely accused:

'Mr. Jones, *we* haven't been doing nothing.'

The Welshman laughed.

'Well, I don't know, Huck, my boy. I don't know about that. Ain't you and the widow good friends?'

'Yes. Well, she's ben good friends to me, anyways.'

'All right, then. What do you want to be afraid for?'

This question was not entirely answered in Huck's slow mind before he found himself pushed, along with Tom, into Mrs. Douglas's drawing-room. Mr. Jones left the waggon near the door and followed.

The place was grandly lighted, and everybody that was of any consequence in the village was there. The Thatchers were there, the Harpers, the Rogerses, Aunt Polly, Sid, Mary, the minister, the editor, and a great many more, and all dressed in their best. The widow received the boys as heartily as anyone could well receive two such-looking beings. They were covered with clay and candle-grease. Aunt Polly blushed crimson with humiliation, and frowned and shook her head at Tom. Nobody suffered half as much as the two boys did, however. Mr. Jones said:

'Tom wasn't at home, yet, so I gave him up; but I stumbled on him and Huck right at my door, and so I just brought them along in a hurry.'

'And you did just right,' said the widow. 'Come with me, boys.'

She took them to a bedchamber and said:

'Now wash and dress yourselves. Here are two new suits of clothes—shirts, socks, everything complete. They're Huck's—no, no thanks, Huck—Mr. Jones bought one and I the other. But they'll fit both of you. Get into them. We'll wait—come down when you are slicked up enough.'

Then she left.

CHAPTER XXXIV

Springing a Secret—Mr. Jones's Surprise a Failure

Huck said: 'Tom, we can slope if we can find a rope. The window ain't high from the ground.'

'Shucks! what do you want to slope for?'

'Well, I ain't used to that kind of a crowd. I can't stand it. I ain't going down there, Tom.'

'Oh, bother! It ain't anything. I don't mind it a bit. I'll take care of you.'

Sid appeared.

'Tom,' said he, 'auntie has been waiting for you all the afternoon. Mary got your Sunday clothes ready, and everybody's been fretting about you. Say, ain't this grease and clay on your clothes?'

'Now, Mr. Siddy, you jist 'tend to your own business. What's all this blow-out about, anyway?'

'It's one of the widow's parties that she's always having. This time it's for the Welshman and his sons, on account of the scrape they helped her out of the other night. And say—I can tell you something, if you want to know.'

'Well, what?'

'Why, old Mr. Jones is going to try to spring something on the people here to-night, but I overheard him tell auntie to-day about it, as a secret, but I reckon it's not much of a secret *now*. Everybody knows—the widow, too, for all she tries to let on she don't. Mr. Jones was bound Huck should be here—couldn't get along with his grand secret without Huck, you know!'

'Secret about what, Sid?'

'About Huck tracking the robbers to the widow's. I reckon Mr. Jones was going to make a grand time over his surprise, but I bet you it will drop pretty flat.'

Sid chuckled in a very contented and satisfied way.

'Sid, was it you that told?'

'Oh, never mind who it was. *Somebody* told, that's enough.'

'Sid, there's only one person in this town mean enough to do that, and that's you. If you had been in Huck's place you'd 'a' sneaked down the hill and never told anybody on the robbers. You can't do any but mean things, and you can't bear to see anybody praised for doing good ones. There—no thanks, as the widow says.' And Tom cuffed Sid's ears and helped him to the door with several kicks. 'Now go and tell auntie if you dare, and to-morrow you'll catch it!'

Some minutes later the widow's guests were at the supper table, and a dozen children were propped up at little side tables in the same room, after the fashion of that country and that day. At the proper time Mr. Jones made his little speech, in which he thanked the widow for the honour she was doing himself and his sons, but said that there was another person whose modesty——

And so forth and so on. He sprang his secret about Huck's share in the adventure in the finest dramatic manner he was master of, but the surprise it occasioned was largely counterfeits and not as clamorous and effusive as it might have been under happier circumstances. However, the widow made a pretty fair show of astonishment, and heaped so many compliments and so much gratitude upon Huck, that he almost forgot the nearly intolerable discomfort of his new clothes in the entirely intolerable discomfort of being set up as a target for everybody's gaze and everybody's laudations.

The widow said she meant to give Huck a home under her roof and have him educated; and that when she could spare the money she would start him in business in a modest way. Tom's chance was come. He said:

'Huck don't need it. Huck's rich!'

Nothing but a heavy strain upon the good manners of the company kept back the due and proper complimentary laugh at this pleasant joke. But the silence was a little awkward. Tom broke it:

'Huck's got money. Maybe you don't believe it, but he's got lots of it. Oh, you needn't smile; I reckon I can show you. You just wait a minute.'

Tom ran out of doors. The company looked at each other with a perplexed interest, and inquiringly at Huck, who was tongue-tied.

'Sid, what ails Tom?' said Aunt Polly. 'He—well, there ain't ever any making of that boy out. I never——'

Tom entered, struggling with the weight of his sacks, and Aunt Polly did not finish her sentence. Tom poured the mass of yellow coin upon the table and said:

'There—what did I tell you? Half of it's Huck's, and half of it's mine!'

The spectacle took the general breath away. All gazed, nobody spoke for a moment. Then there was an unanimous call for an explanation. Tom said he could furnish it, and he did. The tale was long, but brimful of interest. There was scarcely an interruption from anyone to break the charm of its flow. When he had finished, Mr. Jones said:

'I thought I had fixed up a little surprise for this occasion, but it don't amount to anything now. This makes it sing mighty small, I'm willing to allow.'

The money was counted. The sum amounted to a little over twelve thousand dollars. It was more than anyone present had ever seen at one time before, though several persons were there who were worth considerably more than that in property.

CHAPTER XXXV

A New Order of Things—Poor Huck—New Adventures planned

THE reader may rest satisfied that Tom's and Huck's windfall made a mighty stir in the poor little village of St. Petersburg. So vast a sum, all in actual cash, seemed next to incredible. It was talked about, gloated over, glorified, until the reason of many of the citizens tottered under the strain of the unhealthy excitement. Every 'haunted' house in St. Petersburg and the neighbouring villages was dissected, plank by plank, and its foundations dug up and ransacked for hidden treasure—and not by boys, but men—pretty grave, unromantic men, too, some of them. Wherever Tom and Huck appeared they were courted, admired, stared at. The boys were not able to remember that their remarks had possessed weight before; but now their sayings were treasured and repeated; everything they did seemed somehow to be regarded as remarkable; they had evidently lost the power of doing and saying common-place things; moreover, their past history was raked up and discovered to bear marks of conspicuous originality. The village paper published biographical sketches of the boys.

The Widow Douglas put Huck's money out at six per cent., and Judge Thatcher did the same with Tom's at Aunt Polly's request. Each lad had an income now that was simply prodigious —a dollar for every week-day in the year and half of the Sundays. It was just what the minister got—no, it was what he was promised—he generally couldn't collect it. A dollar and a quarter a week would board, lodge, and school a boy in those old simple days—and clothe him and wash him, too, for that matter.

241

Judge Thatcher had conceived a great opinion of Tom. He said that no common-place boy would ever have got his daughter out of the cave. When Becky told her father, in strict confidence, how Tom had taken her whipping at school, the Judge was visibly moved; and when she pleaded grace for the mighty lie which Tom had told in order to shift that whipping from her shoulders to his own, the Judge said with a fine outburst that it was a noble, a generous, a magnanimous lie—a lie that was worthy to hold up its head and march down through history breast to breast with George Washington's lauded Truth about the hatchet! Becky thought her father had never looked so tall and so superb as when he walked the floor and stamped his foot and said that. She went straight off and told Tom about it.

Judge Thatcher hoped to see Tom a great lawyer or a great soldier some day. He said he meant to look to it that Tom should be admitted to the National Military Academy, and afterwards trained in the best law-school in the country, in order that he might be ready for either career, or both.

Huck Finn's wealth, and the fact that he was now under the Widow Douglas's protection, introduced him into society—no, dragged him into it, hurled him into it—and his sufferings were almost more than he could bear. The widow's servants kept him clean and neat, combed and brushed, and they bedded him nightly in unsympathetic sheets that had not one little spot or stain which he could press to his heart and know for a friend. He had to eat with knife and fork; he had to use napkin, cup and plate; he had to learn his book; he had to go to church; he had to talk so properly that his speech was become insipid in his mouth; whithersoever he turned, the bars and shackles of civilization shut him in and bound him hand and foot.

He bravely bore his miseries three weeks, and then one day turned up missing. For forty-eight hours the widow hunted for him everywhere in great distress. The public were profoundly concerned; they searched high and low, they dragged the river for his body. Early the third morning Tom Sawyer wisely went poking among some old empty hogsheads down behind the abandoned slaughter-house, and in one of them he found the refugee. Huck had slept there; he had just breakfasted upon some stolen odds and ends of food, and was lying off now, in comfort with his pipe. He was unkempt, uncombed, and clad in the same old ruin of rags that had made him picturesque in the days when he was free and happy. Tom routed him out, told him the trouble he had been causing, and urged him to go home. Huck's face lost its tranquil content, and took a melancholy cast. He said:

'Don't talk about it, Tom. I've tried it, and it don't work; it don't work, Tom. It ain't for me; I ain't used to it. The widder's good to me, and friendly; but I can't stand them ways. She makes me git up just at the same time every morning; she makes me wash, they comb me all to thunder; she won't let me sleep in the wood-shed; I got to wear them blamed clothes that just smothers me, Tom; they don't seem to any air git through 'em, somehow; and they're so rotten nice that I can't set down, nor lay down, nor roll around anywheres; I ain't slid on a cellar-door for—well, it 'pears to be years; I got to go to church, and sweat and sweat—I hate them ornery sermons! I can't ketch a fly in there, I can't chaw, I got to wear shoes all Sunday. The widder eats by a bell; she goes to bed by a bell; she gets up by a bell—everything's so awful reg'lar a body can't stand it.'

'Well, everybody does that way, Huck.'

'Tom, it don't make no difference. I ain't everybody, and I can't *stand* it. It's awful to be tied up so. And grub comes too easy—I don't take no interest in vittles that way. I got to ask to go a fishing; I got to ask to go in a swimming—dern'd if I ain't got to ask to do everything. Well, I'd got to talk so nice it wasn't no comfort; I'd got to go up in the attic and rip out a while every day to git a taste in my mouth, or I'd a died, Tom. The widder wouldn't let me smoke, she wouldn't let me yell, she wouldn't let me gape, nor stretch, nor scratch before folks.'

[Then with a spasm of special irritation and injury:] 'And dad fetch it, she prayed all the time! I never *see* such a woman! I *had* to shove, Tom, I just had to. And besides, that school's going to open, and I'd a had to go to it; well, I wouldn't stand *that*, Tom. Looky here, Tom, being rich ain't what it's cracked up to be. It's just worry and worry, and sweat and sweat, and a wishing you was dead all the time. Now these clothes suits me, and this bar'l suits me, and I ain't ever going to shake 'em any more. Tom, I wouldn't ever got into all this trouble if it hadn't 'a' ben for that money; now you just take my sheer of it along with your'n, and gimme a ten-center sometimes—not many times, becuz I don't give a dern for a thing 'thout it's tollable hard to git—and you go and beg off for me with the widder.'

'Oh, Huck, you know I can't do that. 'Tain't fair; and besides, you'll try this thing just a while longer you'll come to like it.'

'Like it! Yes—the way I'd like a hot stove if I was to set on it long enough. No, Tom, I won't be rich, and I won't live in them cussed smothery houses. I like the woods and the river, and hogsheads, and I'll stick to 'em too. Blame it all! just as we'd got guns, and a cave, and all just fixed to rob, here this dern foolishness has got to come up and spile it all!'

Tom saw his opportunity:

'Looky here, Huck, being rich ain't going to keep me back from turning robber.'

'No! Oh, good licks, are you in real deadwood earnest, Tom?'

'Just as dead earnest as I'm a sitting here. But, Huck, we can't let you into the Gang if you ain't respectable, you know.'

Huck's joy was quenched.

'Can't let me in, Tom? Didn't you let me go for a pirate?'

'Yes, but that's different. A robber is more high-toned than what a pirate is—as a general thing. In most countries they're awful high up in the nobility—dukes and such.'

'Now, Tom, ain't you always ben friendly to me? You wouldn't shet me out, would you, Tom? You wouldn't do that, now, *would* you, Tom?'

'Huck, I wouldn't want to, and I *don't* want to, but what would people say? Why they'd say, "Mph! Tom Sawyer's Gang! pretty low characters in it!" They'd mean you, Huck. You wouldn't like that, and I wouldn't.'

Huck was silent for some time, engaged in a mental struggle. Finally he said:

'Well, I'll go back to the widder for a month and tackle it, and see if I can come to stand it, if you'll let me b'long to the Gang, Tom.'

'All right, Huck, it's a whiz! Come along, old chap, and I'll ask the widow to let up on you a little, Huck.'

'Will you, Tom, now will you? That's good. If she'll let up on some of the roughest things, I'll smoke private and cuss private, and crowd through or bust. When you going to start the Gang and turn robbers?'

'Oh, right off. We'll get the boys together, and have the initiation to-night, maybe.'

'Have the which?'

'Have the initiation.'

'What's that?'

'It's to swear to stand by one another, and never tell the Gang's secrets, even if you're chopped all to flinders, and kill anybody and all his family that hurts one of the Gang.'

'That's gay—that's mighty gay, Tom, I tell you.'

'Well, I bet it is. And all that swearing's got to be done at midnight, in the lonesomest, awfullest place you can find—a ha'nted house is the best, but they're all ripped up, now.'

'Well, midnight's good, any way, Tom.'

'Yes, so it is. And you've got to swear on a coffin, and sign it with blood.'

'Now, that's something *like*! Why, it's a million times bullier

245

than pirating. I'll stick to the widder till I rot, Tom; and if I git to be a reg'lar ripper of a robber, and everybody talking 'bout it, I reckon she'll be proud she snaked me in out of the wet.'

Conclusion

So endeth this chronicle. It being strictly a history of a *boy*, it must stop here; the story could not go much further without becoming the history of a *man*. When one writes a novel about grown people, he knows exactly where to stop—that is, with a marriage; but when he writes of juveniles, he must stop where he best can.

Most of the characters that perform in this book still live, and are prosperous and happy. Some day it may seem worth while to take up the story of the younger ones again, and see what sort of men and women they turned out to be; therefore it will be wisest not to reveal any of that part of their lives at present.

EXPLANATORY NOTES

THESE notes explain simple matters of reference and are not intended to be interpretive. For a more exhaustive account of textual issues (and especially of the connection between fictional episodes and Samuel Clemens's autobiographical experiences), readers should refer to the definitive edition of the novel edited by John Gerber *et al.*, upon which the following notes are based (Volume 4 of *The Works of Mark Twain*, ed. John C. Gerber, Paul Baender, and Terry Firkins (Berkeley and Los Angeles: Univ. of California Press, 1980)).

10 *roundabout*: a short, close-fitting jacket.

   Old Scratch: Satan, or the Devil.

18 *'Buffalo Gals'*: song copyrighted in 1844 as 'Lubly Fan will You cum out To Night' by Cool White (John Hodges), an early black-faced minstrel.

19 *marvel*: dialect version of 'marble'.

   alley: probable diminutive of 'alabaster'.

   taw: a choice marble used for shooting.

22 *they came to jeer, but remained to whitewash*: a variation on line 180 of Oliver Goldsmith's 'The Deserted Village': 'And fools, who came to scoff, remain'd to pray.'

23 *spool-cannon*: a toy made by attaching rubber over an empty spool, which is then used to fire projectiles.

31 *Blessed are the*: Tom is recalling the Beatitudes, Matthew 5: 3–11.

35 *Doré Bible*: a folio edition of the Bible illustrated by Paul Gustave Doré, French painter and illustrator, first published in the mid-1860s.

45 *percussion-cap box*: a small box for holding caps used in firing the percussion lock rifle.

69 *Black Avenger of the Spanish Main*: *The Black Avenger of the Spanish Main, or The Fiend of Blood* (Boston: F. Gleason,

1847) was a popular boy's book by Ned Buntline (E. Z. C. Judson).

75 *devil-fire*: a phosphorescence or flame caused by spontaneous combustion of gas from decaying materials (also called *ignis fatuus*, friar's lantern, or St Elmo's fire).

90 *wound bled a little*: the belief that a murderer's proximity is revealed by the bleeding of a corpse's wound dates to the story of Cain and Abel (Genesis 4: 10).

93 *'whistle her down the wind'*: to dismiss her. The saying is probably older than its appearance in *Othello*, III. iii. 262.

111 *shoot a cannon over the water*: a common belief was that a cannon's concussion would break a drowned corpse's gall-bladder and cause it to float. This incident is repeated in *The Adventures of Huckleberry Finn*, ch. 8.

put quicksilver in 'em: another common belief was that a hollowed-out loaf of bread filled with mercury would come to rest over the spot where a drowned person lay.

120 *'knucks' and 'ring-taw' and 'keeps'*: 'knucks' is a game of marbles in which the shooter must keep knuckles on the ground. 'Ring-taw' involves shooting at marbles in a circle to knock them out. 'Keeps' is any game in which the winner keeps the marbles won.

136 *Milum apple*: the Milam apple was a popular dessert apple.

153 *'The Boy stood on the Burning Deck'*: the first line of Felicia D. Hemans's 'Casabianca'.

'The Assyrian Came Down': this is from Byron's 'Destruction of Sennacherib'.

154 *'In the common walks of life'*: all of the compositions read aloud come from Mary Ann Harris Gay's *Pastor's Story and Other Pieces; or, Prose and Poetry* (Memphis: Goodwyn & Co., 1871).

159 *Mr. Benton*: Thomas Hart Benton was United States Senator from Missouri from 1821 to 1851.

EXPLANATORY NOTES

185 *Murrel's gang*: the outlaws led by John A. Murrell, whose bloody acts were part of the tradition of most Mississippi river towns during Samuel Clemens's boyhood.

231 *'lucifer-matches'*: the popular friction match invented in 1830, according to the so-called Lucifer formula, was tipped with potassium chlorate and white phosphorus (Phosphorus being the Greek name for Lucifer, or 'the Light-Bearer').

LOUISA MAY ALCOTT	**Little Women**
SHERWOOD ANDERSON	**Winesburg, Ohio**
CHARLES BROCKDEN BROWN	**Wieland; or The Transformation and Memoirs of Carwin, The Biloquist**
WILLA CATHER	**Alexander's Bridge**
JAMES FENIMORE COOPER	**The Deerslayer** **The Last of the Mohicans** **The Pathfinder** **The Pioneers** **The Prairie**
STEPHEN CRANE	**The Red Badge of Courage**
J. HECTOR ST. JEAN DE CRÈVECŒUR	**Letters from an American Farmer**
THEODORE DREISER	**Jennie Gerhardt** **Sister Carrie**
F. SCOTT FITZGERALD	**The Great Gatsby** **The Beautiful and Damned**
BENJAMIN FRANKLIN	**Autobiography and Other Writings**
MARGARET FULLER	**Woman in the Nineteenth Century and Other Writings**
CHARLOTTE PERKINS GILMAN	**The Yellow Wall-Paper and Other Stories**
ZANE GREY	**Riders of the Purple Sage**
BRET HARTE	**Selected Stories and Sketches**
NATHANIEL HAWTHORNE	**The Blithedale Romance** **The House of the Seven Gables** **The Scarlet Letter** **Young Goodman Brown and Other Tales**
WILLIAM DEAN HOWELLS	**The Rise of Silas Lapham**

JANE AUSTEN	**Catharine and Other Writings**
	Emma
	Mansfield Park
	Northanger Abbey, Lady Susan, The Watsons, and Sanditon
	Persuasion
	Pride and Prejudice
	Sense and Sensibility
ANNE BRONTË	**Agnes Grey**
	The Tenant of Wildfell Hall
CHARLOTTE BRONTË	**Jane Eyre**
	The Professor
	Shirley
	Villette
EMILY BRONTË	**Wuthering Heights**
WILKIE COLLINS	**The Moonstone**
	No Name
	The Woman in White
CHARLES DARWIN	**The Origin of Species**
CHARLES DICKENS	**The Adventures of Oliver Twist**
	Bleak House
	David Copperfield
	Great Expectations
	Hard Times
	Little Dorrit
	Martin Chuzzlewit
	Nicholas Nickleby
	The Old Curiosity Shop
	Our Mutual Friend
	The Pickwick Papers
	A Tale of Two Cities

BLAISE PASCAL   **Pensées and Other Writings**

JEAN RACINE   **Britannicus, Phaedra, and Athaliah**

EDMOND ROSTAND   **Cyrano de Bergerac**

MARQUIS DE SADE   **The Misfortunes of Virtue and Other Early Tales**

GEORGE SAND   **Indiana**
The Master Pipers
Mauprat
The Miller of Angibault

STENDHAL   **The Red and the Black**
The Charterhouse of Parma

JULES VERNE   **Around the World in Eighty Days**
Journey to the Centre of the Earth
Twenty Thousand Leagues under the Sea

VOLTAIRE   **Candide and Other Stories**
Letters concerning the English Nation

ÉMILE ZOLA   **L'Assommoir**
The Attack on the Mill
La Bête humaine
Germinal
The Ladies' Paradise
The Masterpiece
Nana
Thérèse Raquin

SERGEI AKSAKOV	A Russian Gentleman
ANTON CHEKHOV	Early Stories
	Five Plays
	The Princess and Other Stories
	The Russian Master and Other Stories
	The Steppe and Other Stories
	Twelve Plays
	Ward Number Six and Other Stories
	A Woman's Kingdom and Other Stories
FYODOR DOSTOEVSKY	An Accidental Family
	Crime and Punishment
	Devils
	A Gentle Creature and Other Stories
	The Idiot
	The Karamazov Brothers
	Memoirs from the House of the Dead
	Notes from the Underground and The Gambler
NIKOLAI GOGOL	Village Evenings Near Dikanka and Mirgorod
	Plays and Petersburg
ALEXANDER HERZEN	Childhood, Youth, and Exile
MIKHAIL LERMONTOV	A Hero of our Time
ALEXANDER PUSHKIN	Eugene Onegin
	The Queen of Spades and Other Stories
LEO TOLSTOY	Anna Karenina
	The Kreutzer Sonata and Other Stories
	The Raid and Other Stories
	Resurrection
	War and Peace
IVAN TURGENEV	Fathers and Sons
	First Love and Other Stories
	A Month in the Country

The Oxford World's Classics Website

www.worldsclassics.co.uk

- Information about new titles
- Explore the full range of Oxford World's Classics
- Links to other literary sites and the main OUP webpage
- Imaginative competitions, with bookish prizes
- Peruse *Compass*, the Oxford World's Classics magazine
- Articles by editors
- Extracts from Introductions
- A forum for discussion and feedback on the series
- Special information for teachers and lecturers

www.worldsclassics.co.uk

American Literature

British and Irish Literature

Children's Literature

Classics and Ancient Literature

Colonial Literature

Eastern Literature

European Literature

History

Medieval Literature

Oxford English Drama

Poetry

Philosophy

Politics

Religion

The Oxford Shakespeare

A complete list of Oxford Paperbacks, including Oxford World's Classics, OPUS, Past Masters, Oxford Authors, Oxford Shakespeare, Oxford Drama, and Oxford Paperback Reference, is available in the UK from the Academic Division Publicity Department, Oxford University Press, Great Clarendon Street, Oxford OX2 6DP.

In the USA, complete lists are available from the Paperbacks Marketing Manager, Oxford University Press, 198 Madison Avenue, New York, NY 10016.

Oxford Paperbacks are available from all good bookshops. In case of difficulty, customers in the UK can order direct from Oxford University Press Bookshop, Freepost, 116 High Street, Oxford OX1 4BR, enclosing full payment. Please add 10 per cent of published price for postage and packing.